Arcane

Patricia Donner

Contents

o n e

You got that Princess Complex,She ain't gonna play that shit,Princess Complex, she ain't gonna play that shitPrincess Complex, she always gets what she wants.She always get what she wants.

"Sweetie hurry up." My mother called from the living room. I said nothing as I looked around my now empty room. I grumbled underneath my breath as I dragged the two heavy suitcases downstairs. We were moving to America, it was currently 5:13AM in England. I didn't want to move, and I sure as fucking hell didn't know WHY we were moving.

Something about, change being good for the body? I don't know, and I do not care. I didn't want to move, my life was in England, not America.

"Domenica! If you don't get your pathetic ass downstairs I swear to God I'll-" I cut her off by shouting, "What are you gonna do mum? Slap me? Kick me? Insult me? Sorry mother but that shit doesn't work on me no more. A* for trying though!" I said sarcastically. It was quiet as I dragged my suitcases downstairs.

"Cars waiting for us outside." She said, not moving an inch. I pursed my lips and nodded quietly. I ran back upstairs to grab my backpack, my headphones, my phone, and my sketchbook & diary. I sighed as I glanced around the room once again.

Whoops, bad of me. Hi, I'm Domenica Romero and I am moving to America for some fucked up reason. I'm 18. I'm in my last year of Sixth Form, but since we've moved in September it means I'll start in America a few weeks in. I'll be a senior is it? Not sure. My dad is somewhere in the world and my mother is with me. I skidaddled downstairs, looking once again back at my old room.

'Move the fuck on you idiot are you going to stand here the whole day? Fucking hell.' The voice in my head thundered. I kissed my teeth and ran downstairs, nearly falling flat on my face in the process. The house was empty. I had not many friends here but I had already bid my farewell to my friends that I had. My bestfriend though, she was crying and all, and I'm not good with criers. My bestfriend since birth, Xenia. We were polar opposites, that's why we were best friends.

She is loud and bubbly, I am quiet and calm.She is extremely sociable, whereas I am anti-social.She's 5'0 whereas I am 5'10.She wears bright colours, whereas I wear dark colours.She has a boyfriend, whereas I don't believe in love.She has a warm heart, I had a cold heart.She loves, I don't.

And we balanced each other out well.

As if on que, I heard her battle cry as I winced.

"OH MY DOM. I AM GOING TO MISS YOU SO MUCH. Anyways, stay updated on Snapchat, and also snap me all those sexy American boys. Also don't forget, if you get a new bestfriend I will fly over and skin you alive, don't forget to call me everyday, we also face time everyday. Also, please don't forget me, also don't forget that you're fucking beautiful with a great heart, and that I absolutely adore you. Also, please don't punch anyone straight away." She started out so loud, then ended softly, with eyes full of tears. She flung herself onto me as I stumbled back. For such a short girl, she was damn well strong. I snorted at her last sentence, quietly.

"I'd never forget you Xenia. And you know that." I said softly, kissing the top of her head. She was a few months younger than me, and also felt like a younger sister. I had an older brother, he was 27 but was abroad and was studying somewhere. We had a tight bond, we were there for each other when no one was there for us. I loved the death out of my brother and Xenia, no one else, actually I lied there is a few more people, but you'll meet them later.

Anyways I'm rambling.

I pulled away from the hug and smiled at her, complimenting her in my head because this girl don't need an ego boost.

"Gotta go. Mum will tear my head off if I stay any longer." She nodded and pulled something out of her pocket.

"I bought you this. You wear it everywhere and take it off only in the shower or else I'll fuck you up." She said, opening a small purple box.

It had two bracelets with best on one side and friend on the other. I felt tears build up but I pushed them back as I glanced down at her. I smiled softly, took best out and wrapped it around her wrist, as she did the same for me.

"Love you X." I mumbled as she smiled brightly replying, "I know you do Don Dom. I love you too." She said side hugging me. We finally pulled away as I got into the car. It was going to be a long ride. The driver started the car as we slowly started setting off, but not without Xenia waiting and waving until the car was out of sight.

I didn't do well with change. And moving to America was change. Maybe if we moved to another town in England, I wouldn't be so...so angry. But we're moving to a whole different country, and I wasn't informed about it until around 2 weeks ago. My mother expected me to drop everything and pack my bags up and dash. It was so silly of her, and I hate her for it.

She glanced back at me as I put in my headphones and opened up Spotify. I put on 'Princess Complex' by Blackbear. I hummed along to the beat, drumming my fingers against my thigh. I soon landed in a world of misery, as slumber over took me. I couldn't sleep normally, but overthinking about the whole moving situation made me tired.

I couldn't help but feel like bad things would happen there, and I always go with my gut feeling.

As soon as we land, I'm looking for a gym.

I told my mum to wake me up once we reach the airport, and she did.

TIME SKIP

I was woken up just as we reached Heathrow Airport in London. I sighed and pulled my bags out, and my headphones out as we waited for our plane tickets. After a good hour, we got our plane tickets when I spotted a shady looking man staring right at me. I tilted my head in confusion, and ignored it. I didn't really care. I smirked at him, pulling up my jumper sleeves. I had tattoos all over both my arms, one on my neck and a few on my leg and thigh. I had a rose on one hand, the back of my hand, and the mouth down of a skull on the other. Where the skull was, on my fingers I had cold, each letter on each finger excluding my thumb. I was always fascinated by tattoos, and got my first one at 15. I've built them up over the years.

We boarded the plane, and set off on a 8 hour flight, something like that. I sat next to a little girl, who was staring at my hands intently as I gripped the side bar of the seat. I closed my eyes, and took deep breaths in and out. I always had mad anxiety on planes, my mother was sitting far from me, and it wasn't like she;d do anything to help me either.

The little girl put her hand over mine, squeezing it. My eyes instantly flew open as I looked at her wearily.

"My brother told me when people get nervous it's good to hold their hands. Sorry for holding your hand without asking you Miss. My brother has anz-ity too." She said softly, giving me a soft toothy grin. I chuckled in my head at her mispronunciation, wondering what it was like if I had a younger sister like her. I smiled softly, and blew out a breath.

"Your brother is a cool kid." I replied, turning my hand over so she could hold it properly.

We were a few hours into the flight, and she didn't leave my hand, even though she had fell asleep. I felt myself drifting off into a deep slumber, and I let it overtake me and my train of thoughts for a few hours.

I would wake up when we landed in America.

Edited Chapter.

t w o

And I drown it out, Like I always do, Dancing through our house, With the ghost of you.　　　　And I chase it down,　　　　With a shot of truth,　　　　That my feet wont dance,　　　　Like they did with you.

I felt slight, soft nudging on my arm, quickly gripping the persons hand that was touching and realised it was unusually small and soft. I pried my eyes awake as the little girl poked me repeatedly.

"It's time to wake up Miss." She said, smiling fully at me.

"What's your name kid?" I said, slowly getting out of her grip. She raised her eyebrows at me, as if she was deep in thought. She made a funny face, and the sighed quietly.

"Rosella, what's yours?" She said, now smiling.

"Do you have a lot of friends Miss? I don't. The girls at school don't like playing with me." She said, saddened. Bursts of anger shot through me, she was such a sweet girl.

"They say I'm weird because I remember everything. I have photograph memory? Mommy told me that I do, and that I'm special. You're also special." She said, now happy.

"Dom. My name is Dom. And I'll be your friend." I said, quietly. The flight attendant said we were landing in around 5 minutes, Rosella looking alarmed.

"Rose who did you come with?" I asked quietly. Her eyes widened as she looked at me in panic.

"Uh, well y-you see the thing i-is-" She stuttered quickly, I looked at her amused.

"Rose, did you come here alone? Why are you on the plane alone? Does your family know?" I asked, as we landed. People started to get up and move when her eyes started getting glossy. Her bottom lip wobbled as she attempted to speak.

"It's okay Rose, come with me and my mum and we'll notify your parents okay?" I said, smiling holding her hand. I never liked it when people touched me, but I felt like I had a connection with this little girl. She smiled gratefully.

"Rose do you know your mums number?" I asked and she nodded excitedly.

"It's +44 07745 47395." (DISCLAIMER: THAT IS AN ENGLISH NUMBER, I DON'T KNOW HOW AMERICAN ONES WORK, I ALSO DON'T KNOW WHETHER IT IS A REAL NUMBER, I MADE IT UP. PLEASE DON't TRY TO CALL IT JUST IN CASE IT GOES TO SOMEONE LMAO!).

I took my phone out, and took my hand luggage down, got out of the plane and saw my mum waiting for me. Her eyes landed on the little girl as she frowned in disgust. I glared at her and pulled my sleeves up.

"Rose, here, type your mums number in." I handed her my phone, looking at her cautiously, if this little girl broke my phone, God help me. She typed it in quickly and gave it back to me as it rang.

"Hello?" A woman said, she had a sweet voice, and an American accent. Why did she have an English number? I also just realised, we were going from England to America, and she had an American accent. What the fuck? Did she leave from England

"Hi, is this Rosella's mother?" I said emotionlessly. She gasped and, hiccuped? It sounded like hiccups?

"Ma'am? Are you okay? She's with me at the airport, in America. Why is she here by herself, with all due respect ma'am she isn't with anyone, and she is such a sweet girl, something back could have happened to her." I said, annoyance lacing my tone.

"Thank you so much, you're such a sweet girl. I'll be at the airport in around 30 minutes, I don't live too far. I'll explain when I get there." She said nicely, in a comforting way.

"I'll wait with here. Thanks." I said, cutting the call.

My mum looked at me weirdly.

"We need to leave now." She said, as I shook my head.

"I'm not leaving Rosella. You go, I'll find my way." I said, nodded towards the exit of the airport.

The glared at me then shrugged her shoulders.

"Suit yourself, our house is in New York, I'll text you the address." I nodded and she grabbed her bags and left. I looked at Rosella and crouched down to her height. She was a tiny girl, and being 5'10 didn't make it any better.

"You hungry kid?" I asked, while she nodded her head excitedly. There was a McDonald's right across us. I held her hand as she followed behind me.

We stood in the queue as she told me what she wanted.

"Chicken nuggets and fries please!" She asked. It was weird not calling chips fries. Chips was what we called it back in England. Luckily, I had already transferred my money from pounds to dollars. I wanted a Big Mac. It was our turn, and she told the waiter our order, I payed and found us a booth to sit in.

"Rose how old are you?" I asked. She held up 6 fingers.

"What about you Dom?" She asked as our food came.

"I'm 18. Do you live here? What were you doing on the plane?" I asked.

"I live here, and I wanted to go on an adventure, no one wanted to come with me so I went by myself." I frowned, while she looked down and fiddled with her food.

"Rosella look at me. You're not allowed to go out by yourself kid okay? There are a lot of bad people in the world. Not all people are nice." I leaned back. "Anything could happen to you when you're by yourself kid. Make sure it doesn't happen again. I don't wanna come back to the airport and see a little Rosella going on an adventure by herself. If you really want to go on an adventure, ask your mum to call me. I'll come kid." I finished, cracking a crooked grin as she leaped over the table and hugged me.

"I promise I'll never do that again, and I'll always tell mommy where I'm going. Only if we go on adventures together." She stated cheekily.

Time flew as we were talking about her school, there was a boy called Mason in her kindergarten. They're best friends. She blushed when she spoke about him, which made me laugh. My phone started blaring, as I saw Rosella's mothers number on the screen.

"Hello? I'm outside, please bring Rosella." She asked kindly. I hummed in response and walked out with Rose.

We walked all the way out, and saw a woman, not looking a day over 25, standing with two buff guys. Bodyguards? Their postures were stiff, and looked around her as if there was threat. They came in a black SUV which also confirmed my suspicion. What the fuck? Why did she have bodyguards?

"MOMMY!" Rosella screamed, letting go of my hand that I didn't know she was holding and ran towards her mother. I walked behind her, pulling my sleeves down. I smiled a small smile, as she came towards me and hugged me.

"Thank you so much, she goes off like that sometimes, claiming she wants to go on adventures." I nodded at her quietly, and pursed my lips.

"I told her if she ever wants to go on adventures, you can call me. Do that please? I don't want her to wander by herself." I said lowly. She smiled at me, while the two buff men stood in front of the protectively. I could easily take them down.

I had put in a pocket knife in my boot earlier, just in case anything happens. My guns weren't with me, I'd have to buy new ones here.

"How can I repay you? Also, my name is Rebecca. Thank you darling. Are you here on holiday?" She asked, probably because me accent was different. I shook my head and opened my mouth to speak.

"Moved from England forever." I said, as Rose tugged on my arm.

"Mommy can Dom come to dinner with us? Please?! She's my only friend!" She said enthusiastically, her mum nodding her head in agreement.

"Ah I'd have to get going, sorry. My mother would be waiting." She flinched when I said 'mother'. I eyed her guards as they said something briefly between them. Her eyes glanced towards my hands, studying the tattoos, and my ring. I shoved them in my pockets, making her look back up at me.

"Nonsense! Please come along, it's the least I could do!"

"Please Dom! Please! Please!" Rosella chanted. I eventually gave in, and got into the black SUV they had, and noticed there was one in front, and one behind. We got into the car, as Rosella sat with me and her mother across us. I remembered we used to travel like this when my dad was around. One day he just packed up and left. He left me his necklace, and a letter. Anyways,

"What's your name sweetie?" She asked, smiling gracefully.

"Dom." I said quietly.

"Why so many cars? One in front, one at the back. Two bodyguards here too. Is everything alright?" I said lowly, leaning back into the chair. She seemed to fidget nervously.

"Safety precautions darling. Anyways, the maids would have whipped something nice up." I nodded but said nothing.

"I'm sorry mommy. I wont go off again like that, I promise." Rose said quietly. Her mother looked at her with wide eyes.

"It's okay sweetie, just please don't do it again. You know daddy gets angry and scared when that happens okay?" Rosella nodded.

Soon we pulled up to a massive mansion, like it was MASSIVE.

We got out the car, and I noticed there was armed men everywhere, talking in Italian. I was half Italian, and could speak, read and write in the language. I walked behind them, not so closely when Rosella tugged on my hand.

"Come on! I want to show you my room!" She said, clapping.

"É il capo indietro? Ad ogni modo, cosa sta ancora con i Russi?" (Is the boss back? Anyways, what's he still doing with the Russians?)

The Russians? Boss? What type of business did they run?

I slowly walked into the house, and through the gates to see one of the metal detectors.

Shit.

My knife.

I walked through it hoping it wouldn't go off, but luck wasn't on my side.

In a flash, men came charging at me as I craned my neck, smirking slightly. They didn't have guns. I stood still as Rebecca suddenly shouted, "Arresto!" (Halt).

I looked at her weirdly, as the sirens shut off and the men backed away. She eye me suspiciously.

"Where's the metal? Rosella go upstairs. Now." The tone she used had no space for arguments.

I pulled out the knife from my boot and flicked it open. It was a butterfly knife, my favourite. It was sharp, fast and fun. I twirled it between my fingers.

"Dom why do you have a knife." I shrugged.

"Safety precautions. Stuff happened in England with me, ever since then I carried it with me everywhere. I'd never use it unless I have to, hence not pulling it out." I said lowly as she nodded, and her eyes softened. She told the men to go back to what they were doing.

"Sorry about that." She chuckled nervously as I shrugged again.

Rosella came back downstairs as we ate dinner. There was a lot of people around the table, as I walked in. Around 19 pairs of eyes were trained on me, immediately guns were pulled out pointing towards my head.

I didn't flinch, I had been in this situation before.

I cocked my head and sagged my shoulders.

"Metti gíu quelle armi ora prima che ti schiaffeggi tutti." (Put those weapons down before I slap all of you!)

Instantly, they were down as they looked at me suspiciously. I shoved my hands in my pockets.

"Rosella, Dom, come sit. Eat." I sat next to Rosella and Rebecca.

I waited for the questions to fly at me as I took a deep breath in and out.

three

One minute he was running his mouth on his celly to me,An hour later he can just about speak,We addicted to diamonds,We ain't scared of no sirens.

I sat down, and glanced at everyone. There was 19 of them, 10 men, 5 women, 2 teenagers and 2 kids. My eyes ran over all of them as I took in each feature of their faces. The kids were around 10 years old, twins, boys. The women were young looking, they had either brown or blonde hair. The men, were most definitely handsome.

"Excuse me Rebecca, where is the toilet?" I asked politely, but quietly.

"I'll show you!" Rosella exclaimed as Rebecca smiled and nodded. As I got up, a boy, barely a man, he looked 18, slapped my butt. I immediately gripped his wrist, flipped him over and dug my knee into his stomach.

"Touch me like that again, I'll break every bone in your body without breaking a sweat. Actually, scratch that, touch anyone like that again, I'll rip your shoulders out of your sockets and break your wrists simply because that slap was lousy too." I said, sharp as a knife. He gaped at me, as did everyone else, as I followed Rosella upstairs. We walked through a massive corridor, until we reached a white door, half way down.

"Here it is! This is the guest restroom, none of us are allowed to use it." She said, opening the door for me. I smiled and walked inside, but not before turning around and telling her to wait for me. She nodded and stood perfectly.

I locked the door and immediately looked in the mirror. My black hair was pulled into a slick ponytail. The scar above my cheekbone had somehow become so prominent. My dull eyes glazed over my jumper as I shook out of the stance I was in. I threw some cold water onto my face as I took a deep breath.

Suddenly gunshots went off as I opened the door immediately, pulling a scared Rosella in.

"Rosella, listen to me, I'm gonna leave you here, and I want you to lock the door and not open it for anyone. Not even me, unless I say the password. The password is 'cupcakes.' When I say cupcakes you can open the door, only to me okay, remember my voice." More gunshots went off as I studied the door, it had a bulletproof clear glass on it. I looked underneath the toilet to see a gun there, I quickly grabbed it and shoved it in my pocket as the gunshots got louder and closer.

"Rosella, stay here, don't move, sit in the corner okay." I kissed her forehead as she nodded, and did what I told her to do.

I slipped out, making sure to lock the door behind my with my pin just in case Rose didn't. I pulled out my knife and slowly walked downstairs.

"Dov'e Rosella e Dom?" (Where's Rosella and Dom?) Rebecca's panicked voice thundered throughout my ears. More gunshots went off as I crept downstairs to see a man, that actually looked Russian. He turned around and looked at me like a piece of meat. Windows were shattered and blood was on the carpets.

"I'm Dom, nice to meet you." He walked towards me, suddenly glaring.

"Don't get smart little girl." He sneered.

"I'm 18." I said, tilting my head. He growled as I saw Rebecca run towards us.

His eyes suddenly lit up, as if he had found something out.

"You're not Don Dom are you?" He asked slyly. I clenched my jaw and put my hand in my pocket.

I held up my hand, signalling not to come any closer, and that I've got this. It was two fingers below my waist, only the Mafia clans knew what it meant. Luckily, this Russian didn't understand. She looked at me with wide eyes, trying to figure me out.

He walked towards me, taking his gun out.

"Since I'm going to kill you, I might as well tell you anyway. Yep, it's me, Don Dom and I am a girl." I smiled, sarcastically.

"You're a girl, what's the most you can do? Shouldn't you be in the kitchen cooking or something? Don't get mixed into stuff you don't understand. And you? You are Don Dom? Don't play yourself little gorl." He said, as if he was talking to a five year old. His accent came through THICK, it was like I was talking to the guy from those Minion movies.

(Lil' bit of gory stuff).

I whipped my knife out and threw it directly at his eye, his hands flew up and dropped the gun as he moaned in pain. I kicked the gun towards Rebecca as she turned around.

"You dumb bitch!" He glowered, getting up again.

"You know, I don't like that way you walk. I'm going to break both of your ankles." I said, smiling again. The blood poured out of his eyes, his hands now covered in blood. I kicked his left ankle as hard as I could, then taking my knife out of his eye and stabbing it directly in his ankle. He screamed out in pain as great pleasure was given to me while him being in pain. I loved hearing the cries of people that thought they were better than everyone else. I took my knife out, stabbed his shoulder, took the gun out and shot his right ankle twice. I was built for this, I was born into the Mafia. My father told me in the letter.

"Yo-you cr-crazy b-b-itch. You r-really are D-Don Do-Dom." He wheezed as I pointed my gun to his heart.

"Last words?" I questions, raising my eyebrow.

"He'll get to you before he gets to any of these Italian bastards. He'll kill you first, without a doubt." He said, not stuttering at all. I payed no heed to what he said, and shot him right in the centre of his heart.

It suddenly quietened down, blood was everywhere, Rebecca was shaking, 19 pairs of eyes were gone and there was only 13 staring back at me.

(Gory shit over).

"Get this cleaned up." I said, hoisting Rebecca upstairs with me.

I got to the bathroom and saw that it was shot a couple of times, but nothing went in.

"Cupcakes." I said, when Rose opened the door quickly and flung herself onto me. There was blood all over me, as I pushed her away softly towards her mum.

"I'll be leaving. Call me, I'd like to have a word with you tomorrow Rebecca." I said, heading out the door. I left the gun there, and shoved my knife back into my pocket.

I called a taxi home, when around 8 SUV's pulled up as I pulled my hoodie up, hearing a mixture of swearing. I dashed towards the end of the road, and called up a taxi, to take me home. Mother texted me the address. I bet she was sleeping.

I got to the address, and it was a big house, not as big as Rosella's though.

I walked in quietly, looking around. It was still empty, and I looked at the clock.

46 minutes past 10. Was I at their house for that long? I decided to explore the house tomorrow. Our luggage was already in the middle of the main room as I got out the one with all my clothes in it, and pulled out a plain tee and some shorts. I waddled to the bathroom taking in my appearance again.

Blood over my jumper, my boots covered in muck, my hair messy, my face sunken.

I sighed and hopped into the shower and cleansed myself, thinking about everything. I also washed my knife.

It was obviously that these guys were in the Mafia, no doubt. But what did that Russian mean about someone getting to me first?

I got out of the shower, put my jumper and all of the clothes I was wearing into a black bag and chucked it outside into the bin. I slipped on my shorts and plain tee and walked towards one of the doors. Pushing it open I saw my mother lying in the middle of the bed sleeping softly, her slow snores echoing around the empty room. I closed the door quietly and leaned against the wall. There was a flight of stairs, leading towards the top. I climbed up them, and noticed there was a switch, and flicked it open.

I saw a loft, an attic room, decorated entirely, fairylights up, bed made everything.

That was weird, why hadn't the people who lived her before us taken their stuff. I switched off the light and went back downstairs to the main room and sat on the couch, thinking about everything that had happened today.

Of course, they would want answers, but so do I.

I let sleep over take me as a whirlwind of thoughts had created a tornado in my mind.

four

See I just came to relax one time, They be saying young neighbour how you act so fine? She be sweating when it's backshot time, Told her baby slow down, take your time.

A few weeks had passed since the shootout, and I hadn't come into contact with Rosella or her mother, and it was time for me to start school. The house was now organised, my room done up, everything was where it was supposed to be. Our house looked like a home. My car was also shipped from England. It was illegal but hey, who cares. The one upside about American schools, is that you didn't have to wear uniform. Having arms and legs filled with tattoos, didn't look great with plaid skirts and white t-shirts.

Anyways, it was silly o'clock in the morning.

I groaned as I rolled over and stop my alarm clock from blaring in my ears. It was 6:00AM, school started at 8:00AM. I shut it off, lay back down and blew out a breath. I rolled over all the way, and fell on the floor, flat on my face. I groaned at got up and contemplated whether I really wanted to go to school or not. I immediately grabbed my phone, and connected it to my Beats pill, and put on Butterflies by AJ Tracey and Not3s. (English rappers, listen to the song it's fucking bomb). I swayed to the music and made my way to the bathroom and took a quick shower. I finished quickly, and wrapped a towel around myself and stepped out, letting the cook breeze hit my body as small shivers electrocuted me.

I waltzed over to my wardrobe, the song finished and Trill by Dappy started playing. I bobbed me head to the beat, pulling out black and yellow checkered Vans, my leather jacket, a yellow shirt, and black ripped jeans. I threw them on and headed towards my makeup table. I hadn't put my jacket on yet, because I needed to brush my hair out and dry it. I did that and it turned into a curly mess. I slicked my hair back, and put it into a low pony tail. I pulled out my clear mascara, and applied that, and also applied mint flavoured lip balm to my lips. I smacked my lips and put on some hoops, my lion pinky ring on too. I got my butterfly knife and shoved it into my sock, and pulled my jean trouser down and my socks up.

I adjusted it, put my leather jacket on too. I spritzed some Victoria's Secret spray on and headed out the room. It was now around 7:15, and it took half an hour to get to school. I didn't leave my room before grabbing my backpack I had packed the night before, my headphones and my phone.

My mother was already awake, preparing breakfast. She had made eggs and toast, with a few fruits on the side. I gobbled that up as I thanked her and left. My car was already parked outside, it was a black Golf GTI, MK5 with gold rims. I adored my baby.

I squealed in happiness as I saw my keys hanging from the key holder. I grabbed them and headed out the door.

I sat in my car, feeling the leather seats. I inhaled and smiled as started it, hearing the engine roar to life. I set off, not before blasting Playing for Keeps by ASCO & Fredo. (English rappers).

My GPS was on, so I made my way to school. As soon as I pulled in, eyes were dead set on my car, my music still blaring. I shut the music off, smirked to myself and parked right in the centre of the parking lot.

I got out of the car, adjusted my leather jacket and pulling my sleeves up, my tattoos on display. I walked straight through the doors, people already whispering.

A saw a petite looking girl standing near her locker, her red hair bouncing up and down as she laughed. There was a few more girls and boys with her, their eyes trained on me.

"Mind showing me where the reception is?" I asked lowly, low enough for only her to hear.

'Ew, she looks like a freak.'

'I heard she murdered someone.'

'Didn't she go juvie?'

'She's hot.'

'I would tap that.'

'She parked in Dane Donatti's parking space. She has a death wish.'

I chuckled at the last one, the girl with red hair staring up at me.

I raised my eyebrow at her as she apologised and showed me the way.

"I'm Willow, welcome to Markwell High, where you wont survive a day without someone from the higher class harassing you." She said as I chuckled quietly.

"I'm Dom." I said.

"Where you from? You have an accent?" She asked. I shrugged my shoulders.

We reached the reception, the receptionist looking at me up and down.

"This isn't juvie kid. It's a high school." She popped her bubblegum, fury spreading throughout of me within an instant.

"I know, that's why I'm here. To learn. Give me my schedule." I said lowly, her eyes widening. She glared at me and muttered stuff underneath her breath.

"Jesus Christ, didn't your father teach you any manners? With all those tattoos, I'd be surprised if you even had a fathe-" I immediately cut her off, slapping my hands on the table, an echo spreading through the corridors.

"If you don't give me my fucking schedule right now, I'll pull all of your teeth out because I don't like the way you talk, lady. The name's Dom Romero. " I said deadly quiet as she nodded frantically. Everyone stared at me, I could feel their eyes on my back. Willow looked at me scared as I cracked a crooked grin at her.

"I have maths first with Mr Henderson. Mind showing me were T14 is?" I said as she nodded her head. I walked with her side by side, until she dropped me off at the door. I thanked her and pushed the door open. Immediately eyes were on me, again.

The girls looked at me weirdly, and the boys looked at me as if I was a piece of meat.

"Ah, new student. Domenica?" The teacher said. He looked as if he was in his early 20's, with blonde hair and blue eyes.

"Dom." I said, looking towards the seat next to the window right at the back of the class.

"Mind introducing yourself?" He said, as I shook my head a no. I walked all the way to the back of the class, their eyes moving in sync with every step I took.

I sat down, leaned back and zoned out.

Around halfway through the class, the door slammed open to reveal a hot boy coming in with a boyish grin on his face.

"Sorry I'm late sir, I got a little caught up." He said, winking at the barbies in the front.

Mr Henderson shrugged and gestured to a seat. He took a look around, when his eyes landed on me. I could see he was trying to figure me out, but I put on a poker face. We had a staring contest, until he broke his gaze and smiled. I nodded at him and he sat down.

The class finished, and I headed out the door.

I found my way to the cafeteria as I bought an apple juice and sat down on a table that was far from everyone. From the corner of my eye, I saw some blonde barbies walk up to me.

"Hi, I'm Christie. You are?" A girl said with a nazzaly voice. I looked her up and down, her blonde hair out, 5'6 with heels, slim, blue eyes, had lip fillers. I carried on drinking my apple juice, ignoring her as she scoffed.

"Hello? Juvie girl?" She said as I squeezed my bottle hard. I wasn't from juvie, hell, I'd never been to juvie before.

I looked at her and raised my eyebrows.

"Piss off." I said lowly, low enough for her to hear it. She gasped and a fire blazed in her eyes.

"Listen here juvie, I run this school. You don't get to come in and be the centre of attention all of a sudden. Who did you murder? That's why you got sent to juvie right?" She sneered as the whole of the cafeteria quietened down.

I sighed and groaned in my head.

"I did murder someone. She looked quite like you." I said, standing up to my full height. She cowered a tiny bit. "She had blonde hair, and blue eyes like you. I gauged her eyes out and ripped her hair out and dunked her head into pigs blood. Move out of my way before I do the same to you. You wouldn't want to be my next victim would you Christie?" I asked, looking at her amused. She shook her head rapidly as I stopped in front of her, and leaned down to her ear.

"Scram." I whispered, Christie letting out a shriek with her two dolls. My body shook with laughter as she ran out of the cafeteria.

I walked out the exit towards the parking lot.

I saw a bunch of guys leaning against my car, looking at it weirdly.

There was one guy that stood out though.

Black hair, blue eyes. Strong build, tall, definitely taller than me.

Black shirt, hugging his muscles, a girl hanging off of his arm.

I walked up to them slowly, not having a care in the world, because I didn't.

"Mind getting off of my car?" I said sarcastically, clenching my fists.

They all looked at me for a minute, then bursted out laughing.

I grew impatient as they still leaned against my car, the black hair blue eyes guy staring at me with cold eyes.

"Get the fuck off of my car before I break your nose." I grounded out, gritting my teeth. Instantly, their eyes darkened.

Note to self: they don't seem to like rude behaviour.

The guy with the girl hanging off his arm got off of my car as he took an intimidating step towards me.

I raised my eyebrow at him. I was unfazed, was this supposed to scare me?

His fists clenched and unclenched as he stared at me.

"Staring is rude." I said quietly, as they looked at me in disbelief.

"Does this girl have a death wish?" One boy said. He was black, very handsome.

"I don't know do you? You're still leaning on my car my guy, get off." I said shoving him out of the way. He stumbled back as he laughed humourlessly.

I stepped towards my car as the blue eyes boy gripped my arm, hard. I looked at his hand, then at his face, ripping my arm out of his grasp.

I looked at his stance, he wanted to hit me.

"Hit me then. What are you waiting for?" I said, as his eyes darkened even more.

"We don't hit girls." One boy said with distaste. He had blonde hair and green eyes, looked like a right fuck boy.

"Funny, I was going to say the same thing to you." I replied, some of the boys stiffling their laughter.

The blue eyes dude had aimed to grip me up again when I stopped him.

"Touch me, and I'll punch you." I said, as he chuckled. He touched me anyways.

I shrugged.

"You asked for it."

I punched him square in the face, with all my might.

"If a girl tells you not to touch her, you don't touch her. It's logic." I sneered, glaring at the rest of them.

'Oh my God! She punched Dane Donatti! THE NEW GIRL PUNCHED DANE DONATTI!' Someone screamed as people gathered.

It was only first lesson too, and I already punched someone.

"You know what, this was all so unnecessary. I didn't even need to use my car, all I wanted was for you to get off. But you didn't. Sorry for punching you dude." I said, patting him on the back, and walking back into the school building. Immediately I was pulled aside by Willow.

"DO YOU EVEN KNOW WHO YOU JUST SUCKER PUNCHED? THAT WAS DANE DONATTI! THE MAFIA DON! WHAT ARE YOU DOING DOM, YOU CAN'T JUST COME AND, AND RANDOMLY PUNCH SOMEONE! Oh my Lord, you officially got yourself tied in with the devil." She rambled as I laughed.

"Relax, I ain't scared of him. I don't care who he is. I asked them to get off of my car, they didn't and I punched him. He deserved it." The bell rang as people dispersed.

My school day went about pretty uninteresting and boring, until I got an unexpected call in last period.

five

Momma, I'm so sorry I'm not sober anymore,Daddy please forgive me for the drinks spilled on the floor,To the ones who never left me,We've been down this road before.I'm so sorry, I'm not sober anymore.

Last period I had art, and I enjoyed art. The teacher, Miss Moreno, didn't make me introduce myself, she simply told me to find a seat and I was grateful for that. We were doing free hand painting, and I just let the music and my hand paint whatever I was going to.

Half way through the lesson, I got a call.

It was from a private number, I didn't trust those.

The ring rang throughout the whole class, all of their heads whipped towards me, I glared back at all of them which made the teacher chuckle.

I picked it up, and waited for the other side to speak, when you get these calls, you don't speak first.

I was about to shut it off when Rosella's small voice came through.

"Dom?" She said softly, as if she was whispering.

"Rosella? Are you okay? What phone are you calling from?" I said as I heard her steady breathing.

"Can we go on an adventure? I'm bored at home. Mommy is out and so is Dee Dee." She said as I chuckled at the nickname.

"Who's Dee Dee Rose?" I muttered as she squealed.

"Why are you squealing? Is someone with you?" I questioned as the squeals died down. Muffled laughter was what I heard as I sighed.

"No! I'm all by myself?" She said, with a questioning tone.

"Rosella, don't lie to me. Who are you with?" I said sternly.

"No one!" Her tone was higher which meant she was lying.

"Rosella I'm at school, are you safe?" I said, running a hand down my face. Who knew this fucking kid was such hard work.

"I'm safe, I promise." She said brightly.

"Okay Rose. I'm going to go now." I said as she sighed unhappily.

"Okay, bye Dom! Come round today, I want to show you my room! I never showed you when you came, and also, you can meet Dee Dee!" I assumed Dee Dee was a sister.

I chuckled lightly and nodded, even though she couldn't see me.

"I'll be there." I promised. She laughed and cut off the call.

I sighed and leaned back into the desk, laughing quietly. How did she even private the numbers? Who the fuck is Dee Dee?

It was soon the end of the lesson, and the boy from before that came in late stopped me.

"Hello new girl." He said, grinning at me. I nodded at him and attempted to go outside.

Keyword: attempted.

He stopped me, by standing in front of me, no doubt he was taller, but not as tall as that sexy hunk I punched - wait, why am I even thinking about him. YUCK.

"Hey wait! I'm just saying hello. I'm Luca. And you are?" He pressured, waiting for my answer.

"Not interested. Bye." I said, ducking underneath his arms and walking out towards my car.

As I headed towards it, the same guy was leaning against it, the guys nose crooked. My body shook with laughter as I took in his appearance, he still looked hot as fuck even with that. I sighed as he watched my walk to my car as if he was a predator and I was his prey.

"Move please. This is getting tiring. I don't have time for this, I have a play date with a little girl later, I don't need this right now." I said, heading towards the driver seat door. He stopped me by standing in front of me too.

"That wasn't very nice, when you punched me piccolo. (Little one)." He said, his voice husky. His voice was laced with a thick Italian accent, which was a fucking turn on. It took all of my might not to stare at his plump lips as he spoke. He towered over me, he was around 6'5, and I was 5'10. That was gap, he also called me piccolo, did I look small to this fucking wasteman? (Wasteman is slang in England, use Urban Dictionary if you need).

"Well if you and your boy toys had moved, I wouldn't have needed to punch you." stronzo. (Asshole). I muttered as his eyes darkened. I whispered stronzo, he couldn't know that I spoke Italian. Luckily, he didn't hear it.

"That's disrespectful, and I don't tolerate disrespect. Maybe I'll have to teach you a lesson, hm bambino?" He said leaning towards my ear.

"You know what, I'm down for that. I'm probably going to fail maths since the grades from here and England are different. When are you free to give me lessons? What was your name again? Demarius? OR was it Darius? No wait, Dane wasn't it? Dane right? Some boys were talking about how you're all chat, no action." I tilted my head at him. "I'm starting to think that they're somewhat right." I finished, grinning cynically.

"Stay away from me Dane." I sneered, getting into my car and starting it up. I quickly pulled out of the parking lot, driving recklessly out of the school grounds.

I blew out a breath and pulled a cigarette out. I lit it up, and took a long drag.

I knew that he was going to be bad news for me, that wasn't hard to accept. I had to do some research on him. I pulled out my phone, and dialled a number I hadn't dialled in 5 years.

It rang once.

Twice.

Three times.

"Who's this?" His voice came through. I sighed in content, listening to him breath.

"Long time no see Axel." I muttered as he gasped.

"No way? Don Dom? Is it really you?" He said in disbelief. I chuckled.

"Yes it's me. I need your help." I told him.

"Sure thing, what do you need? It's cool, call me after 5 fucking years, no hello, no bye, no how are you Axel, how was your life the 5 years I was gone. Sure I'll damn well fucking help you Domenica." He grumbled sarcastically, using my full name. I winced at my name and let him calm down.

"Hi Axel, how was your life the 5 years I was gone? I need your help." I said monotonously as he chuckled lightly.

"Still the same old girl I see." I laughed, throwing my head back.

"What do you need boss?" He said, in business mode.

"Everything you have on Dane Donatti." I said as I heard him suck in a breath.

"The Italian Mafia Don Dane?" he said.

"Yep. That's him I think." I muttered.

"Okay, I'll call you back when I get info. Hope your okay Dom. It's not the same without you here. Come visit sometime." He said softly, making my heart swell in pain.

"You know I can't." I said, pained.

"I know. I'll call you back yeah?" He said, I could imagine him nodding.

"Yeah." I said, cutting the call. I called Rebecca up and waited for her to answer.

"Rebecca? Rosella called me before saying she wanted to go on an adventure? Can I come by if that's okay with you?" I asked.

"Sure sweetie. We need to talk anyways. Come down!" She said brightly, laughing.

"I'll be there in 20 ma'am." I said as she chuckled and cut off the call.

--

Soon, I reached the Rebecca's house - no, mansion.

The guards stopped me as they asked why I was here.

"Rebecca invited me." I said lowly.

"Sorry, you're not on the list." The guard said.

"What list? You don't have jackshit in your hands." I grounded out, gripping my steering wheel, this dickhead was pissing me off.

"If you don't fucking let me through I'll find your family and electrocute them. You don't want that do you-" I looked at his tag name. "Roberto. Do you Rob?" I said deadly quiet as his eyes widened. He shook his head frantically, opening up the gates for me.

"Pleasure doing business with you." I smirked.

I drove through and parked my car in an empty space and made my way to the door.

I pressed the bell 3 times when a little Rosella opened it up for me.

"Dommy!" She squealed, jumping into my arms.

"Hey kid." I said, ruffling her hair. I put her down as I saw Rebecca float towards us.

"Hey sweetie." She said, pulling me into a hug. I stiffened at first, then letting myself relax because her hug felt motherly.

Something I hadn't felt in years.

I pulled back, smiling at her, stepping inside and shutting the door behind me.

I was greeted with the same 19 faces from before, only 6 of them were bandaged up in some places. They also cleaned up the house well.

I nodded at all of them, and all except around 5, smiled back.

3 men, and 2 women didn't smile back. I didn't care anyways, because Rosella had already pulled me up the stairs towards her room.

I made a mental note that the first floor had 6 rooms, and one bathroom. Maybe they had en suites.

She pulled me into the third door down. As soon as she opened the door, I was greeted with multi coloured everything.

It was either pink, purple, blue, green, yellow, or white or orange. It was like a splash of colour.

There was posted on the walls, fluffy rugs on the floor, a shit ton of toys.

"Welcome to my room!" She said, giving me a cheeky grin.

I sat down on the floor as she grabbed makeup and dress up clothes.

Shit.

"I'm really good at it." She beamed as I nodded uneasily.

The makeup was kiddie makeup, and was most likely going to leave a ton of spots.

"Can we only do the clothes? I'm not allowed to wear makeup or else my mother will get really angry at me." I said, pouting slightly.

She laughed and nodded.

She gave me a bright pink tutu.

"How was your day Rosella?" I asked as she got two matching tutu's.

"It was okay, I told everyone I had a new friend and they all was jealuz. The girls still don't want to play with me though." She said, a sad look clouding her face. I chuckled at his mispronunciation and took the tutu off of her. It was bright yellow.

"I can be your friend. You don't need them do you?" I asked as she shook her head a no. I grinned.

"How was yours Dommy?" She asked, pulling on a tutu over her sun dress.

I pulled the yellow one over my ripped jeans and took my jacket off, my arms exposed.

"I punched a boy in the face. He pis- sorry - annoyed me." I stumbled over words, trying not to swear in front of her.

Her eyes trailed over my arms, taking in each delicate detail.

"Your tattoos are very pretty. I love this one!" She said, pointing to the roses with thorns that were wrapped around my upper arm.

I smiled at her as she took out neon pink beaded jewellery.

"Rose, you know that day where I told you to stay in the restroom? And only open the door for me? And big bangs went off?" I said as she nodded, focused on untangling the beads.

"Does that happen quite a lot?" I asked, when she looked up at me.

"Sometimes. But normally Dee Dee is home and mommy helps me. They're the bad guys, but I stay where mommy tells me to. One time Dee

Dee got really hurt." She said, her eyes turning glossy. I pulled her into my lap, running my hands through her hair.

"It's okay. I'm here, nothing going to happen to you kid. I promise." I said smiling at her. She had a weak spot in me, and that was really fucking weird because I always stayed away from kids.

"Promise? And Dee Dee and mommy? You're going to help them too?" She looked at me in hope. Something I hadn't seen in people in a long time. Hope.

I sighed and nodded.

"I promise, Dee Dee and your mommy too kid. Who is Dee Dee anyways?" I asked, picking her up and letting her put the jewellery on me.

"My big brother. He always buys me ice cream. He's a big noob." She said evilly. I laughed, nodding.

"Bet he is kiddo." I said, putting on her jewellery. She got out crazy bright green neon fishnet hand things, and made me put them on.

"Dom! Come here please! Bring Rosella with you!" Rebecca shouted from downstairs.

Shit, I'd have to go like this. I shrugged my shoulders and braced myself.

"Come Rose." I said, holding her hand. We walked downstairs, into the same room where they ate, their eyes on me.

As soon as I stepped inside, they started laughing. Guffawing and howling with laughter.

I sent deadly glares to all of them which made them immediately shut up.

I took my phone out and told my mum that I'd be home in a few hours, she didn't reply.

"Rosella, Roman and Rainie, Tyra and Jay go into the next room and stay there. The grownups need to talk." Rebecca said, in an authoritative tone. The 2 kids and 2 teenagers took Rosella and walked into the other room, sending a tiny smile my way.

"Come, sit." Rebecca said, smiling at me.

I sat down right next to her, she was at the head of the table.

" Let's start off with introductions no?" She said, her Italian accent coming out.

f i v e • part two

This the only way we know to go,Squad up never roll alone,And we gone ride on forever,We, ride out together.Pull up right in your zone,Take over the street that's how we roll,And we gone ride on forever,We ride out,To-gether.

There was now 15 people around the table. She started from the left, the men first, then the women.

Note to self: sexism was quite alive.

10 men, 5 women.

We started from the left, going around the table, back to me.

"I'm Luigi." The first man said, was in his maybe, 40's, had a smile on his face.

"Riccardo." The next one said, he was bandaged.

"Dylan." The next one greeted. He didn't smile at me when I walked in.

"Armani." The one after Dylan said, he was good looking, looked around 21, had a scar on his neck, also was bandaged. Smiled at me. I nodded back.

"Hello, I'm Matteo." An old guy said. He smiled, wrinkles at the corner of his eyes, wearing a ruby ring.

"Alessandro, Alex and Andero." The next three were introducing them-selves quickly, a poker face on. Their hands were layed out on the table, knuckles scarred. Definitely fighters. Alessandro and Andero were the 2 more that didn't smile at me.

"I'm Pietro."

"I'm Alonzo."

The last two said. They all had Italian names, except for Dylan.

Now onto the women.

The first one started out, and introduced all of them. The first one didn't smile at me.

"I'm Anastasia, she's Francesca," pointing at one of the women, she smiled and waved at me. Seemed like a mother. "She's Andrea," She pointed at a woman with blonde hair, she seemed timid. She smiled softly. "Then there is Giorgina and Arifa." She pointed at an old woman, with a scowl on her face. I sent her a bright smile, just to piss her off. I think it was, Riccardo, who scoffed.

Arifa waved.

"Dom." I muttered, looking towards Rebecca.

Rebecca clapped her hands and started talking.

"So as you know we had a shoot out a few weeks ago. My son wasn't here, and security wasn't tight. This better not happen again, family or not.

Please be cautious, we have kids here too. They are too young to be thrown into this." She said, finished her little rant, they all nodded.

"Now, Dom. You made a move on the night, that only Mafia families know. Also, you had a knife with you, and seemed skilled in fighting, and you could also shoot a gun. You also have the tattoos of roses and thorns." She questions, with authority.

I nodded.

"The tattoo is a representative of my father. He packed up and left some years before. He was also in the Mafia, hence knowing the code language. I learnt to shoot a gun and use knives in early years of my life. My mother knows nothing. I intend to keep it that way." I said, emotionless looking at everyone.

"Well I wanted to thank you, for helping us out on the night. My son wasn't here, and luckily you had Rosella safe. I'd do anything to repay you." She stated, emotions evident in her voice.

"I'll keep that it mind. Rosella spoke about someone called, Dee Dee? Your daughter?" I asked, confused.

She howled with laughter and shook her head.

"No that's my so-" She was cut off by the slam of a door, immediately, their guns were out, pointing towards the door.

The door slammed open, when the sound of 15 guns were ready to fire.

I was still sitting down, I didn't care who it was.

"Relax it's only me." A voice said. My eyes widened at his voice.

"Shit!" I whispered, Rebecca looking at me weirdly.

"That's Dee Dee." Rebecca said, getting up and walking towards Dane.

I turned around and smiled innocently at him.

His eyes darkened.

"What the fuck is this puttana doing in here?" He roared, making everyone except me and Rebecca flinch. "Why the fuck is she wearing a tutu and this bullshit?" He said, laughing.

I smirked at him and tapped my nose.

"Do not speak to your guests like that! Mafia Don or not, I am your mother and I would like to think I installed some values in you!" Rebecca shouted as he looked away.

I stiffled my laughter as he apologized.

"If it were for Dom, God knows where Rosella or any of us would have been when those Russians came in. You were out doing God knows what while a girl we don't even know what her second name is risked her life for YOUR little sister!" Rebecca said, as I shrugged, him looking at me surprised.

Oh shit! He is Rose's brother?

Rosella Donatti? Fuck my life, why didn't I realise before?!

"Rebecca it's okay, I'd react the same way. It's fine." I said, smiling softly.

She blew out a breath and sat down.

"Now Dom, you've taken the Omerta no?" She asked as I nodded. Omerta was the code of silence for the mafias.

"I believe you are no threat to us." She said as she smiled at me.

"I'm not. I don't care what you guys do as long as it don't bother me my amigos." I said grinning. They laughed, and nodded.

"Where did you get rid of the Russians anyway?" I asked, looking at the boys with bandages.

"We sent the back to the Russians." Alessandro said nonchalantly, shrugging.

Shit then.

"Don Donatti, was is her who punched you when you called me?" Alex asked as I nodded wildly.

"He was leaning on my car. I asked him not to, he refused." I grinned as he scowled at me.

"Why's she still here?" He asked.

"Well, I'm going to get going now anyway. I'm going to say bye to Rose and grab my jacket. Thanks for having me Rebecca." I said, smiling gratefully.

"You're welcome anytime sweetie." I nodded and walked out, brushing past Dane.

"Non penso che possiamo fidarci di lei. Lei sembra cosí fiduciosa." (I don't think we can trust her. She seems too confident). The old woman said quietly. I had good hearing, but walked slowly anyways.

"Sí e occupata della Rosella. Non di interrogarmi su questa Giorgina."(She took care of Rosella, do not question me on this Giorgina). Rebecca said, making my heart swell in happiness. I smiled to myself, asking Rosella to come out and take her tutu and shit.

"Are you leaving?" Rosella said, pouting. I nodded and ruffled her hair.

"I promise, on Saturday we'll go on an adventure." I said, holding my pinky out to her.

"Promise? Can Dee Dee come?" She asked. I sighed and nodded. She squealed and jumped up and down.

"Ella, mi principessa," (My princess). "Can I talk to Dom for a second? Wait outside please? And sure, we can go on an adventure." He said, grinning at me.

Rosella nodded and skipped out the room, shutting the door behind her. I bent down to pick up my jacket, to turn around and see Dane's beautiful face, centimetres away from mine.

Lil' bit of saucy stuff

"W-what are you doing?" I stuttered as he pushed me all the way back into the wall.

"I deserve an apology il mio amore." (My love). His minty breath grazed over my cheeks, and fanned my ear. "That was rude of you, punching my in front of my friends. I hope it doesn't happen again." He said lightly, planting kisses on my neck. My oxygen supply was cut short.

Suddenly, his hand made its way to my throat, gripping it lightly.

Such a fucking turn on.

I was staring into his eyes as he spoke, but I didn't seem to hear anything he said, I was too busy staring at his fine ass.

"If you ever disrespect me again like that, I wont be so nice. You are disobedient, and I don't like people that defy me. If you insist on defying me, I'll have to punish you Domenica." His lips were now trailing down my chest, his big hands running down my arms. He nipped at my neck as I pushed him off of me, a sudden plan coming to mind.

I pushed him onto the small bed, and got on top of him. My warm breath tickled his neck, he sucked in a large amount of oxygen and blew it back out. His tanned neck was exposed to me, and I couldn't help but think how sexy he would look with my hickies all over him.

"I don't like being controlled Dane." I said seductively, trailing kisses down his neck, pressing my body on his.

"I also don't like being told what to do, unless we're in bed." I whispered in his ear. I nibbled on his ear, rubbing his abs through his tight black t-shirt. He groaned and looked straight at me.

"Lastly, you disrespected me first. You should know by now, I'm not one to be following rules darling." I said, pressing my lips to the corner of his mouth. I got off of him quickly, my hand grazing the bulge in his pants.

Saucy stuff ended

I grabbed my jacket and headed out the door. I hugged Rosella, and left him there. Bitch, that's what he gets.

He's messing with the wrong person.

I made my way home, my mother eating dinner.

I smiled at her and ran to my room, completing any bit of work I hadn't in school, then taking a shower and falling to sleep.

s i x

Love is like a rose,Flawless to the eyes,Beautiful at first,But eventually it dies

Sleep was something that didn't sit well with me.

I couldn't sleep most nights. Some nights I could, if I was extremely tired or just exhausted from living. I had a bestfriend, 5 years ago. He was great, he helped me sleep. 5 years later, here I am, sleep deprived.

It's whatever. I was currently lying in my bed, face up towards the ceiling with numerous thoughts running wild. I missed my brother, Damien. I hadn't spoken to him in a very long time, he was abroad, studying. He was 27, and was a heart surgeon, he was still studying because there was 'just so much more to learn about the human heart and body'. He lived in Hawaii, but then moved to Malaysia, to help more people. He's been gone for about 7 years. I hadn't seen him in 5. Since I left...

It was 2:12am at night, well morning, and I decided to take a stroll.

I literally just put a hoodie on, pulled on some tracksuits, socks and shoes. I settled on Nike Air Max 97's in black, and made sure my pocket knife was with me, shoved into my socks.

I jumped out of the window, grabbing my my phone and $20 as I was jumping out that was on my desk. It was a school day, but I reckon I would be back in time.

I let the smell of the night hit me with all its might, letting the wind brush through my long hair. I inhaled and exhaled as I walked down the street my house was on, and onto the Highstreet. It was the street that had all the shops on and stuff, we called it the Highstreet back in England. I hummed to Move Too Fast by Phora while zipping my hoodie up. A few cute little diners were open, but one caught my eye in particular.

It was called Macy's Retro Diner, and it looked cute and homey, so I settled on that.

I pushed the door open, to see a fair amount of people sitting down. They were either teenagers, bikers or just normal couples. There was servers rolling around on skates gracefully, giving people their foods. A few people smiled at me, in which I returned. The smell of grease had over taken my nose as I smiled to myself.

I found a secluded booth and sat down, shoving my hands into my pockets. There was menus already on the table, I grabbed one and let my eyes wander.

The Double Decker burger with some fries sounded sweet, maybe a strawberry milkshake on the side. Yep, that is so what I'm getting. My mouth watered at the food that was being given.

"Hi honey! What can I getcha?" A sweet lady said, maybe in her early 30's. She smiled at me sweetly, it was like a contagious smile. I couldn't help smile back.

"Can I get a Double Decker burger, with some fries and a strawberry milkshake please?" I said lowly.

She nodded and jotted it down.

"I'll be back with ya food in a hot second darlin'." She said, winking at me. I smiled and nodded, and waited for my food.

My eyes scanned over the diner, there were quite a bit of people. It was unusual to me because who sits in a diner at 2 in the morning? I shrugged and got up to go the the toilet.

I stepped in the toilet to see a girl on the floor, crying.

She stared at me with red puffy eyes as I raised my eyebrows at her.

"My boyfriend broke up with me. We've been together for, wait no sorry, we WERE together for 3 years. That's 1095 days wasted. He fucking cheated on me, then had the AUDACITY to tell me I was the problem? What the fuck man? I tried so fucking hard to love him, and cherish every moment with him, and that's what I got thrown back into my face. I walked in on him humping my BEST FUCKING FRIEND. MY FUCK-ING BEST FRIEND, NOT EVEN A GIRL I DIDN'T KNOW. Can you believe it was going on for 9 fucking months? 9 FUCKING MONTHS?" She roared as I winced. I took a step closer to her and hoisted her up from the floor.

"All because I didn't want to have sex with him. Just because I didn't want his penis to meet my vagina. That's why he broke up with me. He said he's a man. and they have needs. I don't fucking get it. Was I not pretty enough for him to wait for me? Am I ugly? Do I stink? 3 fucking years bro. 3 fucking years." She said, quieting down. I pulled her into a hug, she wasn't short. I felt weird hugging her, I rarely hugged anyone. She was pretty. Dark hair, tan skin, large brown eyes, like she was from Asian background.

"He sounds like a dickhead. If he couldn't wait, that means he ain't right for you. He only wanted to get into your pants. You're not ugly, and you don't stink. I- you, well you see-" I stumbled over my words as she chuckled and pulled away.

"You're not good at this stuff huh? Nice accent by the way." She said, smiling softly.

"Come eat with me. Let it out, I'll listen." I mumbled, looking away from her face.

"Thank you. I'm Maliha." She said, walking towards the toilet exit.

"Dom." I muttered, following behind her.

My food was already on the table, as she ordered for herself. I told her I'd pay for her, she refused but eventually gave in.

I didn't start eating until she got her food, in my house, well a few years ago, we'd eat when everyone was served and when my dad had sat down. It was just like a tradition. We exchanged numbers, and I learnt she goes to a college not far from the highschool.

She got the same as me, and as she started eating I did too.

"His name's Luca." She started. I had heard the name before, but can't pinpoint where.

"He's very handsome. 19 years old. He was so good to me at the start of our relationship. He treated me like a princess." She said, smiling softly, biting on a chip. Fries sorry.

I stared at her, sipping my milkshake.

"I don't know what made him do it Dom. I swear I was faithful, I curved every boy, never spoke to no one that he didn't like. I was DOWN FOR HIM. I was down for him, man." She said, her eyes turning glossy again.

"There's plenty of fish in the sea Maliha. You can't expect to be with him forever, even if you thought you would be. And you never know, he could realise his mistake and come back. Maybe? I don't know. Okay whatever, allow him, he don't deserve you." I mumbled, biting my burger as she did too.

"Tell me about you." She said, staring at my hands intently.

I shrugged. "Not much to say to be very honest. Name Dom, I'm 18, I go to this shit school and I kill people."

Her eyes widened at the last statement, she looked like she was deep in thought.

"Kill people?" She squeaked.

I nodded and cracked a crooked grin.

She laughed as did I, little did she know what I was saying was true.

We carried on chatting and eating until we were both finished. I checked my phone for the time, and it had just turned 3:30am. The total of the food came up to like 10 dollars, which was extremely cheap for such a big amount of food. I gave the nice lady the 20 dollar note and told her to keep the change. She smiled gratefully at me.

"Where do you live?" I asked Maliha as she stared at the ground.

"Just round the corner. Havelock drive." She said my eyes widening.

"I live there too. What number?" I mumbled looking across the street, at the dull lamp lights.

"31." She said looking at me.

"You?" She asked. I was going to answer when a scream erupted from a dark alleyway. No one except me was stupid enough to go see what was happening, and of course, it was a feminine scream.

I walked towards the alleyway cautiously, telling Maliha to stay back, and of course she did.

Abusive content, and gory details. Feel free to skip until it's finished :)

"Wait till I'm done with you, you filthy little slut." An old man growled while groping a girls breast. Anger instantly blew up in my as I pulled my butterfly knife out of my sock.

"Help me please! HELP!" The girl screamed as the filthy man slapped her.

His hands wandered down to her pants as she screamed pleading for help.

"No! Please stop! No!" She yelled, kicking him in the shin in the process.

"I'm going to drive my dick so deep inside of you, you'll be screaming with pleasure." He growled, gripping her hair.

"You know, my mother always told me never to touch someone unless they wanted to be touched." I muttered, his eyes snapping towards me.

"Oh another one! Let's have some fun babe." He grinned, his yellow teeth sickening me.

I chuckled and stepped forwards toward shim, my knife now in my pocket.

"Please. P-please hel-help." The girl whimpered as he kicked her side.

"Come here." I whispered seductively, he grinned and made his way towards me.

He was in front of me as I whipped my knife out and drove it into his thigh.

He screamed in agony and pain as I grinned. I pulled the knife out and dug it into his hand, watching the blood gush out of it. I ripped it out of his hands, breaking his hand bones with it and drove it into his neck, his blood spluttering all over the wall.

"If a girl doesn't want to be touched, you don't fucking touch her you disgusting filthy cunt. I'm going to cut all of your fingers off now, then I'm going to cut your tongue off for saying such filthy things. Now you are going to be screaming in pleasure." I said sarcastically, punching his jaw. I looked towards Maliha who was now turned around and shielding her eyes. The night was dark and lifeless, quiet and motionless which was easier for me.

I grabbed his left hand and bent his fingers as far as I could, hearing crunches of his bone, making me smile cynically. He screamed and withered in my grip, I punched his temple not too hard, just that he got a little drowsy.

"See now, if you left her when she asked you to, we wouldn't be in this situation."

I cut his thumbs off first, letting them drop to the floor. He looked at me in horror as all colour left his face. I then cut his ring fingers off, allowing the blood to create havoc on his face. I hummed in content, dropping his hands. I dug my knife inside his mouth, making him open it. I pulled his tongue out while tears streamed down his face, he shook his head furiously and somewhat pleaded me to leave him alone. I let him talk for just a second.

"W-who are you?" He whimpered as I smiled psychotically.

"Don Dom." I whispered, his eyes widening to the max. His eyes rolled to the back of his head as I ripped his tongue out and slashed it off with my knife, blood pouring out as I shielded my face. Luckily, after all of this not one bit of blood got on my clothes, only my hands.

Abusive content and gory stuff over :)

I let him drop to the floor, pulling my hoodie up and shielding my face from the girl.

I looked towards where Maliha was and saw her staring at me with wide eyes.

I motioned to her to come over here as she ran towards us.

"Help the girl get up and get cleaned up." I took a glance at the girl, which made my eyes widen to the max.

"What the fucking hell? Willow?" I whispered to myself as she steadied herself against the wall. Luckily she didn't see me and didn't question me either. I guess she was too shaken up.

"Maliha, I'm going to call you around 7 in the evening. I expect you to pick up and comply or else I wont be responsible for what happens to you. Am I clear?" I said emotionlessly, with my back towards her. I tilted slightly to see her nodding. I thought she would be more shaken up by all of this, yet she seemed like she had seen it before... I shrugged and brushed it off. I nodded at her and muttered a 'good' and made my way home. I shoved my blood filled hands in my pockets and walked out the alleyway, Maliha and Willow following after me. Maliha was muttering soothing words to her, she'd help her out.

I waited for them to get a taxi home, then I started walking home.

"Fucking rapist." I muttered, glaring at the ground. I sighed at myself. Was I really built for this? The mafia world was and always will be my world...but for how long before my life is taken?

A thousand thoughts danced in my mind as I kicked rocks underneath my feet, still glaring at the ground.

A loud screech of tires made me stop in my tracks, my hand flew to my pocket gripping my knife. I steadied myself and carried on walking, it had nothing to do with me, all I wanted to do was sleep. I glanced at my phone, it was 5:30 now, the sun slowly starting to come up.

I walked quickly, hoping to not get into another row. Luckily, I didn't get stopped or nothing and walked home quickly, jumping back through the window. My mother was still sleeping as I went to the toilet and took a long shower, cleaned my knife and just freshened up.

I wonder how Willow was feeling, I can't imagine what she would be going through.

I finished up my shower and got out at around 6:30.

I pulled on a black Gucci jumper, black jeans, black Louboutin sneakers with spikes on them. I pulled my hair up into a pony tail, and put on some black mascara and lipbalm.

I spritzed my normal perfume and headed downstairs, to see my mother drinking tea. I nodded at her and headed out the door. I plugged in my headphones into my phone and played Move Too Fast by Phora, again. I loved his tracks, you could relate to them so well.

Me and my mothers relationship wasn't always so hostile. Since father left, everything went downhill, and to be honest, I blame myself for it.

I reached the school gates earlier than I expected, especially since I walked.

I felt like it was going to be a long day, and boy, was I damn fucking right.

s e v e n

So I get drunk till I can't feelThe love fake, the pain realI get drunk, till I can't seeI love you, but I hate meTrying to be someone I can't beAnd I ain't been myself lately

School always was my number one hatred. Growing up, I rarely made friends. No one really spoke to me, and I didn't make the effort talking to anyone either. Everyone was either too immature or I was too mature.

I waltzed into the school, everyone's eyes on my, a recap of my first day. I thought that by now they would know that I go to the damn school. As I was walking, I couldn't help but overhear some girls conversation.

"Did you hear what happen to that old guy? It was on the news. His thumb, ring and tongue were cut off, and he was stabbed in his thigh and hand? To be honest, he deserved that. He was always a paedophile. Whenever I walked past his house, he'd be staring at me through the window. Apparently there was bloody EVERYWHERE." She said, emphasising everywhere. The other girls looked at her and nodded.

So I did the world a favour.

"Apparently the police had been looking for him too, dead or alive. I can't help but think it involved Dane Donatti and his mafia. Sheesh. They just can't keep themselves to themselves, always in everyone's business." She said, her voice raising an octave.

Now, I'm not normally one to get involved into peoples stuff, but this pissed me off.

"I find it hilarious that you're wanting someone to stay out of 'everyone's' business," I muttered lowly, quoting the everyone with my fingers. "Yet you find it hard to stay out of theirs. Tell me, would you say the same if he was here now?" I stepped towards her, making her take a step back. "N-no." She stuttered, staring at me. I raised my eyebrows at her. This bitch.

"So don't say it behind his back. As you say he's in the mafia no?" I asked looking away from her, and watching Dane stroll in with his friends. He looked so old why was he in school? Axel never got back to me on his over view. "So imagine you got on his bad side. Don't talk down on someone you don't know. I don't know him either, neither do you. Keep to YOURSELF." I snarled, walking towards my first lesson, English. I don't know why I had the sudden urge to 'protect' him from petty little girls words.

I walked into lesson, opening the door quietly, apologising for being late. I sat down near the window and stared outside, watching the dry leaves sway with the wind. Half way through the lesson, many thoughts started clouding my brain. Dane and his 'crew' was sitting on the other side, all of them staring at me intently. I felt it on the side of my head, their eyes glued to me. I put my head on the desk, and closed my eyes.

I sighed and played with my pinky finger ring. What if my life was normal?

What is normal anyway?

What if I never learned how to use a gun, or a knife, or how to hack into computers and banks and shit. What if I never killed anyone and got away with it? Jesus Christ. Tears built up in my eyes. What if father had never left us? What if me and mother had a good relationship. What if we were a fucking family again?

I clenched my jaw as I picked my head up off the desk and leaned back into the seat. I stared at my Loub's intently, acting like they were the most interesting thing in the whole world.

"Miss Romero. Miss Romero?" I heard a distant voice call. I thought it was in my head until two hands slammed down on my table.

"MISS ROMERO. I've been calling you for the past 3 minutes. Care to tell me what's so interesting about your shoes? I bet they don't cost more than 10 dollars anyway." He snarled, looking at my hands in disgust. I sighed and looked at the window. Why do these teachers dislike me because of the way I look?

"My the clothing I'm wearing now costs more than you get in over 6 months combined. Actually scratch that, my ring probably costs your house plus two more. Now, you are working here as a teacher to get money, whereas I've complete what you're talking about years back. I've done this shazam." I muttered lowly, kicking my feet up onto the desk so my red bottoms were on show. "These are red bottoms. Quite expensive if you ask me. 980 dollars in exact. Love the spikes on them, gives 'em a little kick, no?" I said sarcastically, nodding. He gaped at me and then glared at me.

"Where did you get the money from? I bet you're a drug dealer right? I bet you're father is a drug dealer too. Criminals. Look at those tattoos." He said as I nodded, smiling.

"Ask your wife, she'd know whether I'm a drug dealer or not. Bring up my father in any conversation again, I'll get rid of you and no one would notice.

Don't stray out of your lane, Harold." I sneered, grabbing my backpack and walking out. I walked out to the back of the school, putting my head in my hands.

I had just realised Willow hadn't come into school.

I waited for break to come, walking back into school to see where Willow's friends were.

I saw a mop of blonde and black hair, she was with Willow yesterday.

I tapped her shoulder, making her twirl round with wide eyes.

"Where's Willow?" I muttered, looking straight above her head. She shrugged and looked away. She was lying.

"What happened to her?" I asked softly. I knew, but I know she knew too.

Her eyes turned glossy.

"Bathrooms." She whispered, she lead the way and I followed.

She sat down on a stall, the door open while I sat on the sinks. There were a few younger kids, but it didn't take long for them to look at me then dash.

"Willow came home around 4 or something yesterday in the morning. She called me a-and she was a mess. She couldn't speak properly and there was a girl with her called M-maliha? I think it was Maliha. She said t-that Willow nearly got ra-" She stumbled over her words, choking back a sob.

"Is she at her house now?" I asked quietly, she nodded.

"Okay. She'll be fine don't worry. Do you know who the guy was?" I asked, she nodded her head a yes.

"He was on the news. Gregory Howl or something, he's a fucking pedo." She grunted as I smiled.

"I know. We should get going." I jumped off the sink as she wiped her tears.

"You're not too bad. I never thought you were bad anyway, people just have fun making shit up." She muttered. I cracked a grin.

"Name's Ocean." She said, smiling directly at me. I took the time to notice she had light freckles, and jittered a lot. She also had a nicotine patch on her arm, her sleeve lifted involuntarily when she wiped her tears. She had a nose piercing like me, and a few on her ears. Her hair wasn't natural, I think it was naturally blonde.

"Dom. Nice name." I muttered, walking behind her. I saw Dane and Luca was it strolling, talking to each other angrily. Like not a fight angry, like they were friends disagreeing on something. Next lesson was PE and I hated playing sports with the wrong people. You also had a PE kit in this school. Me and Ocean had PE together which was an upside, I wasn't alone, and I preferred her over anyone else.

We both pulled on our kits, that were way too tight. My ass cheeks were hanging out of my shorts, so I exchanged them for track bottoms, I left the top on because I didn't have a spare. The top squished my breasts together, and it really didn't help that I was DD cup.

I sighed and wiggled in the shirt, however, most of the girls seemed fine with it. I shook my head and grumbled profanities as Ocean laughed at.

"Shuddup." I mumbled, my speech muffled since I was looking down.

She stiffled a laugh as I couldn't help but crack a grin. I rarely laughed anyway.

We headed out the changing rooms where the boys had also come out. What pissed me off is that Dane and his amigos had nearly all their lessons with me.

PE went past as a blur until that little queen bitch lobbed a ball at Ocean's face, calling her a freak. I rushed by Ocean as she waved it off saying she's fine, but it was evident that it was going to bruise.

"Ocean I'll take you to the medical office. Come on." I muttered, gripping her arm as the teacher said nothing. I left her there with a cool nurse and came back. The game was restarted and I joined my team. Dane and his friends were on mine too, but we rarely made any contact unless it was "Throw it harder!" or "Catch the fucking ball Romero!". I picked up a ball and launched it directly at her stomach, making her stumble and fall back into her minions.

The whole class roared with laughter.

Even the coach had to cover up his laugh with a cough.

"My f-friends aren't freaks." I mumbled lowly, stuttering at friends. The game ended and she was in tears and I was happy with myself.

School day was over and I was at home, chilling. Me and mother spoke a little bit, she spoke about her job and just life really.

It was nice sitting down with my mother, I felt like a huge weight had been lifted from my shoulders. Then I remembered I had to call Maliha and see how Willow was.

e i g h t

Drinking everyday just to escape the memories of us,You paint me as a villain, but my blood is on your brush,I was in it till the end, you was in it for the rush,See I'm scared of being hurt, and I'm scared of getting closeBecause the closest people to you are the ones that hurt you most.

Watching the clock hit 7 in the evening, I picked up my phone ready to dial Maliha's number. Axel had gotten back to me and told me about Dane, the funny thing was, I hadn't even listened to a word he said. I was s engrossed with staring at the leaves falling from the tree across my house. In that time I had also had asked him for Maliha's number. I also had asked him for Willow's address.

My fingers hovered over the call app as I clicked it and typed the number in. It was on a private number call because I hadn't known what she would do with it.

"Hello?" A timid voice came through. I heard her breathing and slight shuffling over the phone.

"Forget everything that happened on that day. I'd much rather have you alive and well. You also didn't seem so...affected by all of it. Like you had seen it before. Tell me Maliha, have you seen it before?" I grunted as stiffled breaths came through.

"I was caught off guard. And I wont breathe a word about it, plus you were doing the right thing." She mumbled as I thought about it.

"Cool. Grab a tea with me sometime, will you?" I asked not being sarcastic at all. She guffawed and tried catching her breath.

"Shit you re- oh shit my throat." She said, laughing. We exchanged good-bye's as I left my phone on my bed and headed downstairs. I sat down on the kitchen stool, at the bar like table. My mother was still at work as I put some pasta for myself, from what I had made earlier.

I chewed on it slowly, making a mental plan to warm up a plate for my mother when she got back. As I was eating, my mind went back to Dane.

He was so devilishly handsome. Honestly, have never seen someone so... good looking. My throat got dry as indecent thoughts of him clouded my eyes, I laughed at myself.

I was still a virgin.

It's whatever, I cleaned out my plate, made some warm for my mother and left her a little note.

There was a soft, steady breeze outside. I let it hit my face as I played with my ring. Small cries of laughter came from the park across where I was. I saw a tiny face pop out of the little tube like slide, when I recognised who it was.

Of course, it was Rose.

"DOMMY!" She yelled, running across the park towards me. There was a road between us, so I quickly crossed so she didn't need to run across the road. She ran as fast as she could, her arms open wide, her innocent eyes twinkling. She jumped into my arms as I picked her up and twirled her around. At times like this, I felt like I had no care in the world, and to be frank, I loved it.

I laughed as hard as she did, squealing too. I set her down and saw her face twinkling. I loved this kid.

"Who you with kid?" I asked as she pointed to a familiar, muscular back.

"Oh." I mumbled, looking away. I felt blood rush to em cheeks which was really fucking weird because I never ever blushed. As if he knew I was staring at his back, her turned around, and looked me deep in my eye. He smiled, like fucking smiled. HE DIDN'T SMIRK. HE SMILED. LADIES AND GENTLEMEN, he smiled.

I smiled back, letting my dimples show, a show of surprise washed over his face.

"Dommy. You like Dee Dee don't you?" Rosella asked me cheekily.

"What? M-me? No- what. Not him I don't like Da-" I spluttered as an amused voice cut me off.

"You don't like who tesoro?" (Treasure). I coughed loudly and excused myself.

"I need to go! Bye!" I exclaimed rushing off. His deep husky laughter was echoing throughout the street, it was so melodic. He made me feel so fucking confused. I never got nervous, I never blushed and I've known this man a few weeks and he already has me doing exactly that. I DON'T EVEN KNOW HIM THAT WELL! God, what is happening to me?

I reached Willow's house quickly.

I knocked on the door thrice, softly, a small petite woman who had her red hair smiled and me sweetly.

"You alright dear?" She said, still smiling. But it didn't reach her eyes.

"Hi ma'am. Is Willow home? I er, I'm one of her f-friends." I stuttered, she looked at me with wide eyes. My hands were in my pocket.

"Friend? Oh dear! She never brings no friends home! She should have told me I would have whipped up a dinner or something! I'm sorry darling come in! I made a fresh batch of stoopwaffels too just now." She rambled as I smiled softly. I loved stroopwaffels. They were Dutch and simply the best thing ever.

"It's okay ma'am, my visit was unexpected." I mumbled, stepping into the house, the smell of caramel hitting me.

"Ma'am? None of that dear. I'm Pricilla. Are you visiting her dear? Your accent." She said, pulling me into the living room.

"No ma- sorry, Pricilla, I live here now." I said, shortly. She nodded. She wanted to ask more, but she didn't pry, which I was grateful for.

"Willow is upstairs dear. First door on your left." She said, piling the cookies onto a plate. I nodded and headed up the stairs, making no noise.

I knocked thrice again, before I heard her delicate, but now scratchy voice saying 'come in'.

"Oh my word, you look like shit." I muttered, looking at her in disbelief. The mop of red hair was everywhere, her eyes were sunken and her nose red. She looked so...void of life. I looked at her eyes and they were too so fucking lifeless. Anger blew up inside me as I recalled the night of her sexual harassment. I should have slit his neck. I composed myself and sat down on her bed next to her.

"Thank you." She said sarcastically, cracking a smile.

"What happened Willow?" I muttered, as she looked out of it. She looked so dazed, as if she had no clue what was going on. Her bottom lip wobbled as tears fell from her eyes like waterfalls. She leaned into my side, and I put my arm around her letting her cry. This was unusual for me, but I allowed it.

She sobbed for a good hour, while I just muttered soothing words to her, stroking her hair.

"I got you now. No one's going to hurt you Willow." I mumbled. I loved her as a sister, and I don't even know her that well.

"He t-touched me everywhere Dom. Everywhere. He didn't actually, did …it. But it was still..I feel so dirty Dom. So fucking dirty." She trailed off hiding her face into her hands. My heart ached for her.

"It's okay Willow. He got what he deserved no? Don't cry about it. You're a strong, independent girl, and you will get through this, and I'll do everything to help you I swear. Just saying, I trust you now, if you fuck me over it wont be so nice. And I swear on my life, nothing's going to happen to you again. Nothing like this, I promise. And I don't break my promises." I said strongly, she nodded and smiled. It was a sad smile.

"None of my friends came to see me. Only you. And you, you're fucking new. You don't even know my second fucking name. I don't have any friends anymore. I only have you and trust me, I wont ever go against you or nothing." She mumbled, through sobs. I held my hands open wide as she got up and wobbled over to me and hugged me tight.

"You're going to get a prince charming and he's going to sweep you off your feet. How old are you by the way?" I asked. She pulled back and blushed.

"I'm actually 21. I stayed back the years, I couldn't complete them after my dad passed away." She said looking at the ground.

"HELL NO? 21? Girl you don't look a day over 16, what?!" I gaped as she laughed and blushed again.

"Shut up you weirdo." She giggled as I let out a full on laugh.

"You should laugh more Dom." She said, sighing.

"I got nothing to laugh at Wills." I said looking out her window.

We spoke about life, and had stroopwaffels. I stayed with her overnight and we literally had a full on slumber party. It felt nice doing something that was 'normal'. I felt great, and it was even better with her here with me. She was officially my bestfriend, she couldn't back out even if she wanted to.

nine

- -

And I still don't know how I feel about it,And I still don't know but I feel like I'm learning,How to catch my breath when all I'm breathing for is you.I used to wonder what love is,But ever since you've been around,Finally think I have it figure out,But I missed it,I see now.I found out.I know now.

Waking up in Willow's bedroom with half my body off of the bed and half on, while she was a tangled mess wasn't what I wanted for a Friday. I'll admit, yesterday was the day I had smiled, laughed, be saddened the most ever since dad left us. I asked my mom to drive my car here and she did surprisingly.

"Willow. Willow get up. We ain't going school though." I said, shaking her as she said five more minutes five minutes ago.

"Willow if you don't get your ass up on God I'm getting water." I growled as she shot up.

"Up! I'm up, dang woman you fuckin' crazy or what?" She groaned taking the blanket off her feet. "SHIT! I need to text Ocean, she was the only that asked me how I was." She muttered sadly.

"Rise and shine sunshine! We're going shoppin' and having a shit load of fun. Can't be arsed to go to school either." I shrieked, fist pumping the air.

"This is the Dom I love. But what the fuck is can't be arsed?" She said, testing it out on her tongue.

"I can't be bothered." I chuckled at her 'ohh' face. My phone pinged as I looked at who sent me a message, it was on Imessage.

Unknown: Hello.Me: Who's this?Unknown: You know who I amMe: If I knew who you were would I have asked who you are? Idiot.Unknown: Watch your mouth tesoro.

Tesoro? That was Italian. Treasure. Who spoke Italian that had my number?

Me: How did you get my number? Unknown: Sources.Me: Mysterious. I gotta go now, my friend is waiting for me, chat to you later mate! Unknown: Who's with you Domenica?

I gasped at this. Who the fuck knew my full name?

Me: Stop texting me, don't make this into something worse. Fuck off.U nknown: Rillasare. (Relax). God women are so uptight.Me: You're sexist now too?

"DOM! WHO ARE YOU TEXTING? I'VE BEEN CALLING YOU FOR A HOT SECOND NOW!" Willow fumed as she stared at my head. I shrugged, showing her the phone screen.

Unknown: No, never sexist. I was bought into this world by a woman, relax.Me: Okay, bye.Unknown: See you soon, piccolo. (Little one).

I put my phone down and glared at it, curse the media! SHIT! I HADN'T CALLED XENIA AT ALL, and as for what she said about bestfriends I'm sure she's going to welcome Willow with open arms.

"We going shopping, gonna get you a whole wardrobe, then we gonna munch then we're going to go to my house, then we're going to the gym so I can teach you how to defend yourself. Plan?" I asked, looking at her with my eyebrows raised. She nodded.

"Thank you for that day. I know you saved me. I don't know what I'd do if you weren't there. Thank you man." My eyes widened at her statement.

"How'd you know it was me?" I muttered as she smiled.

"Your shoes. No one in our school wears the shoes you do, you Brit." I chuckled.

"I'd like to keep it on a down low about what happened. Seriously if this gets out I'll get rid of you and no one will notice that you're gone." I deadpanned as she nodded frantically.

I slapped my hands on my thighs and got up.

"Right!"

"Get changed. We gotta goes." I shrieked running downstairs.

Pricilla was at the stove cooking breakfast as I smiled at her, and greeted her.

"Mornin' ma'am." I mock saluted as she laughed.

"Sleep well?" She asked while flipping over a pancake.

"I sure did." I grinned, I actually did. That was the first bit of sleep I had got in a long time.

Thuds were heard when we saw Willow groaning rolling on the floor, holding her knees.

"Jesus fucking Christ, goddamn it!" She groaned as I howled with laughter.

"Don't use the lords name in vain Willow!" Pricilla glared as I stiffled my laughter

I helped her off the floor, still laughing. She whacked my arm as I winced, she had a hard ass hit.

"Come eat girls." Pricilla's mum said as we both sat down.

We made small talk and ate nicely. There was pancakes, waffles, tea, coffee, fruits, eggs, sausages and so much more just for three people.

"So where's your dad?" I asked, while chewing on some waffle.

They instantly stiffened at the same time as Pricilla looked away.

"He, er, he died. Few years back. Cancer." Willow mumbled as Pricilla's eyes got glossy.

"Damn, I'm sorry for asking, also sorry for your loss." I said looking at my food.

"It's fine honey. We knew it was going to happen. Eat up!" Pricilla smiled as I nodded. We finished eating and cleared up as we went back up to Willow's room. I looked at the clock and it had just turned 1pm.

She changed into a jumper and jogger.

"Hell to the no. Hell no. Turn your ass right back round. I'm gonna get an outfit for you." I said, as she threw a tantrum.

"No I can't be arsed!" She yelled as I giggled.

"Shut up, move." I pushed her towards her wardrobe and pulled out some clothes.

She had a leather jacket which was good, I pulled out some forest green Vans, a forest green turtleneck top, and black ripped jeans. I shoved them into her chest.

"Go." I motioned towards the door as she grumble. I went to her jewellery box and pulled out a cute necklace with a green stone in it, and a few rings and a chain. She came out as I gave her a once over, she looked pretty. I told her to put the jewellery on as she sat down so I could do her makeup.

I put eyeliner, highlight, mascara, a nude-pink lippy, and waterliner, that would suit her red hair. She looked smokin'. I pulled her hair down and straightened the mop of curls on her head as she totally looked new. To my surprise, she had a nose pierce and put it in.

"Wow. Thanks, I looked hot!"

"Girl you look BAD." I snickered as I adjusted my jacket and grabbed my bag as did she.

We went outside, bade Willow's mum a good bye and got into my car.

"This car is so bad ass gosh." She said, mesmorised. I smiled and nodded. We reached the mall in no time and headed towards the good brands. Our parents were both very loaded, and we did have quite a bit of money on us. We visted Gucci, Prada, Versace and loads more. I helped Willow look for clothes that I would wear, we'd be matching! I never did this with anyone except Xenia, so it was was awkward at first, but later on it got better. We got a shit load of clothes, and new makeup and shoes and so much more. I got these cute rounded sunglasses and so did Willow. We took silly ass pictures too.

We finally sat down in the food court and ordered some food.

"You feelin' okay?" I asked Willow, sipping on my strawberry milkshake.

"Still a little shaken up, but okay cause you're with me." She said, smiling gratefully.

"Did he...?" I trailed off. She shook her head.

"He just harassed my boob. Luckily nothing else happened. I'll get over it." She mumbled.

"It's not about getting over it Willow. We'll all help you, you didn't deserve that. Why the fuck was you out at that time anyway?" I asked as she shrugged.

"Needed air." She said munching on a fry. I nodded, understanding where she came from.

We spoke and chilled for a bit, then we headed home. She got her gym stuff out and we headed towards my house so I could get my stuff.

I felt bad for her, I knew she was hurt be she acted like she wasn't.

She was 21 but that didn't make her feel less. I wish I was there before, as soon as he even looked at her.

I hoped she healed in time.

NOTE: If you are going through any type of abuse, don't hesitate to contact local help lines, or talk to anyone, even me. We're here to help. Yes, I'm young but I'll do everything I can to help people. Coming from a background of help with mental health, I know how hard it is to try and talk to people about your 'problems'. But please, don't hesitate to message me, or call a helpline. Helplines are there to HELP you, girl or boy, part of the LGBTQ or not, trans or not. Help for ANYONE. Young or old. Please put those to use. There are people that care about you, no matter how much you think there isn't one person that cares. I promise, there is. Stay happy, and safe my pookies. I love y'all. -S x.

t e n

- -

I've been tryna do my best,In the worst way,But it all comes back to love.But it all comes back to love.

We reached my house in no time, singing along to the lyrics of Russ. My mother's car was in the driveway, meaning she was home. I knocked 3 times, and she came and opened the door with a smile. I smiled timidly.

"Hello mother." I mumbled, passing through.

"Hi Domenica. Who's your friend?" I winced at my full name when I glared at Willow to introduce herself.

"Hi I'm Willow." Willow said shyly. My mother smiled, invited her in and asked whether she wanted anything to eat, she politely declined as I dragged up to my room.

"Welcome to my room." I declared, entering my humble abode.

"Wow." She gaped at the walls, at my paintings and drawings hanging everywhere. Her eyes skimmed over my music corner, my guitars and piano, then my dreamcatchers and my closet, the posters of cars and bikes on the walls.

"Damn. I thought you room would be way more.." She trailed off. "Darker?" I finished for her as she nodded.

"Draw me sometime." She beamed smiling at me. I chuckled and nodded.

I got out some gym gear for the both of us, we were roughly the same size. She was maybe smaller around the chest area, and the same in the waist. I shoved it all in a bag and told her to follow me.

"Mother we're going to the gym. We'll be back before," I glanced at my phone, "9 latest. Bye." I said, sauntering through the living room.

"Okay honey, stay safe the both of you." My mother said, narrowing her eyes at me. My heart thudded in my chest, but still kept on a 'i-don't-care' facade on.

I jumped into my car, Willow on the passenger seat.

"Wait, I need to FaceTime someone." I mumbled, pulling out my phone and clicking on Xenia's contact.

I let it ring until she picked up.

"DOMENICA!" She shrieked as Willow winced.

"WHERE THE FUCK. Holy shmoly girl how are you? I miss you so much." She said quietening down.

"I'm fine, you?" I asked smiling.

"I'm okay. Just bored. Schools shit. Miss you." She grumbled, making me laugh.

"Miss you too X. I'll come visit you before you know it, fuck that come visit us!" I exclaimed.

"Made any friends?" She asked. I grinned and nodded.

"She's with me now actually. Say hello to our new bestfriend Willow." I grinned and shoved the phone into Willows hands. She looked at me with pleading eyes for me to not give her the phone.

"Don't worry Wills. She wont bite. Hard." I snickered as she glared at me.

"Hi Xenia, I'm Willow." She gave her a nervous smile and Xenia laughed.

"I accept her Dom. I love your hair, the red suits you." Xenia said gleefully. Wills smiled showing her pearly whites and complimented her back.

"WE GOTTA GET GOING BYE X SEE YOU SOON BITCH." I shouted and told Willow to shut it off. She did I and zoomed off to a local gym I had googled when I came here. I parked up and stood outside of it, sizing it up with my eyes.

Santobello Gym.

"Feel like it's going to be penis infested." Willow mumbled as I nodded.

I walked in the gym, testosterone and sweat slapping us both in the face. I walked up to the reception and asked the guy to make us memberships.

"Excuse me." I said, he was still on his phone. He looked around 16.

"Hello." I said again.

"If I have to ask him to listen one more time, he's getting punched." I mumbled to Willow. Her eyes widened and she tried stopping me.

I shot my arm through the little hole and gripped his shirt, jerking him towards the glass that seperated us, making him alarmed.

"I called you twice while you were on your fucking phone. Why are you sitting here if you're not here to help you little shit?" I growled as her muttered frantic sorry's.

"Sorry miss! My family is a tiny bit of a crisis, that was why I was so focused on my phone." He mumbled softly. I didn't care! His job was here, he could deal with family later. I was about to give him a piece of my mind when Willow stopped me.

"It's okay. Can we have the memeberships please darling?" Willow said, smiling, the boy gazed at her.

"Y-yes. What are y-your names?" He stuttered and blushed. I scoffed at him and walked towards the girls changing rooms. A few minutes later, Willow showed up with two cards, grinning at me.

"Sometimes being nice works Dom." She said sarcastically.

"Nice can be shoved where the sun don't fucking shine." I mumbled, taking clothes out of my gym bag.

I pulled out some basketball shorts and t shirts for the both of us. We both changed and put our hair up. I took my ring off, and shoved it in a little pocket I had made in my leather jacket.

We walked out to the gym space, walking directly towards the secluded place where the boxing mats and bags were.

"Right." I muttered, everyones eyes on us.

"Do you know how to punch?" I asked as she shrugged.

Suddenly, a fist came flying towards my face as I quickly dodged it.

"Give me a fucking heads up before you do that you prick." I grumbled making her laugh.

"Okay, I'm going to teach you how to wrap your hands. We'll start out slow, on the punching bags and speedbags then move higher and higher.

Capisce?" She nodded and I quickly ran back into the changing rooms to get the wraps I had picked up before.

My back was suddenly slammed into the wall as I came face to face with Luca.

"What the fuck are you doing you absolute crackhead?" I grumbled, shoving him off me.

"Just wanted to say hi!" He grinned and slung an arm over me.

"Fuck off. This is the girls changing room by the way." I said, grabbing the wraps.

"Stay away from me. Bye." I muttered and made my way towards Willow talking to some sketchy looking guy. He was built well, most definitely handsome.

"Mind introducing me to your friend?" I said keeping a poker face on.

"Yeah sorry, he's not my friend. Armani this is Dom. Dom this is Armani." She said looking between the both of us.

"Pleasure to meet you, Dom. I'm Armani Rodriguez." He said. He had this...aura around him. He was definitely not good. He had this crazy, evil glint in his eyes that I'll admit, made me uncomfortable. His green orbs studied me as I nodded curtly at him.

"I'll be leaving now. Pleasure meeting you, Willow, and Dom." He said somewhat sarcastically.

Willow chirped a bye as I stared at him.

"What did he want?" I muttered wrapping my hands up, then doing hers.

"Not sure. He asked me who you were." She mumbled. Why would he want to know who I was? Weird. Need Axel again.

"Whatever, lets start."

I taught her some easy punches and kicks until she was really worn out. It was fun but she did get tired quickly. We got changed, and headed home quickly, it was around 8:45pm. I dropped Willow off, she thanked me and left for my house.

I took a shower and freshened up, I had a few miss calls from someone but I was way too tired to notice. I hit the bed and knocked out fully.

I slept quickly, surprisingly. And it felt nice.

e l e v e n

Needing it all we be playing for keeps, No changing for money we'll stay in the streets,I'm sinning while my mummy's praying for me,Don't hide how you feel pussy say it to me

Dreams are something that I don't like, good or bad. Bad, because well, they're bad, and good because it gives me hopeless amounts of hope that something good would actually happen. Guess who I dreamt about though. Of course, it was Dane. We were at the carnival, he got me candyfloss then the whole place got shot up. Love it.

It was now Monday, meaning school. The weekend went by quickly, me and mother just had a catchup, nothing serious.

I got out a red t shirt and blue ripped jeans, with of course, my leather jacket and red checkered Vans. I had already showered and all, I just slipped on my clothes and applied the same makeup I do everyday. I decided to do my hair half up half down, leaving them in their curls.

I was picking Willow up today. I ran downstairs grabbing an apple and a bottle of apple juice, thanking my mother and skipped out to my car.

I was in a good mood, literally skipped.

I revved the car and zoomed off, putting music on.

I reached Willow's house quickly, she was waiting outside for me. She hopped in and I zoomed to school.

We walked in, everyone looking at us in disgust. Did I forget to mention Willow had dressed like me today, so did Ocean but she lived near the school. I saw Ocean out of the corner of my eye, she grinned at my and raced towards us.

"What is going on my people?!" She shrieked into our ears.

"Girl shout like that again and I'll rip your tongue out." I grumbled as she stuck her tongue out at me. She was wearing a leather jacket, so was I, so was Wills. We were like the three Musketeers, girls version. We all had AP maths first, so we made our way there.

Maths was so fucking boring, so I decided to spice it up a little. Dane and his groupie were sitting behind us, but we payed no attention to them.

"Ocean, are you a parking ticket, cause you got fine written all over you." I said, winking.

"Hell yeah I'm a parking ticket. Willow are you from Tennessee? Cause you're the only ten I see." Ocean whispered in Willow's ear making her cough violently. I snickered quietly, watching my maths teacher glare at the three of us.

"Ahem, Dom, can you take me to the doctors? Cause I think I broke my leg falling for you, baby." She said, winking. I bursted out laughing, clutching my stomach, the oxygen in me leaving.

"Miss Romero! Care to explain what's so funny?" He said, glaring at me. I smirked and shook my head no.

"I'm not asking you, I'm telling you." He said, narrowing his eyes at me. I shrugged and said nothing, but still grinned cynically.

"Hey piccolo,I lost my phone number, can I have yours?" (Little one). His breath fanned my ear, making me shiver in delight. I stiffled my laughter but it didn't work.

I laughed so hard, I wheezed and started coughing violently. Everyone looked at me in disbelief, but I was still laughing.

"Damn she has a sexy laugh." Dane groaned behind me. Immediately I stopped laughing, when I saw the teachers face red and bothered.

"Get. Out." He said calmly, making everyones eyes widen.

"GET OUT! GET OUT RIGHT NOW YOU DISRESPECTFUL LIT-TLE GIRL." He yelled as I howled with laughter.

"Dom what are you playing at, get out!" Wills shrieked next to me.

"No." I said between laughs.

"NO?" She questions as if he life depended on it. I shook my head.

"I can't be bothered. The laughing made me tired." I let out a breath to emphasis my statement.

A cute boy was sitting next me between the rows, he gave me a flirty smile as I winked back.

"Sorry sir, I'll take her. She doesn't know how to act sometimes." Dane's velvety voice cut through my ears.

"Thank you Mr D-donatti." The teacher stuttered. Dane gripped my fore-arm and dragged me outside.

"Why are you dragging me?" I asked tiredly, inspecting my nails. He pushed me into the janitors closet, cliché. I laughed mentally, knowing I was about to get some good good. Know what I'm saying? Wink wink?

He glowered at me, his eyes seemed darker than usual. His body posture was stiff and tense which made me furrow my eyebrows in confusion.

"What was that back there? With that boy? Are you guys dating?" He said with disgust, pushing me up against the wall.

"No we aren't why do you care if we were?" I asked, raising my eyebrow.

"You're mine, and mine only. No other guy, man, boy, hell even girl, is allowed to look or touch you unless it's me. You're all mine. Il mio." (Mine). His breathing became heavier, his dark hair fell over his eyes, his muscles flexed as he moved. My eyes dropped from his and down to his lips.

"Do I sense some jealousy?" I teased as he nodded without hesitation.

"I'm a possessive man, darling." He muttered, looking me in the eye.

Fuck it.

I grabbed the back of his neck, pushing it down softly towards my face as I entangled my lips with his. He immediately started kissing me back, our lips fought for dominance but he won. The kiss was filled with passion and lust, and love. Honestly, it was love, from him though, not me. I just wanted a kiss.

He pulled away and panted, "Jump princess." And I did. He trailed kisses down my jaw to my neck, making me bite back a moan. I met his lips again and tangled my fingers in his soft hair, the smell of axe and cigarettes consumed me as I moaned in bliss. He put me back down and his hands travelled down, gripping my butt making me moan, again.

"Dane." I mumbled, pulling away. He smashed his lips back to mine, biting my low lip ever so softly. I let out a hearty moan, immediately blushing red at what noise I had just made.

"If I can get you to moan like this for me just by kissing you, imagine how you're going to be moaning while my dick is bruising your cervix babygirl." He said huskily, his deep, rough voice clouding my senses. I kissed him with just as much passion, licking his bottom lip for entry, which of course he denied. He pulled away and rested his forehead against mine.

"As good as that was, we have a lesson to go to." I said, hearing the corridors filled with chatter. My cheeks were burning red, and I couldn't help but look at anything but his face. He chuckled while gripping my chin with his fingers, making me look at him.

"You're so cute when you're shy. Mi amore." He mumbled pressing a soft kiss to my forehead. How could he have called me his love so quickly? Weird.

"This isn't finished cupcake." He growled, snapping back into reality. He began kissing me aggressively again, then pulled away after one more kiss. He walked out the janitors closet, making me touch my lips. My lips still tingled from the kiss, and I sure as hell wasn't getting over it either.

It was my first kiss, and boy was it fucking great.

The door suddenly slammed open, making me immediately remove my hands from my lips.

"We're going on a date at 7. Come to my house. Dress fancy." He said, staring into my soul. I smiled and blushed. I walked out, leaving him behind.

"Out the closet with Dane Donatti hm?" Willow and Ocean teased me as I flipped them off.

For the first time in a long time, I could say I was happy. I hope my mother was happy too. I hoped my dad was happy too, where ever he was.

He said he left us for our safety, but I think that was utter bullshit.

He was my father nonetheless, and I didn't not love him.

I loved him, I sure did. I just wish he was here again, with me, my brother and mother. Then we'd all be happy.

I couldn't suppress the feeling of happiness and excitement in me, making my stomach swirl with butterflies.

I hope this doesn't turn out badly.

But somewhere deep down, I knew there wasn't going to be a happy ending to this night.

twelve

You don't understand,how much you really mean to me,I need you in my life, you're my necessity, But believe me you're everything that makes my worldComplete.

Silk and velvet gowns were my favourite. It was currently 6 in the evening, and Willow was me, helping me to get ready for my date with Mr Donatti.

I had picked out my gown, it was a velvet blue gown, by Jovani. There was a V cut between my breast, and a split at the bottom, showing off my legs. It was simple, with gold embellishements around the waist and neck. I paired it with gold heels and blue and gold eye makeup, and a gold clutch.

"Hurry up! He'll be here in no time! I need to do your hair, you idiot." She shrieked, sitting me down on the chair.

"Straight or curly?" She asked.

"Is crimped an option?" I asked, monotonously.

"HELL NO. Are you mad?" She asked incredulously as I chuckled.

"Straight then." I said. My hair was curly anyway, so why not. She got to work, burning me a couple of times. After half an hour of severe yanking, pulling, swearing and even tears, I was finally done.

I looked in the mirror, staring at my arms. They were covered, but the tattoos on my hands and legs were out.

I smiled at myself when I glanced at the clock.

"FUCKING HELL!" It was 6:55 and I was panicking. Why was I panicking? I was Don Dom, I knew what I was doing...right?

I took deep breaths in and out to normalise my breathing, rubbing my sweaty palms on my dress. I spritzed on some perfume and make my way down the stairs, just as the doorbell rang.

"He's here!" Willow said with excitement. I smiled softly.

"Hey Willow, is Domenica read-" I stepped out from the stairs and his jaw dropped.

Literally.

"Damn." I heard him whispered.

"You look so...beautiful. So gorgeous." I blushed hard at this, I had ever really only gotten 'sexy' and 'hot' or 'bangable.'

"Thank you. You cleaned up pretty well to." I mumbled, looking at his suit. His suit hugged his muscles tightly, a few buttons open near his chest. His black hair was messy, but styled. He had a gold watch on and his phone was in his hands.

"Shall we?" He said, holding out an arm. I forgot my knife and gun! Shit.

"Wait, I need to get something quickly." I walked back upstairs quickly, grabbing my gun and putting it in the strap around my thigh, my dress covering it. I put my knife in my bra and straightened myself out.

I walked back down, Willow smiling at me.

"Take care, be safe, and don't do anything that isn't safe. And for God's sake, come back unharmed." She said seriously. "Suck his dick bitch love you." She shrieked, shoving me outside, slamming the door behind me.

I glared at the door, facing back towards an amused Dane.

"Suck my dick? I wouldn't mind that." He smirked.

"Whatever." I grumbled, taking a seat in his black Rolls Royce.

"So it wasn't a no?" He said, gleefully.

I smiled seductively, and held up a finger, motioning for him to come closer.

He did, and I took hold of his jaw and brang his ears to my lips.

I kissed it softly.

"I will bite your little dick off you cunt." I growled, pushing him back away from me, huffing looking out the window.

He let on a full blown laugh escape his mouth, making me twitch my my mouth into a smile.

"You really are something Domenica." He said lowly, looking out the window.

"Maybe I am." I mumbled, leaning back into the seat.

We soon reached the restaurant, and to say it was for rich people was the least. It was crowded by men in suits and women in beautiful ballgowns. The car stopped and Dane got out quickly and jogged round to my side. He opened the door for me and held out a hand.

"Mia signora." (My lady). He said, staring at me. I took his hand, and he helped me out of the car.

"Well chivalry isn't as dead as I thought it was Mr Donatti." I mused.

"Only for you, Miss Romero. Soon to be Miss.." He said, saying the last part quietly. I didn't catch it fully. I shrugged it off and let on a smiled.

We walked into the restaurant, light classical music playing. The interior was gold and white, massive beautiful chandeliers hanging from the ceiling. It was called ' Il Palazzo Delgi Angeli' -'The Angels Palace', and the name definitely suits. It was - not so surprisingly, - an Italian restaurant.

"Wow." I gaped, looking at the paintings that were on the side.

My favourite one was by Claud Monét, The Artist's Garden at Giverny. It had the most delicate, softest details, and had my favourite colours in it. He painted it in the 1900's, an oil painting in Paris.

A hand against my lower back pulled me out of my thoughts, just as I was about to turn around and punch who ever touched me's face.

"It's only me bambina." (Baby). Dane muttered, pulling my into the inside room.

"Sorry, caught me off guard." I mumbled as he smiled. He pulled me into a booth, I sat across him and he sat across me.

"What do you want?" He asked me. Luckily the menus were in English and Italian so it was easier for me.

"Can I get the alfredo fettuccine please, and rosé." I said sweetly, smiling.

"Sure." He said calling over a waitress. The waitress literally ignored me.

"Can I have the canelloni with chicken, and for my girlfriend, alfedo fettuc-cine." He said, not looking at her. She glared at me when he said girlfriend, and I glared at his head for saying that.

"Also, a bottle of the best rosé you have." He finished, closing the menu.

"Is that all sir?" She said, smiling a little too friendly for my liking.

For your liking? The voice in my head said. I shook it off and smiled at her.

"That would be all," I looked at her name tag, "Ella. That's all." I said sharply as she nodded slightly and left.

"It's pretty sexy seeing you all possessive and jealous." He smirked at me, leaning forwards.

"I-" My sentence was cut off by him. "I'm only here for you. I'm all yours, as you are mine." He said, softly, sitting normally.

"Why'd you call me your girlfriend?" I asked, sipping on water. "You don't even know me."I stated, putting my glass down.

"I know more than you think Domenica." He said, smiling crookedly.

t h i r t e e n

M y foolish heart, turns at the stars, All that I am, is all I let you see, You don't need nobody else, And you're putting this all on me.

"Domenica 'Don Dom' Romero, daughter of Alonzo Romero and Katerina Romero. You're favourite colour is yellow, you moved here from England for some reason, your dad left to 'protect' you. You have anger issues, but rarely get too riled up. You box, you can drive, you've crashed 5 cars, your bestfriend is Xenia, and you left a gang 5 years ago, in England. Also tell Axel that if he's going to do a background check on me, make it discreet." My heart fell, and I honestly couldn't speak. "You have an older brother, and your little sister had died when she was 8, in 2009." He finished, making my slam my glass on the table.

"I can't just allow my mother to let you into my house without no background check, it was just a safety precaution." He stated, I sighed and nodded.

He only missed out one reason.

Why I had left.

And I didn't intend on telling him either.

"That's all true. Do you know anything about my dad?" I asked, the waitress setting out food down.

"More than you know. He was involved in the mafia no? Him and my dad were best friends." I tried recalling anyone my dad was with, but they were all just blurry images.

"I also need to talk to you about something. It's pretty serious, but don't freak out just yet." His Italian accent intoxicating me.

I studied him for a minute. Like literally just stared at him.

"Is there something on my face Domenica?" He asked, raising a perfect eyebrow.

I shook my head. "Nothing." I mumbled taking a bite from my pasta.

"What's the serious thing?" I asked as he glanced at his phone, his eyes hardening. He looked around, his eyes settling on an unfamiliar couple at the booth. I then studied them, they guy had stiff posture and the woman smirked. I looked around a little more, and saw four men in suits, standing around, not looking very bodyguard like. The woman looked Russian.

"Dane. I have a bad feeling. There are four men in suits, standing weirdly and a couple a few booths away from us. Please tell me you brang a weapon, because this isn't going to go down well." I said quietly, and discreetly, sipping my rosé.

"You have a good eye. They are from the Russians. Apparently we killed one of their bosses right hand men, Viktor. Viktor Ivanovic's right hand." He stated, taking a bite of his cannelloni.

"Shit. Was he big and bulky and Russian?" I took an uneasy glance at the two, staring right back at me.

"Yes. Why?" He pondered.

"Well you see...I may or may not have accidentally inserted my knife into him." I said, shrugging my shoulders.

"He was on my list anyway, thank you." He stated, still eating.

My eyes widened.

"You're not mad?" I asked, gaping.

He shook his head a no.

Can he kiss me already? The reason that these Russians were here was because of me, and he said the guy was on his list? God.

"I can kiss you anytime actually." He stated.

I furrowed my eyebrows, did I say that out loud?

"Yes, you did." He said, grinning.

"Oh. Ha ha." I choked.

Suddenly, multiple gun shots went off, zooming right past Danes head.

"Get down!" I urged as he did.

Screams and sobs of the people in the restaurant echoed throughout the place, the deafening sound of bullets overtook it. I pulled out my gun from my thigh strap, gripping it strongly. The four men immediately came towards us, shooting, narrowly missing us.

"That's not nice is it?" I mused, shooting the guy in the forehead.

Dane shot the other two while the couple started clapping.

I shot any camera that I saw.

"Well done. You have killed my four most skilled men." The woman said, with a Russian accent.

"They weren't that skilled if you ask me. There was open space for them to shoot us straight actually." I muttered, inspecting my nails.

"Andrei! It's great to see you buddy. How you doin'?" Dane said sarcastically to the man. He wasn't ugly, he was most definitely handsome.

Not as handsome as Dane, though.

"I can finally kill you, and sleep in peace." The guy said cynically.

Dane let out a full blown laugh, slapping his knees and holding onto the barrister for support.

He wiped a fake tear.

"I guess you need to go sleep again, because you aren't killing me Andrei." Dane growled lowly.

"You killed my father, it's only even that I kill you." The woman and man said at the same time.

Me and Dane looked at eachother, trying to stiffle a laugh.

"Did you guys rehearse that? I must say, it was in sync." I guffawed.

The woman pulled out a gun, waving it in the air.

"Shut up you bitch." She sneered, as I sighed heavily.

"Shoot me already please." I said, shifting my weight onto my other leg.

"Gladly." She said, cocking her gun.

"WAIT." I shrieked, going back to my booth, gulping the rosé down.

"Can't let a good wine go to waste can I?" I said, while pulling my knife out and chucking it directly into her chest as Dane shot Andrei. Immediately, Dane's men came running in, taking care of the bodies. The woman wasn't dead yet though.

"Don Dom aren't you. He'll come for you first, don't forget that. He will come for you first." She choked out, blood splattering everywhere.

"Send him my greetings babe." I said, smiling. I pulled my knife out of her neck as her eyes rolled to the back of her head. I didn't have any blood on my dress, nor did Dane on his suit.

"All I wanted, was a simple nice dinner with my woman, and I get interrupted while eating cannelloni. FUCKING CANNELLONI." He yelled, picking up a whole ass table and chucking it at the wall.

"Hey it's okay Dane. We can do it another time." I said, holding his face in my hands, my thumb grazing his cheek.

"You might as well leave bambina. I'll never be the perfect boyfriend, husband or even friend. This happens with me everywhere, and I can't risk loosing you." He mumbled, kissing my palm.

"We're in this together. I don't care, I'm not perfect either, but I will sure as hell help you as much as I fucking can. I'm here for you Dane, don't forget that." I mumbled, pressing my lips to his softly.

He led me outside to the same Rolls Royce, but not before shouting at his men to clear everything up. We sat in the car, he intertwined out hands, kissing mine softly.

"Also, the thing I wanted to tell you was," He said, looking at me uneasily.

"Go on." I encouraged.

"Your dad signed a contract for when you turn 19, you have to marry me." He said, gripping my hand.

He what?

My dad what?

My 19th birthday...was..

"What date is it?" I asked him calmly.

"I just told you that you need to marry me and your asking me about the date?" He said, confused.

"GIVE ME THE DAMN DATE." I yelled, making him wince.

"November 30'th damn girl." He mumbled.

November 30th...my birthday was December 9th.

That means...

"9 FUCKING DAYS?" I shrieked, glaring at Dane.

"I TURN 19 IN 9 DAYS AND I HAVE TO MARRY YOU. WHAT THE FUCK?" I groaned, tears building up in my eyes.

"I'll explain everything when we get home. I promise." He said, pulling my into a hug.

He better.

Did my mother know about this?

First a shooting and now I'm going to marry a mafia don?

My life can't get any better can it?

fourteen

And it's so hard to stay afloat,When you make monsters out your thoughts,And you're chained up now,And everyone around you,Is too far away to notice.

Rain was my favourite type of weather. I loved the sound of the rain hitting the floor, the smell of rain water. I absolutely loved it. There was no doubt that from September till January was my favourite time of year. It was currently 9 in the morning, and it was definitely raining. I was just staring outside my window, watching the rain fall.

A few days had passed, Dane telling me to marry him. 3 days have passed, meaning I have 6 days left. And my father did sign a contract. It was near to Christmas as well, and well since dad left, it wasn't a big Christmas no more. I wanted my brother to come home, I wish my sister was alive and I wished my dad was still with us, and didn't sign a contract for me to get married to a mafia don. I hadn't spoken to Dane after that, he knew that this isn't what I wanted. Well it was, just not like this.

I knew eventually, it would go down, I knew that I was going to get married to Dane. But not under these circumstances. I wanted to fall in love with him naturally, I wanted to all come to me normally.

Just, normally.

I hadn't ask my mother yet. And that's what I was going to do now. I was in my pyjamas, my hair in a messy bun.

"Morning mother." I greeted her, sending her a little smile.

"Morning Domenica. Breakfast?" She asked, turning around.

"Please." I sent her a small smile.

"Come up and help me." She asked, I nodded and started getting stuff out that she needed. Eventually we finished and I had now eggs, bread and coffee with some fruit in front of me.

I ate slowly, and it was quiet. It wasn't an awkward silence.

"Mother." I said, in a soft tone.

"Yes?" She said, looking at me.

"Did father sign a contract for me to get married to Dane Donatti when I turn 19?" I asked, sipping my coffee. Her eyes immediately widened, and her head snapped towards me.

"Why?" She said, sharply.

"I have 6 days mother. Get talking." I said, coldly. The demeanour had changed, and the atmosphere had now turned intense. The soft patter of rain helped me relax and calm down.

"He did. How do you know?" She whispered, looking at the floor in guilt.

"He told me. We know each other." I said curtly, not expanding on my point.

"He said it would be for protection from bad people, just like when he left us. I tried so hard, I swear Domenica my darling, I tried so hard to convince him to let you move with your aunt and have a normal life. Have a normal childhood. I tried to convince him to let you make the decision for yourself, when you got older.

But he didn't listen. Of course he didn't. Alonzo Romero didn't listen to anyone." She said bitterly, laughing humourlessly.

"Protection from what mother? All I hear is you need protection, but from what?" I asked, still sipping on my coffee.

"Your father was in the mafia. You know that. He was head, the don. The don's daughter couldn't be harmed in anyway. Your sisters death wasn't an accident. It was a murder. And in all honesty, not because I'm a mother and I carried her for 9 months, I feel she is still around. Honestly I feel it." She said, a tear falling.

"Me too." I admitted. My little sister Diana wasn't a weak girl. Hell, she packed a good punch at her tender age.

"I don't know who's body was in the coffin that day either. I swear. How old would she be now?" She asked herself, smiling sadly.

"17." I mumbled.

"I'm sorry Domenica. I tried to stop him I really did. He told me he loved me before he left, but he chose the business over the family. I tried, and I failed as a mother. I couldn't keep him here. I'm sorry. I failed all 3 of you, you, your brother and your sister." She said, now sobbing.

I hugged her tightly, sighing sadly. I had no idea my mother felt this way. I was so absorbed in my own problems I hadn't once thought about her.

"It's fine, don't worry. What are the consequences if I don't marry Dane?" I mumbled, rubbing her back.

"Death. Once you take an oath to be part of the mafia deals, you can't go back. Death meaning me, and your brother, since we are the family of his." She muttered. Anger flared up in my as I thought back to my dad. How selfish of him, he didn't even think about this once? I'm glad he left.

"No one is going to die. I'll marry him ma." I said, using an old name I used to call her.

"No it's fine, you don't want to." She mumbled. "I need to step up and be a better mother." She said, wiping her tears.

"No mother, I don't mind. He took me out on a date yesterday. I also met his mum already." I said meekily as she jumped up from her seat.

"WHAT?!" She yelled, shaking my shoulders,

"Are you sure? He isn't pressuring you or anything is her?" She said suspiciously as I laughed,

"No ma, it's good. He told me." I said, putting our dishes in the dishwasher. She looked at me in surprise.

"I mean, if you are happy with it." She trailed off as I chuckled.

"Whens Damien coming?" I asked, cleaning the table top.

"Not sure, I miss my little boy." She said. I'm probably going to call him today and ask him to come over.

The rest of the day went by as a blur, I had invited Willow over just to chill. We watched movies, and I told her about Dane. Surprisingly I trusted her a lot. We also FaceTimed Xenia, and her babes. It was a good day, and she was planning to sleep over.

It was now night time, and me and Willow were snuggled up in front of the TV with ice cream.

"Dom I have a question." Willow said, looking at me.

"Shoot." I mumbled, taking a spoon of cookie dough ice cream.

"Why are you so...cold towards so many people? I'm sorry if it offends you, but I just wish you weren't because you're so amazing and funny, and people would love you to be their friends." She said, smiling sadly.

"Are you confessing your undying love for me?" I asked, gasping, holding a hand over my heart dramatically.

"Yes. Where for art thou Domiet?" She said, getting on her knees. I chuckled and ate more ice cream.

"I've been betrayed, used, hurt and so much more shit a ton. I find it hard to trust people because it's been broken too many times, and I'm cold towards a lot of people because I get attached easily, and eventually, they'll leave. And I know they will." I mumbled, staring at the wall.

"That is bollocks, because I ain't leaving." She said, slapping my head. She had picked up my English lingo, and it was funny when she used it.

"We'll see Wills." I said, leaning back into the sofa.

"What's your brother like?" She asked, staring at the TV. The Duff was currently playing.

"He's a fucking moronic idiotic twa-" My sentence was cut off when a few knocks on the door had startled us both. It was 11pm in the night, so who the fuck was here?

"Willow, you know how to fight now, go get me a knife from the kitchen." I said cautiously moving towards the door. She chucked it at me and I caught it with ease.

I looked through the peephole, and it was a guy.

I opened the door slowly, my jaw dropping at the sight of who was on the other side.

<h1 style="text-align:center">fifteen</h1>

We're like fire and rain, You can drive me insane, But I can't stay mad at you for anything. We're like Venus and Mars, We're like different stars, But you're the harmony to every song I sing, And I wouldn't change a thing.

Slow, unsteady breathing came from the person standing in front of me. He was covered in blood, his face scattered with little cuts, his knuckles bruised and bleeding. But that wasn't what even caught my eye. It was the fact that there was a little girl behind him, who looked a lot like Rosella, crying and whimpering.

"Come inside." I mumbled, stepping aside as he limped into the room, as I picked up Rosella, giving her a hug. I muttered soothing words in her ears as she slowly calmed down.

"Willow, do me a favour and look after Rosella. There is a bathroom through the kitchen and to your left, give her a bath. Then put her to sleep, I bet she's tired." I asked her softly, pushing Rosella over to Willow.

"Come on Rosella, let's get you cleaned up, then I'll make you my favourite hot chocolate." Willow grinned as Rosella nodded and hugged her leg. I took Dane by the hand and led him upstairs to my bedroom.

"I haven't even asked you out yet and I'm already in your room, let's slow it down I have feelings too." He rasped, smirking at me. I slapped his shoulder. He muttered an ow as I led into him into my bathroom. I told him to sit on the table as I got a bottle of vodka and a first aid kit. I pushed his thighs apart, standing in between them, close to his chest. I poured the vodka into the bowl, dipping a paper towel in it, cleaning up the cuts on his knuckles, a comfortable silence falling towards us. I moved on to his face, staring up into his eyes. His pupils dilated as he hissed in pain when I dabbed at each of the cuts.

"Sorry." I whispered, finishing up the last one. I put the paper towel down, when both of his big hands cupped my face. He leaned down and crashed his soft lips to mine, both of us moving in sync. He bit my lip, as I moaned softly in pleasure. I pulled away and stared into his eyes.

"What was that for?" I asked panting heavily, his eyes turning glossy.

"I come home with a shaken up little sister, and myself covered in bruises and cuts and you didn't even ask me what happened. You helped us both. This marriage based on a contract or not, you are the person I want to marry. No doubt." He said, resting his forehead against mine.

"Maybe I don't want to marry you. I have a boyfriend." I teased, stepping away from him.

"Yeah, you do, and I'm your boyfriend." He growled, wrapping an arm around my waist pulling my closer. His head rested on my shoulder as I rested my head against his hard chest, listening to the beating of his heart.

"What happened Dane?" I asked as he sucked in a breath.

"It was a random attack. I didn't notice the cars following us until Rosella pointed it out. I took her for ice cream, she missed my papa and had a full on tantrum." He mumbled chuckling. "We got the ice cream when one of them had the decency to threaten me in front of my little sister. We got into a fight and..yeah." He said, clenching his fists.

"Didn't you think that Rosella was there with you, and it's extremely traumatising to see that?" I said softly. His eyes clouded with guilt as he shamefully glazed at the floor.

"Just don't let it happen again Dane. Learn from your mistakes." I said, pressing my lips to his.

"I want you to come with me to a meeting tomorrow. These disgusting Spanish dons had made a sex trafficking ring with a shit ton of underage girls working for them, they've all been kidnapped. I'm going to go there, act like I want the ring then kill him. His name is Armani Rodriguez." He said, as my eyes widened.

"Wait here, don't move." I instructed as he raised a brow at me.

"You honestly question my manliness. Dominance is kinda hot on you though." He said winking as I rolled my eyes and went downstairs.

I saw Rosella snuggled up on the couch sleeping soundly as Willow sipped on hot chocolate.

"Wills come upstairs." I told her as she followed me.

"The guy we met at the gym, what was his name?" I asked, as I pulled her into the bathroom. She glanced at Dane and I.

"Armarni Rodriguez I think." She stated. "Why? Is everything okay?" She asked looking worried.

"Yes it's fine, thank you. Go sleep in the guess room or with Rosella. You must be tired, we'll be down in a second too." I said, smiling softly as she nodded her head. It was currently 1:04am.

"You know him?" Dane asked, looking a little shocked.

"I wouldn't necessarily use the term 'know'. He came up to Willow at the gym, asking about me. He had this like, this aura, a bad one too around him. Gave off really bad vibes." I said as I shuddered.

"Fuck." He whispered.

"What's wrong?" I said, pulling him out of his thoughts. He looked down at me, then back up to my eyes.

"Nothing. I'm glad I have you." He said, pulling my into his chest again. I sighed and wrapped my arms around him.

"Come, sleep here tonight. Call your mother, I'll bring my phone." I mumbled, pulling away, going into my room. I unlocked my phone and gave it to him and gave him some privacy.

"You okay Dom?" Willow asked mumbling, sleep evident in her voice, snuggled against Rosella. I nodded mutely and waited for him to come downstairs. There was no doubt he was looking through my phone, but there was literally nothing he could find. I didn't have any social media or nothing. I only had 4 contacts, Willow, Ocean, Damion and my mother. Eventually, the stairs creaked and he popped his face through the door. Willow had already fallen asleep by now. He came and sat on the other couch, leaning back into it.

"Thank you." He whispered, looking at me sincerely. It slowly turned into lust and love, he looked so good. His muscles bulged out of his vest and literally made me drool."Like what you see?" He said, smirking as I nodded my head a yes. I got up and cat walked my way over to him and straddled his lap. His hands immediately rested on my hips, with a slight grip. I kissed him slowly, my hands made their way to his curly hair, softly gripping it as our tongues fought. I grinded on his lap, pressing our areas together. Goosebumps littered my skin, as he dragged his finger up my arm. He quickly flipped us over so he was on top of me, while gazing down at me with a certain fire in his eyes. He started kissing my neck, making his way down between my breasts. He gripped and massaged my left breast, while biting lightly on the the other one. "All mine." He muttered as I sighed in bliss while playing with his hair. He caressed my skin until he got to the waistband of my booty shorts. He looked up at me for confirmation as I nodded. Butterflies erupted in my stomach as he pulled down my shorts slowly, kissing every inch of me.

My red lacy panties had come in handy today.

"Red's one of my favourite colours babygirl." He mumbled, rubbing me through the fabric. I gasped softly, the feeling making me blush. He bit the inside of my thigh, making me moan quietly. I was definitely wet as fuck. He slid my panties down, lust clouding his eyes.

"My baby is so wet for me hmm?" He said, rubbing my clit lightly, my wetness soaking his fingers. I gasped lightly and threw my head back as he carried on working his magic on me. He licked up my slit, circling my swollen nub with his wet tongue. He paced it at first, but started to move faster. "Oh fuck." I moaned as a sensation built up in my stomach. He carried on licking my sensitive spot until I felt a burst of bliss. He carried on licking until he made my legs shake, he held them down and didn't stop. Not that I wanted him to anyway.

"D-Dane, I can't take it." I gasped as he carried on. My hands gripped his hair tightly as my body shook. He gave me one last lick and pulled away, my juices all over his mouth.

"You did so well for me baby. Good girl. You taste sk sweet. All mine." He muttered as he lifted me bridal style and took me to the bathroom. He cleaned me up with gentle fingers, and himself and carried me back to the couch. It was clean, nothing got anywhere.

My eyelids started to droop. He lay down and told me to get on top of him. He was so big and tall and heavy so he literally took up all of the couch. He wrapped his strong arms around me, and kissed the top of my hair. I listened to his slow and steady heartbeat beating, and smiled to myself. He stroked my hair softly, breathing in and out. My face was pressed against his hard chest, as I kissed it lightly through the fabric of his shirt.

I was happy. I was so happy with the people I had in my life, but I knew it would eventually come to an end.

I heard a small 'goodnight Mrs Donatti' as slumber finally over took me.

sixteen

They say that I am the sick boy, Easy to miss when you don't take the risk boy, Welcome to the narcissism, We're united under our indifference.

Strong hands were wrapped around my waist as I tried moving and failed. I pried my eyes open to see Rosella staring at the TV, Willow with my mother giggling and me on top of somebody.

Shit.

"FUCK!" I yelped jumping off of Dane and to the other side of the room, banging my head in the process. I groaned and held my head in my hands as my mother and Willow laughed. Rosella giggled too.

His eyes were open, he was still lying down, grinning at me.

"I know I'm hot, relax. I don't burn that much." He said with arrogance as I narrowed my eyes as him.

Suddenly all the memories of last night came rushing back to me. My face went beet red.

"I don't burn that much." I mimicked him while he sat up and chuckled. His morning voice was a turn on, it was so husky and...nice. He got up and stretched, his shirt riding riding up as all of us averted our eyes. I coughed and made my way upstairs. I went into the bathroom, did my business and washed my face. I stared at myself for a few minutes, I don't know why. I got my tooth brush and started brushing my teeth, obviously. I spat the foam out and when I looked up through the mirror I saw Dane grinning at me.

"Jesus." I yelped, holding a hand over my heart.

"Good morning bellissimo."(Beautiful). He mumbled, kissing my shoulder. I mumbled a 'morning' and carried on brushing my teeth, handing him a new one.

"Join me for a shower?" He said, taking his shirt off.

"In your dreams darling." I said smiling, grabbing him a towel.

"We're going to the ring today. Are you sure you want to come?" He asked seriously. I nodded and smiled softly.

"I have a good, and a bad feeling about it." I mumbled, hugging him.

"Don't worry. I'll be there to protect you." He said, puffing out his chest.

"I don't need protection big boy." I mumbled, pulling away.

"I need to go home, change, and drop Rosella off. Come with me." He said, running the water.

"Yeah I'll get ready at yours, I'll bring my clothes. What time are you looking to leave?" I asked, combing my fingers through my hair.

"Five maybe?" He said, smiling. I nodded and shut the door behind me.

"Not up for that shower?" He shouted, making me blush. Luckily he wasn't there to see it.

"Shut up, you stink." I yelled back making my way downstairs. It was 2pm, and yes, we woke up at 2pm.

I saw mother cooking something up, Willow grinning at me.

"I better be your bridesmaid. Bride of honour actually." She said, sipping her tea. I flipped her off.

"You like him don't you?" My mother asked, setting a plate of waffles in front of me.

"Maybe." I mumbled through a mouth full of waffles.

"DOMMY LIKES DEE DEE? WOW! I CAN HAVE LITTLE BROTH-ERS AND SISTERS NOW!" Rosella yelled in glee as I choked on my waffles, my mother laughing and Willow howling, tapping my on the back. My violent cough died down as Dane entered the room, looking fresh.

"What was all that about?" He said with a twinkle in his eye. I glared at him and my mother set a plate of waffles down in front of him, smiling.

"It's been long Dane." My mother said smiling.

"I know Mrs Romero. You're still looking pretty as ever." He said, thanking her for the plate. She smiled and patted his shoulder.

"Still going through with the wedding?" She asked, sipping on her coffee.

He swallowed his bite of waffle and started speaking. "Yes. Even if there wasn't a contract, I'd marry your daughter anyway." He said, smiling at me. It was a genuine smile. Blood rushed to my cheeks as I looked away again.

"Thank you for letting us stay Mrs Romero." He said, finished with his waffles, he fucking ate them quickly.

"I'm gonna go home. I need to change and get studying for school. Bye guys, bye Rosella." Willow said, tapping Rosella on her nose.

"Bye." We all chimed. As she was leaving, she smirked at me and made the 'call me' hand gesture and sent me a flying kiss. I pretended to catch it and put it in my pocket as we bursted out laughing.

"We're gonna go too. Domenica is coming too." He told my mother. She nodded and told us to be safe.

He called his friend to come get them two, as I went upstairs to grab some clothes.

"Should I wear a dress or what? Formal?" I asked him, he nodded. I sighed heavily and got to me closet. I pulled out a creamy coloured strapped silk dress, floor length, which also had a slit in it. I paired it with silver heels. I put out my makeup bag and put in my foundation, eyeliner, lipstick, eye shadow pallet, contour and highlighter pallet and mascara, and setting powder. It was minimal makeup but I didn't need that much either. I shove it all into a backpack, grabbing my perfume too, and a sparkly set of earring and necklace. I raced downstairs to see one of his friends that I saw when I punched him. His name was something I forgot. I also got my gun strap and knife.

"Hi I'm Jordan." He said, grinning. Dane and Rosella were already in the car as I got in too.

"Dom." I mumbled, as he started driving. The drive wasn't too long, and we were listening to soft music. Eventually we reached at around 4, I had an hour to get ready which was okay.

We walked in the house, greeting Rebecca and the others. He took me to his room, where both of us started getting ready.

"Black or grey?" He asked, holding up two suits.

"Black." I said, taking off my clothes. I slipped on my dress, and walked over to the bathroom with my jewellery, gun strap and makeup. I put my gun in my makeup bag, it was quite big so it fit, and my knife was, of course, in my bag.

I started on my face, and applied everything I needed to. I opted with red lipstick. I put on my earrings and my necklace, and I strapped the strap to my thigh and put my gun and knife in it.

I walked back out to him fully dressed, combing his hair.

I put on my heels and spritzed some perfume on my neck and wrist.

"I'm done." I mumbled, grabbing my phone. It was now 5.

"Coming." He said, turning around. He stared at me for a hot second before smiling.

"You look beautiful." He said, wrapping an arm around my shoulders.

"Lets go." I said, chuckling.

His school friends that were leaning on my car were also there. They were all in the mafia? So was Luca. He grinned at me and waved. I nodded at him and proceeded to listen to Dane, when he round up the guys.

"Here is the plan. We secure the area, killing the guards QUIETLY." He said, giving a pointed look at Luca, to which he shrugged and winked. "Then, me, Dom, Jordan and Ali are gonna go to talk to Rodriguez. I kill him quickly, fight off anything there. Secure all the doors to the girls room, and if there is anyone there trying to take them, get rid of them. Round all the girls up, they will most probably be bare, so I got clothes for all of them, all sizes. I will not tolerate ANY disrespect towards them. They are women and deserve much more than they have, some are as young as ten, and are probably frightened. I have food stocked, clothes, water and all of that in the third van." My heart swelled with pride as I fought back a smile.

"Are we ready?" He asked, we all nodded.

"Let's get going then. Dom is in my car, the coach is coming to pick up the girls, and no girl should be harmed. Ali, Jordan and Luca ride together. Raquel, Tio and Gio ride together." He pointed at two twins and the black guy from school. He was hot. "More of my men will be there too. Let's get rolling guys." He said, clapping his hands. Everyone grabbed all their weapons as he slung an arm over my shoulder.

"Stay safe, and stay by my side." He mumbled, kissing my temple. I nodded, but knew I wasn't going to stay by his side.

seventeen

I try to tell 'em not to mess with my gang, gang, gangWe do what we gotta do and don't complain-plain-plainI'm on the road, I'm probably fresh up off the plane, plane, planeKnow you heard about me, I do my thang, thang, thang

'TRIGGER WARNING: This chapter is mainly filled with helpless girls and rape. If you don't like reading this type of writing, please skip the chapter. Love, S."

Fixing my dress, I stepped out of the car, flipping my hair. I scanned the place, there was guards everywhere. The ring looked disgusting, there was literally no air anywhere, the air was complete polluted and it stank.

"Mr Donatti! It's a pleasure." Armarni grinned, shaking his hand.

I stepped out, walking up to Dane. "Did Kai shut off the CCTV system?" I asked, leaning towards his ear. He nodded mutely and smiled at Armarni.

"Ah! Domenica, it is most definitely a pleasure too." He said, cracking a crooked grin. I smiled back, muttering a hello.

"Lets go in shall we?" He said, bringing us inside. The insides stank like alcohol and old men. There was lights everywhere, it looked like a strip club.

There was a few girls dancing on the poles, that looked so uncomfortable. I clenched my hands into fists, regulating my breathing. One girl made eye contact with me, mouthing a 'help'. It was like she knew we were coming. I smiled and mouthed a 'wait' back. I winked at her as she held a hand over her mouth, her eyes going glossy. I held a finger over my mouth, telling her to be quiet. She nodded and got back to doing what she was.

"We have over 300 girls. We also have this club front. Come, I'll take you to the girls." He said, grinning at one of the old men touching one of the girls. It was disgusting, you could see she didn't want to be touched. I gripped Dane's hand as he shot me a reassuring smile.

He led us through the back, and into a big warehouse kind of thing. All I heard were cries and wails of girls, screaming for us to help them, yet they couldn't see us. It was completely dark as he flicked on the lights.

To say I was shocked was an understatement.

There was a glass wall, and behind the wall was around 250 girls screaming, and crying. They looked so thin and malnourished. Most of them had cuts and bruises on them. They were sectioned into age groups, and my heart fell looking at the 10 year olds. A few girls were being dragged by their hair by grubby looking men as I tried keeping my anger in check. They were only in their bras and pants.

"Just sign this contract, and all of this is yours. The club, the girls, the booze. Everything." He said. "For 5 million dollars." He added, making me scoff in my head.

"Get me a pen." Dane said, smiling.

"Pleasure doing business with you Mr Donatti." He turned around and snapped his fingers, asking one of his guards to get a pen. A few shots went off, he looked around frantically.

"I hope that isn't you Mr Donatti." He said in fear.

"And if it is?" Dane said, stepping towards him and raising his eyebrows. Armarni looked over Dane, widening his eyes at one of the guards. He slowly pulled his gun out as I smirked.

Let the fun begin.

I shot the guard in his thigh, more shots going off. Dane had punched Armarni and he was on the floor. I shot all of the guards in the room, Jordan helping. I immediately ran towards the girls, knocking on the glass wall. It could easily be broken. I didn't want to break it because they were barefooted and would have to walk on the glass.

I ran back towards Armarni, Dane beating the shit out of him. More shouts went off, and their screams had escalated. Ali, Gio and Tio had pushed in all the girls that were in the club, most of them crying violently.

"We killed everyone in the club, and took most of their stuff. Hey, I got a Rolex." Gio grinned, waving the watch around. I rolled my eyes at him and bent down to Armarni's level.

"How do I open the wall?" I asked, twirling my knife in my hands.

"I'm not telling you. You're a girl, know your worth." He said, looking at me disgustedly. Dane was about to punch him but I stopped him.

"My worth is more than yours. Tell me before I stab your eye." I said lowly as his eyes widened. He looked at me as if I wouldn't do it.

"You asked for it." I said, shrugging. I dipped my knife into his eye slowly, making him scream and wither in Dane's hold.

"I promise, if you tell me, I'll let you go. Girl scouts honour." I said, grinning, holding up my hands.

"Really." I added, making it look believable.

"There is a button on the right side of the wall. It's red, press it twice." He mumbled.

"If it's wrong, I'll kill you." I seethed, walking over to the wall. I walked over to it cautiously, one of the girls shouting and shaking her head at me.

"Don't! It's on the other side! It's green! Press it twice! Don't press it the red one, it's going to blow us all up!" She cried, her voice muffled. I sent a dirty glare at Armarni, walking over the the other side, pressing the green button twice. Funnily enough, it did open up.

"Stay put. Stay there, we need to deal with him first. We'll get you all clothes and water. Wait please." I smiled softly. One girl in the 17 category caught my eye. She was staring at me intently. She looked like me. I raised my eyebrows at her. She didn't move. At all.

I walked back over to Armarni.

"Why did you have to lie! I could have let you go." I pouted, walking around him.

"S-sorry. You can still l-let me go." He begged.

"Now why would I do that? Did you let all of these girls go when they asked you to?" I asked, digging my heel into his chest.

"DID YOU?" I roared, pressing it harder.

"Dane finish him off, I'll go in fucking sane if I keep looking at him." I kicked the side of his head, making him cry in pain. I walked back to the girls, the van arrived. The gates to the back had opened, and I hadn't noticed they were there.

"Thank you so much." One of the girls wailed, hugging me. I stiffened immediately but patted her back awkwardly.

"Do you all have homes?" I asked, looking at all of them. The 10 year olds looked so fragile. The van had come in with food, water, and clothes. Most of them shook their heads a no. We had a summer house, not too far from here. We used to come with my father and my mother's families in summer, but now, no one used it, since father left. It was massive, because our whole family line used to come there for summer.

I told them to go get stuff by category of age, and they listened well. Soon enough all of them were clothed and Dane was finished with Armarni. They were all eating food, some of them smiling, but I noticed the girl who looked like me was shaking.

"We did it hm. Since they're homeless and know eachother, I'm going to buy a big penthouse and let them stay in it until they get onto their feets." He mumbled in my ear as I nodded.

"I have a summer house they can go to." I mumbled. "I will be back." I said, walking towards the girl

"You okay kid?" I said, looking at her. She shook her head a no and jumped into my arms, hugging me tightly.

"What's your name?" I asked, pulling away.

"Roxy." She mumbled, playing with her fingers. She was lying. She didn't look at me when she said that

"Your real name." I deadpanned as her eyes widened.

"Diana." She mumbled. My heart rate quickened, and the circulation of air in my body had stopped.

"Diana what?" I asked.

"Romero." She said, glancing at me. I couldn't believe it. Was it really her? We had a whole funeral for her! It couldn't be.

"D-did you have an older brother and sister?" I asked, tears building up in my eyes.

"Yes." She said, smiling at the floor.

"What were their names?" I asked, to confirm. My mother would be so... ecstatic.

"Demonica and Damien. They were so good to me. I loved them both with my heart. I don't know where they are right now. I bet Damien is in some other country." She said, still smiling and shaking her head.

"What happened the day you were taken?" I asked, wiping my hands on my dress.

"Car crash." She said, sighing. "I woke up to being chained in a room. I was 8 I think." She mumbled, tears falling.

"Do you know where my sister is or my brother?" She asked, looking at me with hope.

"Your sister is right here Ana." I said, using my old nickname I called her.

Her eyes widened and she sucked in a breath.

"Monica!" She said, sobbing, hugging me.

"Shh, I'm here now." I mumbled, stroking her hair, a tear falling. I wiped it away quickly as Dane came up to me. He raised his eyebrows at me and looked confused.

"I'll explain at home." I said, pulling away.

"You're safe. You're with me now." I muttered, pulling her outside and into Dane's car.

"Stay there, don't move." I ordered as she nodded mutely.

I went back into the ring and saw all the girls getting onto the coach with food, they were all fully clothed. I saw Jordan stare at one of the girls intently, and she was very pretty. All of them were pretty. I laughed in my head, knowing that something would sprout between them.

The coach was being driven by Ali and Gio and Tio were gonna be there as backup, in case anything went wrong.

"Take them to SunnyVille summer house. The code to get in is 6578. There are around 40 rooms in it, and all of the rooms have bathrooms, it has a massive kitchen and is probably stocked up with food. Tell the girls to clean up and get into groups so they can all fit in the rooms. I'll come tomorrow to see how they are doing. And also, tell them, if they mess anything up, they need to clean it up immediately. I don't want to see any mess." I said, all three of them mock saluting me. "Dane, I want you to put a few of your men around the area too. I don't want no one in contact with Armarni to contact the girls." I said softly, smiling.

Everything went to plan. And everything worked out well, hell I found my sister. Now I just had to go home and tell my mother about her.

I hugged Dane, and kissed him softly. If it wasn't for him, we wouldn't have found her.

"Thank you." I whispered, gripping his hand. He pulled me into his chest as siren sounds cut through the silenced place, as we left. We made sure to leave no evidence of us being there.

<h1 style="text-align:right">eighteen</h1>

And everybody gone run,And you can call it what you want,But I call it moving on,And I'm so done,With singing words I don't believe in no more.

The ride home was quiet. Diana had her head on my shoulder, sleeping, Jordan in the front and Dane driving. We dropped Jordan off, and drove to my house. Luca had gone with the twins and Ali. I was just worried about how mother would take this all in. She never wanted me to meddle in mafia affairs. What confused me was, we moved from England to America. And she was born in England, and the crash happened in England. How the fuck did she get here? I slapped my forehead. Of course Armarni would have scouted her and sent her here on a private jet or something. My poor sister. But at the funeral, who's body was that? I had no idea how this had worked out.

We reached home and I woke Diana up.

"Ana. Wake up. We're home." I mumbled. She opened her eyes and smiled.

"Home?" She repeated as I nodded.

"Home." I confirmed, getting out the car.

"Babe, I'm going to go home. See how ma is doing. Stay safe okay, call me if you need anything." He said, kissing my cheek. I nodded and bid him goodbye, opening the door quietly. It was around 10 in the evening. It did take that long to get all the girls to the house and get them cleaned up etc.

"Mother?" I said, walking inside.

"In here." She said.

I held Diana's hand and showed her inside.

"Mother don't freak out. I found...someone." I muttered. She stared at me intently.

"Who?" She asked as I pulled Ana inside.

Her eyes immediately widened, she placed her hand over her mouth.

"Is that...is she?" Mother stumbled over her words, wobbling towards us. I nodded, pushing Diana towards her.

"Turn around." She croaked. Ana did so. She lifted her hair up a bit to show a birth mark. I didn't even know she had it.

"Oh my beautiful princess Diana." She wailed, throwing her arms around her. Diana sobbed in her shoulder. I moved upstairs to give them some space, changing and taking a shower. Ana soon came up and showered too. I lent her a pair of clothes, and it was around 12 now, we sat down at the table.

"Diana. My darling daughter. You've grown up so much." Mother said, wiping her tears.

"Diana I'm gonna ask you a few questions okay, if you feel like I'm being too pushy, tell me to stop." I said seriously. I sounded like a cop.

"What year did you go missing?" I asked. She furrowed her eye brows.

"What year is it now?" She said sipping on some hot chocolate.

"2018." I mumbled.

"09." She mumbled. I nodded, that was the correct date.

"Did you ever...get..you know?" I asked softly.

Her eyes watered and her hands started shaking. I studied her properly, she had mothers hair and dads eyes.

"I never got r-raped in the years I was there. No one asked for me, I made myself the ugliest. I always fought back, and no one took me. I had been t-touched before though. Not... properly. Just inappropriately." She stuttered. I nodded.

"And those girls. When did they come?" I asked as she blew out a breath.

"Different times." She said as I nodded again.

"Mother I gave the summer house to the rest of the girls." I pursed my lips and she nodded.

"How did you find her?" My mother asked.

"She was in a sex ring Dane shut down. I found her there along with around 300 girls." I said, not elaborating on the matter.

"Where's Damien?" She asked.

"He's coming home tomorrow." I said, knowing that I was going to call him tonight.

"I think you should get some rest darling. Tomorrow we'll sort everything out." Mother said smiling softly.

I nodded and took her upstairs the the attic room. She immediately loved it, it was for her.

"Thank you Monica. I wouldn't be here if it wasn't for you." She said, hugging me tightly.

"You need to go to school by the way." I said chuckling as she groaned.

I left her room and went back to mine, snuggling up in my covers. I had less than 5 days till I got married and I had done 0 preparations. Maybe I could persuade Dane to let this go, so we could get married properly. There was no doubt that I wanted to be with him, I just think this was all too much. I grabbed my phone and dialled Damien's number.

"Hello?" He said, his voice low.

"Damien. You need to come home. Tomorrow, latest. I have a surprise." I mumbled smiling.

"Why is everything okay D?" He asked worried.

"Yes, just make sure you're home tomorrow. No if's or but's. Home. Tomorrow. Goodnight." I said, shutting off the call.

A lot of thoughts had floated around in my mind. Tomorrow I had to go see the girls, and Damien had to buy a house for them.

How did Armarni find her?

Who was in the casket at the funeral?

Why did they take her to America?

I sighed heavily and stared at the ceiling.

I wonder where my father was. Was he okay? Was he dead? Did he have a different family? It was Monday tomorrow anyway, missing a day of school wouldn't hurt. I also had to get Ana's enrolment papers.

A tear rolled down the side of my face. I wiped it and closed my eyes, letting myself sleep soundly.

nineteen

Stay, you're not gonna leave me, This place is right where you need to be, Why your words gotta mean so much to them? They mean nothing to me.

Glancing at my alarm that read 7:46 in the morning, I got up steadily and wobbled over to the toilet. I retched and sat down in front of the toilet bowl, trying to regulate my breathing. I retched again and let my body push out the waste. Sweat beads started forming on my forehead, my breathing becoming dishevelled again as I tried to stand up. I sat the in front of the bowl for a good 40 minutes. I eventually became calmer, and rested my head on the tub. I took deep breaths in and out as I clenched and unclenched my fingers.

I wasn't going to school, and I like getting stuff done early. Me and Dane had to scout for houses, and also visit the girls, and also get Ana into school. I had already gotten her papers sent in the mail, I just need mother to fill them out and send them back.

I got off the floor and place both of my hands on either side of the sink, steadying myself. My throat had suddenly gotten drier and drier as I violently started coughing. I saw a tiny speck of red. It didn't worry me much, so I stumbled over to the the door, closing it so my mother and Ana wouldn't wake up. I wobbled over to the sink, again, and splashed cold water on my face. I dried it off and sat on my bed. I grabbed my phone and called Dane.

It rang thrice before he picked up.

"Is everything okay?" He said immediately as I chuckled lightly, coughing. He didn't sound like he just woke up, which I was grateful for.

"Did I wake you up?" I asked, lying flat on the bed.

"No, I went out for a jog. I always do. You know me, gotta keep my sexy body in tact to attract the ladies." He said arrogantly. "Are you okay?" He then asked.

"I'm fine. I just wanted to tell you we're leaving to see the girls at 9. Have you found a house?" I said, my voice scratchy.

"Yeah, a couple of houses. I figured they all wouldn't want to live together but near to each other. Are you sure you're okay? Your voice sounds scratchy tesoro. Are you ill?" (Treasure). He questioned as I chuckled again.

"I'm fine. Get ready I'm coming over to yours in," I glanced at the clock, "An hour." I said lazily, smiling.

"Okay Domenica. See you then." He cut off the call as I smiled at my phone. I left it on my bed and headed downstairs. I trekked into the kitchen, pulling out eggs and peppers to make a cute little omelette thing. Don't ask why I put peppers in it, it tastes beautiful. I quickly finished that up and drank a cup of coffee. It was now 8:30, and I headed back to my room to get ready. I showered in like 2 minutes, and pulled out a Thrasher crop top, some black ripped jeans as always, a red bandanna and red Vans. I got my knife just in case. I put it all on, and my pinky finger ring and a silver necklace. I left the house and headed towards Dane's.

I saw him standing outside wearing of course, a suit. He ran up the the passenger seat and grinned at me.

"Hi baby." He said as I cringed.

"Name's Dom. Not baby." I mumbled, setting off.

"Sorry...baby." He said, giving me a cheeky wink. I tightened my grip on the wheel.

"Dom."

"Baby."

"D - O - M. Dom."

"B - A - B - Y. Baby."

"I'm going to rip your throat out." I muttered, glaring at him.

"Kinky, I like tha-"

"With my fucking teeth you little asshole." I glowered making his eyes widen.

He winked. He literally winked.

His eyes hardened for a brief second as A sly smile etched across his face. He leaned towards me, I could feel my heart rate going up.

"W-what are you doing?" I stuttered. Why the fuck did I stutter?

He nibbled on my ear as I inhaled sharply. He moved down to my neck, and up my jawline.

His hand suddenly gripped my jaw, making me look at him. His eyes had definitely gone a shade darker as I stared at me. We were driving and my eyes weren't on the road, panic built up in my body.

"I don't like disobedience." He said, his minty breath fanning my face.

"You sound like a teacher." I said muffled.

"I could teach you a few things." He mumbled, tracing his thumb over my lips.

I immediately looked back at the road, turning the music volume up. Really up. His chuckles were now drowned out by One Acen.

The drive to the summer house was relatively quick, since I was speeding and could not wait to get out of the car. As we were driving, we settled into a comfortable silence.

We reached there, I pulled in quickly, stopping at the gates.

"My my, is that you little D?" The gatekeeper said, smiling in glee.

"Sure is Uncle S. How have the girls been? Any of the gone out?" I asked as he shook his head.

"They all seemed really frightened little D. Are they okay?" He asked, frowning.

I nodded and smiled tightly as he let us through. The summer house was definitely my favourite place to come.

Not now, not anymore though.

It was surrounded by the crystal blue sea, and the beach, pretty palm trees and great weather.

I had my key on me, so I walked in unannounced.

twenty

Oh, you know I've been alone for quite a while,Haven't I?I thought I knew it all, Found love but I was wrong,More times than enough, Since you came along..

Pushing the door open and walking in, I was immediately, I was pinned up against the wall by my neck. The girl had definitely had a strong grip, but I was stronger. I punched her jaw lightly making her stumble. She held her jaw and then looked at me. She was tall with raven black hair, and pretty brown eyes, she was very skinny though.

"Oh my gosh! I'm so sorry I thought you were someone else. I'm so sorry!" She said panicking as I laughed lightly.

"You have a strong grip girl." I said smiling. She smiled back.

"Round up the girls in the living room. Need to talk to all of you." I said, Dane resting his chin on my shoulder. I walked into the room and it was still as I remembered it. It was very clean which I was grateful for. I sat on the couch with Dane, waiting for all of them to come down.

Eventually, they were all either standing, sitting on the floor or sitting on the couches in front of me. There was around 250 girls.

"As you guys know, the ring has now been shut down and you guys are free. Dane has looked for a few homes because I know I can't cram so many of you girls into this little summer house. So please stand next to anyone you are related to, or want to stay with." I said, standing up. Some of the girls shuffled towards others, some towards their related people. Eventually I had quite a few groups, and no one was left out.

"Does anyone here have beef with anyone else?" I asked,walking around.

"We're a family ma'am. None of us fight with each other." A girl spoke up. She had pretty blonde hair and blue eyes.

"That's what I like to hear. Now who is the oldest?" I mumbled gazing at each of the girls.

One girl with brown hair and green eyes that kind of looked like a girl version of Dylan O'Brien raised her hands.

"I'm 25, the oldest." She muttered, smiling slightly.

"Who has family here? Can you contact them?" I asked as quite a few girls raised their hands. Around 100 of them, which made it easier for me.

"If you have family and are able to go back to them, you can do so." Slight chatter filled out the room before I asked them to be quiet again.

"Who want's to go to school?" I asked as nearly all the girls raised their hands. Around 8 girls hadn't raised their hands.

"We've already finished. We're quite clever if I must say." One girl with glasses said, she was petite and nerd like.

"Okay. Well, we have found houses for you guys. Some of you can stay here. All of you can enroll into the schools if you want. I go to school here too. There are many colleges and universities for the older girls. And for the younger girls, there are middle schools too. Who wants to move out of here into a house?" I asked. The groups they got into had roughly 7 people in them. And the house were 3 bedroomed with 2 toilets and a big living room. It worked, they could sleep in the same rooms.

"Who ever wants to leave to go back to their families please go upstairs to the room on your left. Who ever wants to stay here, stay in this room, and who ever wants the houses, upstairs to the room on your right. Go." I said, waiting for them to disperse.

Around 50 girls stayed here, which was okay. The summer house was big, and the rooms were most definitely enough.

"Right girls I have no objection in you guys staying here. You girls can go to school if you want to. If anything happens to any of you, my phone number is already engraved into the fridge. Don't ask why. I want this house spotless. It is my families and we have a ton of good memories here. I don't want any parties, and trust me, I'll get to know if there are parties here. There will be guards surrounding you guys, for your own safety. And I expect the older girls to get jobs to pay off for daily supplies such as food and stuff like that. None of you are allowed to smoke anything other than regular cigarettes, and alcohol is a no for girls younger than 17. I'll also get to know i any of you have disobeyed my rules. No drugs allowed, no alcohol or cigarettes for the younger girls, no parties and definitely no boys until I meet the boys. All of you are now under my wing. All of you, the younger and olders, will train to learn how to protect yourself at the gym we have in the house. I'm sending a friend of mine, she's a great trainer but she wont go easy on you. If anything breaks in the house, I want it repaired quickly. I'll also be sending 600 a month until you guys get on your feet for food, hygiene stuff, clothes and more essentials. And remember girls, if you tell anyone what I've done for you, trust me it wont be nice for you anymore. If any one of you leak out information about where you guys will be staying and I find out, I'll kill you. No hesitation whatsoever. And please, don't fight with each other. You guys are a family now." I finished as muffled sobs echoed throughout the room.

"I still don't know all of your names. I'll come back another day for that. Thank you girls." I said curtly, walking upstairs.

"Babe I have to make a call, mafia shit." Dane mumbled, kissing my cheek. I nodded and headed upstairs to the room on the left. I opened it to around 150 girls. I was glad they had families.

"Do you guys know where your families all live?" They all nodded except for one young girl.

"There are phones in each of the rooms, so do your thing and leave by tomorrow if you can. If anything happens, my number is engraved on the fridge for any of you that can't seem to find your families. I hope that all of you get your lives back together. I'll send a driver today to pick all of you up. Sound good?" They all nodded, smiling at me gratefully. I smiled back and left the room, and headed towards the room on the right.

I pushed the door open quietly to see the girls huddled together. There was around 35 of them.

"She's nice. I get a good feeling off of her." One girl said.

"No! We can't trust her? What if she is working for them? She will give us back to him! I know she will! She will." Another girl starting thrashing around, holding her head in her hands. MY heart was crushed in pain, it was no doubt that bad stuff had happened to her.

"Hey, hey. I'm not going to hurt you. I promise I'm not with Armarni or none of them. He's dead. I'm here to help you." I said slowly, holding her shoulders. She broke down and cried in my shoulders as I rubbed her back.

"I'm sorry f-for her. My sister - she's been...hurt. A lot. She's not stable. I need to help her but I can't find someone to help her, and I don't have the money either." A girl the resembled her said.

"Don't worry. I'll pay for her therapist. She'll get what she needs." I said, letting go of the girl. I stood up awkwardly and brushed myself off.

"You guys will leave for the houses tomorrow. I will also send a driver. I'll send 400 a month to each of you for stuff you need. The older girls I expect you to get jobs. The houses must and will be kept tidy. The majority of the younger girls are here, so no alcohol, no parties, definitely no boys until I meet them and NO DRUGS. Any sign, smell, or use of drugs will have you out of the house immediately. Each of you will be able to go to school, but do not breathe a word about who saved you or what happened. I can't have the feds knocking at my door. Stay safe girls. If you need anything, my phone number is on the fridge. Sleep well tonight." I mumbled, closing the door.

"Girls! Can you all come down here once more please!" I yelled. I heard a thunder of footsteps as all the girls showed again.

"Right sorry for calling you guys down but quickly, you cannot tell anyone that I've taken you in. NO ONE." I said seriously, looking them all in the eye. "If I find out that any of you have, I'll kill you. No one will even notice." I said coldly, making them flinch. "You all know what's happening now, and where you guys are going. I hope it all turns out well for you. All of you are strong women. Don't let anyone hurt you or nothing. As for training, I've changed my mind. Santobello gym, be there everyday at 8, and my friend will be there. I'll pop in time to time, as I will checking up on all of you. And remember, you can't hide from me. I know where you are, who you're with and what you are doing at all times. I wont pry unless I have to. Let me tell you once more, no one can know that I've helped you. If you dare to double cross me, trust me, it wont be in your favours at all. Good day girls." I said grinning, walking out. I saw Dane leaning against my car.

"Everything okay?" He asked as I felt nauseous.

"I'll drive baby." He said, taking the keys.

"Fine, Dane." I said getting in. We set off, waving at the guard and pulling out of the area.

"Dane." I said, looking at him, fiddling with my fingers.

"Can we postpone the marriage please?" I asked, staring at the trees we passed.

"Why? Don't you want to marry me?" He said sounding hurt.

"No it's not that! It's just that..I found my sister and I need to help her too. Also the girls, I need to help them. We're not even going out yet. I just want to slow it down, and then we get married when the time is right you know? I don't want to rush it and hate myself for it when everything turns out wrong. Please just postpone it, it's not like I don't want to marry you, I do, just not now." I said, gripping his hand. He sighed and nodded.

"Okay il mio amore. I'll wait, for you. I agree, it seems to be moving fast. Also, your birthday is coming. Do you want anything?" (My love). He asked, smiling at me.

"No. I have my family. That's all I need. Thank you Dane." I said, kissing his cheek. He cheeking whipped his head so our lips met.

"Cheeky cunt." I mumbled, sitting back down. It was now 11, ans we reached home quickly.

Dane came in with me, and greeted my mum and sister.

"SHIT! Damien is coming home today!" I shrieked as my mother widened her eyes.

"Who's Damien?" Dane said confused.

"Damien?" Ana said, looking happy.

I totally forgot.

twenty-one

I didn't think it would be true,Let alone that it would be you,I think I'm in love again.

Dane had said hello to my mother before I had dragged him upstairs.

"Who the fuck is Damien?" He asked, glaring at the wall.

"Relax hot shot, Damien is my brother." I said, laughing.

"Oh." Pink tinted the tips of his ears as I laughed harder.

"Stay here, I need to go talk to my mother really quick." I mumbled, trekking downstairs.

"MOTHER!" I yelled, even though she was right in front of me.

"Dom honey, I'm right in front of you. No need to yell. What's up?" She asked.

I looked around the living room and it was all tidy, that was good. "What're you making for dinner?" I asked. "Damien's gonna be coming at like probably 8 or something." I added.

"I'll whip something up. Go check on your sister." She said smiling as I nodded. I headed back upstairs to my sisters room, and obviously, I knocked before going in.

"Ana banana?" I called, walking inside.

"Hey." She croaked.

She sat on the far left edge of the bed, staring at the wall.

"What's wrong?" I asked sitting down next to her. We did look very much alike, and I hadn't noticed it until now.

"What if he doesn't accept me? What if he thinks I'm a...slut or something?" She said sadly, her eyes filled with tears.

"Remember when you punched that boy in the nose for pushing that girl in lower school?" I asked, laying flat on her bed. (A/N: Lower school is equivalent to to the third grade I think, it's what we call it here in England - you would be 8-9 years old).

"Yeah, he cried." She said, laughing.

"What did Damien tell you?" I asked.

"He said well done. Do it again if you have to." She said quietly.

"So why would he think you're a slut or anything? You've done absolutely nothing wrong. If anyone thinks that, send them my way." I mumbled, throwing a sloppy arm over her shoulder and giving her a lazy smile. She smiled back but then glanced at the door.

"Is that your boyfriend?" She asked, whispering.

"No. He's just someone I know." I whispered back, grinning because I knew her was standing at the door.

"He looks like he's about to murder you." She mumbled, smiling slightly.

"My boyfriend is Dylan." I said loudly. "O'Brien." I whispered in her ear. She started laughing as I did too.

"Hell no we're going to have a talk about this." Dane glowered, gripping my forearm lightly and dragging me out the room.

"Love you sis." I yelled dramatically, Dane pulling my into my room. MY ROOM.

"Who is Dylan?" He mumbled, sitting on my desk chair.

"My boyfriend." I answered.

"Where does he live?" He asked.

"Not telling you."

"Why?"

"Because."

"Tell me."

"No."

"Why?"

"Because."

"Because why?"

"Because I forgot."

"What do you mean your forgot?" He asked incredulous.

"Well it slipped my mind." I mumbled.

I was still standing up as he stood up too.

"You don't have a boyfriend." He said slowly.

"Hey! Maybe I do." I said, crossing my arms.

"Maybe you do." He took one step forwards, as I took one back. I sort of already noticed where this was going to go.

"Maybe I do?" I muttered as he came forwards again and I moved back.

"Yep. Guess what his name is?" He said, as my back hit the wall.

"Shit." I mumbled.

"His name isn't shit Domenica." Dane said laughing.

He put either of his hands on each side of my head against the wall, basically trapping me.

"Mother! Are you calling me? I'm coming down now!" I yelled, trying to get out of his hostage.

"Dom! I ain't calling you. When I call you, you don't reply! When I ain't calling you, you act like I'm calling you!" She yelled back.

Shit.

His loud chuckles echoed throughout the room.

"Hey yes, I'd like to get out of this. It's a kidnapping." I mumbled as he looked at me, with a twinkle in his eye.

"Nope." He said, popping the p.

"Toilet break!" I yelled, slipping out of his grasp and heading towards the toilet, locking myself in.

"I'll be here when you come out, you know that right?" He said amused as I groaned.

"My big scary brother is coming! Go home before he throttles you!" I shrieked.

"No can do." He said as I groaned again.

Suddenly, a loud knock pierced the silence we were in.

"It's him. He's here." I said horrified. I was only shitting myself because Dane was here, and my brother never allowed me near boys. Trust me. He went all big over protective brother mode whenever he saw me within 5 feet of a boy.

"Ana! Come here." I whisper yelled.

"What?" She whisper yelled back, walking into my room.

"Damien! My baby boy how are you?!" We heard my mothers voice.

"We need to go downstairs." I mumbled.

"Wheres my baby sister and her surprise?" He asked grinning.

I held Ana's hand and went downstairs. Dane still was upstairs, looking confused.

"Hey bro. Here is the surprise." I chuckled awkwardly, pushing Ana forwards. He stopped dead in his tracks, staring at Ana for a minute.

"Diana?" He mumbled. She nodded and hugged him. She was crying, and he looked contipated trying to hold his tears in.

"Where the fuck have you even been?" He mumbled, stroking her hair. They pulled away and sat down, as I slipped back upstairs.

"Dane?" I called, walking into my room.

"Here." He mumbled, looking at my paintings and drawings.

"Come, I'll introduce you to my brother." I mumbled, holding his hand.

"Wait!" He yelled, spinning me around into his chest.

"Do you want to be my girlfriend?" He asked, pink tinting his ears. I chuckled and nodded.

"Now I can introduce you as my girlfriend. Lucky me." He mumbled. I pulled him down the stairs, and into the living room.

"Damien, this is my boyfriend Dane." I muttered, not looking at him. And when I did, his eyebrows were raised and his mouth was set in a straight line. He then took a glance at Dane, when his eyes widened.

"This is your boyfriend?" He asked, gaping. I nodded a confused yes. "I accept." He said smiling, giving him a man brother hug male thing.

"You what?" I gaped, staring at the both of them.

"He helped me out one time when I was in Paris was it? My car had broken down and he actually took me to where I needed to be AND payed for my car to be fixed." Damien said happily as I nodded shocked. Dane sent a cheeky wink to my as I stuck my tongue out at him.

The evening went past slowly, we all just sat and chat, Ana and Damien had brother and sister bonding time while me, Dane and mother were discussing her school things and protection at school for her.

Night came quickly and Dane stayed round and we were currently in my room.

I got into my bed after brushing my teeth and all, so did he.

"Erm, who said you could sleep in my bed?" I said with an accusing tone.

He grinned at me and plopped down next to me. His arms snaked around my waist, pulling me into his chest.

"We have school tomorrow." I mumbled, snuggling into his chest.

"I can't be bothered." He groaned making me laugh.

"How old are you?" I asked, looking at him.

"21. I had to stay back and do years because of when I lived in Italy for the years I missed." He said, kissing my cheek.

"My birthday is in 2 days." I said, turning around and wrapping my arms around his waist.

"I know bambino. I have something planned for you. You're gonna love it." He said, grinning widely. I nodded and yawned.

I slowly started slipping away, but not before I felt lips on my forehead and an 'I love you'.

twenty-two

But you can leave if you really want to, And you can run if you feel you have to, And I'll be fine if you ever ask me, I know it's hard but no one said it's easy, Falling's easy, but there's only one way out.

Waking up with Dane was my favourite thing, and today we had school. I woke up at six, and so did he, but he left to go home get clothes and all that jazz. I took a quick ass shower, and woke up Ana because she was starting today too.

"Ana. Wake up, you have school." I mumbled, shaking her. She groaned and told me to fuck off.

"ANA! ANA THERE IS A SPIDER RIGHT ON YOUR FACE ANA WAKE UP!" I shrieked, as she jumped up off the bed, rolling around slapping herself. I howled in laughter as her eyes zeroed in slits at me. I back up slightly.

"Time for school Ana Banana." I cheered, running off to my room.

"I'm going to fucking KILL YOU DOMENICA!" She roared, slamming her door. I laughed loudly and went back into my room. I pulled out a white tee, black ripped jeans of course, and for shoes I chose some black

Doc Martens, and my leather jacket. I pulled up my hair into a messy ponytail, and put on mascara, lipbalm and highlight. I spritzed my perfume and put on my ring and shoved my knife into my boot. I grabbed my backpack and my phone and my headphones and headed downstairs.

Ana was already sitting there, looking pretty. She was wearing a white floral of the shoulder top, with some blue skinny jeans and white Vans. Her makeup was minimal like mine, and she also had her hair down.

"You're lookin' pretty Ana." I said, winking. "Stay away from the boys, they all have herpes okay." I said seriously making her laugh.

"Come let's go. Bye Damien!" I muttered waving at him and ma. We left and got into my car.

"There will be a shit ton of stares, ignore them all. They just remind you that you're better lookin' than everyone else. Keep your phone on at all times and if anything happens, call me straight away." I mumbled, looking at her directly. She nodded and sighed.

"What if they think I'm a...freak? Or something like that." She mumbled looking down.

"Why would they?" I asked. "Are you a freak?" I added, pulling into the school

"No." She muttered as I gave her a pointed look.

"Exactly Diana. You'll be fine, don't worry." I said, parking in my usual space. I saw Dane and his friends hanging out near his car. As we got out, their jaws dropped, well not Dane's but his friends.

"Who in everything Holy is that?" Jordan gaped, looking at Ali. I had just realised they also come to the school. I winked at her and headed towards Dane. She shifted uncomfortably, heading into the school.

"Jordan you're going to be in all of her classes. Keep an eye on her please." I said, patting his back. He nodded and smiled.

"Sir yes sir!" He mocked saluted making Dane slap the back of his head.

"Ciao bambino." (Hello baby). He leaned down and pressed a chaste kiss on my lips.

"Hi." I mumbled awkwardly. He held my hand and we walked together, as a couple, into the school. Everyone was looking at us and it made me uncomfortable. I spotted Ana talking to some girls, with a smile on her face. I smiled at that and headed to my first lesson, which was with Dane.

The day passed by pretty quick, then lunch came. Walking into the cafeteria, it was loud, chattery just as a school cafeteria is. I saw Natalie and her cronies come in, their heels clicking the floor. Everyone was doing what they were doing, I was sitting with Ocean and Willow.

"Ew." Ocean and Willow said in unison.

"I agree." I said chuckling. Suddenly all I heard was fight, fight, fight. And of course, I had to go see what was happening.

All I saw was Natalie on a girl. I sighed and turned around till I noticed what she was wearing, a white floral top...blue jeans and white Vans.

"Shit." I mumbled, ripping Natalie off of Ana. Ana took this as a chance to get up and punch Natalie repeatedly, making her bleed.

"Ana come, calm down." I said pulling Ana towards me.

"I'LL FUCKING KILL YOU." Ana roared at her, making me wince. I left her with Jordan going up to Natalie.

"Why were you fighting with her?" I asked lazily.

"What's it to you?" She sneered, holding her nose.

"She's my sister." I sighed.

Her eyes widened and there was something in her eyes that just put me off.

"Why did you hit my sister?" I asked, stepping towards her. Threateningly, obviously.

"Both of you are psychos." She said, running out. I shrugged and went back to Ana. She was sitting down, with her head in her hands.

"Get up." I said. It was her first day and she was already in a fight? Hell no.

She looked up at me, with her eyebrows raised.

"Did I stutter? Get. Up." I said, glaring. She got up and sighed.

"What was that all about? It's your first day and you're already having fights?" I asked. "You are supposed to be the better sister. Stop trying to end up like me. Focus on your grades, not fighting pathetic little twats like her. Fix this shit up, next time I wont be able to help you." I mumbled, the principle coming inside.

"Diana Romero? To my office!" He said, turning around.

"No. It wasn't her fault, it was mine. I'm coming." I said, picking my bag up.

"That's good enough for me. I should have known it was you." He glared at me and led me away. Natalie was already sitting outside, and her eyes widened when she saw me. I winked and headed inside his office.

"Care to tell me what happened girls?" He asked, glaring at us.

I looked at Natalie and waited for her to speak.

"It was a misunderstanding actually sir. I'm sorry. Wont happen again." She said, not looking at me. I nodded and said nothing.

"Okay well whatever. If I find out you two are in a fight again, both of you are getting kicked out. Ya here me? Kicked out!" He shouted. "Now get outta my office. Don't wanna see you guys here until the end of the year." He shouted again, shooing us out.

The corridors were empty as she headed into the toilet.

"Why did you two fight?" I asked as she shrugged.

"Fine whatever. Put some ice on that nose." I mumbled, walking out to my class.

The rest of the day turned out as a big ass blur. Ana went straight home not talking to me, I couldn't care less. If she wanted to act like a kid I'd treat her like one.

I had to go to a mafia meeting with Dane and that was what I was getting ready for right now.

Only lord knows how much I dreaded this meeting.

twenty-three

Pulling out a long forest green dress, with a V cut in the back, I decided that I would leave my hair curly, in it's natural habitat. I chose some back Choca Lux 100 Louboutin's to go with it. They were open cut with spikes on them. Dane had told me over 20 mafia lords would be there with their wives/husbands, girlfriends/boyfriends and that it was a formal event. It would go under a big charity ball, but really we would be underground talking business. I made sure to grab my knife and two guns and put the thigh strap on.

For makeup, I didn't do anything heavy. I did a smokey green eye shadow, bold red lips and of course, mascara, foundation, eye liner and all that jazz. Willow was over helping me, curling my hair and stuff.

"If I was a boy I'd totally dip my dick in you." She said staring at me. I laughed and flipped her off.

I looked hot. I looked really pretty actually.

"Where are you going?" Damien said, standing at my door way.

"Date with Dane." I looked at Willow and her eyes were stuck on Damien.

"Is your friend alright?" He asked, looking concerned. Her jaw was literally on the floor. He stepped in getting a good look at her, his eyes widening. He looked like he knew or had seen her before.

"Yeah she's fine. Shoo." I mumbled shutting the door on him as he chuckled.

"Is that..is he your brother?" She asked, still gaping.

"Yeah why?" I mumbled, putting in black earrings and a black statement necklace.

"We fucked." She blurted out.

"You what?" I said uneasily.

"Fucked. We had sexual intercourse. He dipped his dick in me." She mumbled as I laughed.

"WAIT! You and my brother had.." I trailed off staring at the wall.

"Yeah."

"How come?"

"I was horny and alone."

"How old are you again?"

"21."

"Oh. He's 27."

"Age is just a number, and jail is just a cell." She mumbled smiling

"Well hope it goes on well! Welcome to the family sister." I said, throwing my arms around her. She chuckled when the doorbell rang.

"Dane look after my sister. I'll kill you if she comes back harmed." Damien said quietly, but I heard.

"She wont get hurt Damien, promise." Dane said giving him a bro man hug. Willow helped me down the stairs because I'd probably fall in these heels. Dane was talking to my mother when he stopped and his jaw dropped at me. Diana was standing on the side, she sent me a small smile.

"Wow." He gaped making me blush. "You look so stunning." He mumbled, kissing my cheek. He was wearing a black suit with a bow tie, making him look a tad bit younger. I just realised he had grown a little stubble, his hair was gelled back swiftly. He was wearing a few rings too.

"Don't want to ruin your lipstick." He mumbled, hugging me. He inter-twined our fingers and headed out.

"Bye Willow, Damien." I said slyly making her blush.

"Bye mother, bye Ana Banana." I said, smiling.

"Bye Monica." She said quietly.

We went in a limo. Pretty cool.

He kissed my knuckles when we reached, even held the door open for me. It was held at some big ass hall. There was a lot of people that looked expensive. Everyone looked uptight and rich, snobby. Yes I was judging books by their covers.

"Whatever you do, do not leave my side Domenica. You have guns on you no?" He said, his accent seeping through.

I nodded and gripped his hands. We sat down at our designated table, Jordan and Ali there too, with two beautiful girls. One was black and the other one was Asian, South Asian I think. She had brown skin and prominent features.

"Hey." I said smiling at the both of them. They smiled back, which I was thankful for.

"Both of you look extremely pretty." I said still smiling.

"And you." The black one said. "What's your name?" She asked as Jordan, Ali and Dane spoke between them.

"Dom, and yours?" I asked looking at both of them. The black one was wearing red, and it really looked good on her. The Asian one was wearing a royal blue, that also looked really good. I felt a tad bit self conscious because the girls were so pretty.

"I'm Raeni, and that's Darya." She said pointing at the Asian one while saying Darya. "Where are you from?" She asked, smiling.

"I'm Italian, and yourselves?" I asked sipping on champagne.

"I'm from Barbados." Raeni said.

"I'm from Afghanistan." Darya said smiling.

"How do you find Jordan and Ali?" I said chuckling.

"Ali is hard work, he's my bestfriend. Nothing romantic between us, he just took me because he had no girl to go with him." Raeni snickered.

"Jordan and I are also bestfriends. No romance there whatsoever, I have a husband actually. But him and Jordan are like brothers and Jordan is like a brother to me too, so I could come." Darya said laughing.

"You're with Dane I see?" Raeni said, smiling. I nodded and blushed.

"Yeah, my boyfriend." I said, spotting him with a cup of scotch talking to someone. Like he sensed I was looking at him, he looked straight at me, winking.

I blushed AGAIN and looked away, Raeni and Darya laughing.

"We're definitely going to be good friends." Raeni said smiling.

"Yeah, I have two bestfriends and you guys will definitely get on well. How old are you guys?" I asked

"I'm 21, and Raeni is 20." Darya said as my eyes widened.

"What! Really? I'm so probably the youngest here." I mumbled to myself.

"Yourself?" Raeni said.

"I'm 18, 19 in...tomorrow!" I said shocked, I literally forgot my birthday.

"Girl what? Are you not doing anything for your birthday?" Darya asked, frowning.

"I shrugged. Dane's taking me somewhere, but I'm not doing nothing with the girls. Maybe we'll have a cute girls only dinner." I mumbled. "Yes! Then you can meet Willow and Ocean!" I said happy with my discovery. They agreed and we exchanged numbers. Dane dragged me somewhere, it was probably time for the meeting.

I put on a poker face, bracing myself.

We walked in the room, two guards on either side. Dane looked powerful and very scary. There was around 30 people in the room, a large ass table in the middle, they were all sitting around it. There was one old guy right at the top of the table.

"Mr Donatti! Nice of you to join us. Who is the beauty next to you?" He asked, looking at me. Dane's arm snaked around my waist, pulling me close.

"My girlfriend, Domenica Romero."

A gasp from the other side of the room was heard. I didn't look there because I was uninterested.

"Take a seat Mr Donatti." The old guy said, him pulling out a chair for me, and then sitting down. I thanked him quietly, looking around the room. Everyone seemed pretty ordinary people, the women were beautiful the men were handsome. Except for the old ones. Ew.

My eyes stopped at a man, who was looking at me intently. I raised my eyebrows and he looked away.

The men were talking about how to get cartels across the boarder easily when a thought circled my mind. I didn't say anything though.

"Does anyone else have anything else? Any other methods?" The guy at the top of the table muttered, sipping on some whiskey.

"Dane I have one." I whispered in his ear. He nodded and told me to go ahead.

"If I may." I piped up, making everyone looked surprised.

I straightened out my back and blew out a breath.

"Take the cars apart. The cartels are small, and easy to hide no? Taking the inside of the cars apart and putting them back together makes it seem like it wasn't even tampered with. The easiest way to get them is from the Mexican and America boarder." I said, looking at the Mexican mafia lord who nodded his head in agreement. "It's a simple way, and I'm pretty sure it's risk free." I finished. Everyone started clapping, but I still had a poker face on. Dane looked at me smiling, with pride.

"Well done Miss Romero." The guy at the top said.

"You aren't related to Don Romero are you?" He asked, raising his eyebrows. "Alonzo Romero to be specific." My breath hitched in my throat. I didn't know whether to tell him or not.

"Just because my second name is the same as someone else, doesn't mean that we are related sir." I said coldly. He nodded and raised his hands in surrender.

"Why are we trusting this girl? She's a girl, she shouldn't be here. Mafia is for men, hence the mafia started with the letter m." Some guy sitting across me said. They woman next to him shot me a sorry smile. She looked unhappy and was definitely hiding bruises under that makeup. He had an accent, it sounded Russian or something.

"I'm sorry Mr Aleksiev but is there a problem with my girlfriend being here?" Dane said, shooting him a glare. "As far as I know, she was the one who made actual contribution, not you. So I suggest you keep your mouth shut thank you." Dane finished, gripping my hand. I squeezed it lightly to tell him that it was okay.

"You are losing an ally here Mr Donatti." He said.

"My mafia is bigger than yours. I'm not losing anything." He said coldly. Aleksiev shot him an icy glare.

"Well anyway, this meeting is dismissed. Go back to having a good party, donate if you can, it's going towards the children cancer program." The guy at the head said leaving. I sighed and leaned back into the chair.

Aleksiev pulled out a gun and pointed it at me.

"I got embarrassed in front of everyone because of you. Dane immediately went to stand up but I stopped him.

"Who? Me?" I pointed at myself, looking around as if I was looking for someone.

"Yes you, you slut." He roared making me laugh.

"Honey. It's not my fault you say dumb things." I said, flicking my hair. "Had you chosen to keep your mouth shut none of this would have had happened." I mumbled, putting my hand on my gun ready to take it out.

A loud bang echoed off of the walls, it fell deadly quiet. A burning sensation built up in my arm as pain electrocuted my arm. It was like a bloody 2 in 1.

I stood up slowly, trying to regulate my breathing. Everyone in the room had now stood up and had their guns pointed at him. I was shocked. Why were they even backing me?

"Thank you guys, but please put down your guns." The woman next to him had a scared face as she stood up. She slowly relaxed and pulled a gun out too, pointing it at me. Dane had his gun out, pointing at her, also everyone else was pointing their guns at her too.

I sat back into my chair.

"What are you waiting for? Shoot." I said, gripping my arm trying to stop the blood flow. She smiled cynically, swiftly aiming the gun at Aleksiev's head, shooting him dead directly. I winced and smiled. I got up leaning on Dane.

"Well done." I mumbled, walking towards the door.

"It was nice talking to all of you, and thank you for backing. I wont forget it." I mumbled, feeling dizzy.

I was about to walk out, but my hands were covered in blood so was my arm.

Then I blacked out.

twenty-four

Devoted to destruction,A full dose of detrimental dysfunction,I'm dying slow but the Devil tryna rush me,See I'm a fool for pain, I'm a dummy.

Bright lights filled my vision. Everything seemed louder than it was. I tried talking but I couldn't. I tried moving but I also couldn't.

"She's waking up! Call the doctor!" A male voice roared. I wanted to cover my ears and tell him to shut the fuck up.

"It's okay Domenica you're okay. Il mio regina. Questo non ti succedera mai piu, lo prometto." (My queen. This will never happen to you again, I promise). Soft lips graced my forehead as I smiled slightly.

I opened my eyes and everything was fuzzy. I squinted my eyes to try make out who the people were moving around rapidly.

"Domenica it's me your doctor. Can you hear me?" A sweet girls voice asked.

I nodded, unable to speak.

"W-water." I croaked, trying to sit up.

Someone put a bottle to my lips, making my gulp the water down greedily. I could now see a tiny bit clearer. Dane was sitting there across me with a worried look on their faces, so was Jordan, Ali, Raeni, Darya, Willow and Ocean. The girls had tears streaming down their faces.

I sat up but winced, a pain shot through my arm.

"Fuck me." I muttered, looking at my arm.

"What happened?" I asked, leaning against the hospital bed, looking around. "Did I get shot or somethin'? Why you guys crying. I don't do well with tears." I mumbled. They let out awkward laughs.

"You were shot actually." Dane said without emotion. "It was my fault, I shouldn't have made you tag along." Then, all the events came rushing back to me.

"I remember now. Well, it's okay, I'm alive aren't I?" I joked.

"I'm fine. Now get me off this dang bed." I mumbled, ripping the IV thing out of my arm. It hurt but whatever. My arm was bandaged tightly.

"Sit you can leave tomorrow. Sit down before I make you." Dane said glaring.

"Kinky." I said, groaning at the pain that had shot up my arm again.

"You guys should go home. Get yourselves cleaned up and stuff. Are you guys okay though? You guys look like you haven't slept. What time is it?" I asked.

"12 in the morning." Jordan mumbled. Luca came stumbling in with bags of food.

"I'm here! Sorry I got late, some man harassed me, he said I was too pretty to be walking around the streets at night." He shuddered as I laughed. "You're awake!" He exclaimed throwing his arms around me.

"Alright kid off me now." I said patting his back.

"Not gonna lie, I do have a pretty face." He said thinking. "But holy shmoly he was like 50! Touched my arm and everything. Had to punch his nose." He said, glaring at the wall.

"Alright Luca we get it." Dane muttered, looking amused.

"Guys go home, go get some sleep. We have plans tomorrow. It's my birthday tomorrow ain't it?" I said confused.

"It is." Willow said. "And I don't want to leave you here by yourself." She said frowning. "You looked so..pale and.." She choked as Ocean and Darya hugged her.

"I'm fine. And tomorrow we have a girls meal so go home get some sleep all of that, and we'll see each other soon. You as well, Raeni and Darya and Ocean. Go now. Jordan, Ali and Luca take them home safely please." I said smiling.

They nodded and headed out.

"Get well soon Dom." They all said, leaving.

"What you waiting for? Go as well." I said, closing my eyes.

"Hell no. I'm staying with you." Dane said, glaring. I shrugged my shoulders as he went to grab the food.

"I got Chinese. I didn't know what you wanted. So I just told Luca to get Chinese. I'm sorry I should have gotten something else, you don't have to eat it if you don't want t-" I cut him off my grabbing the food out of his hands.

"Chinese is fine. And you were rambling." I mumbled, taking a bite of prawn fried rice.

"I was so scared when he pulled his gun out Dom. I love you, I don't want to lose you not when I just found you." He said, with a pained voice. My breath hitched at the L word.

"I'm here, it's okay. I'm not going anywhere." I said, holding his hand. "How come they all backed me?" I mumbled taking another bite.

"Our mafia is the biggest, and they also owe me favours. Also they like you. They think you're a strong woman, fit enough to be a mafia don's wife." He said smiling proudly. I blushed and looked down.

"After you go out with the girls, I'm taking you out." He said, kissing my forehead.

"What time can I leave tomorrow?" I asked, now eating stir fry.

"7 in the morning. Sound okay?" He asked, staring at me.

I nodded and said nothing. He wasn't eating so I pushed a tin in front of him.

"Eat Dane." I said, holding out the stir fry.

"Not hungry." He said, pushing it away.

"Eat." I said sternly.

"No."

"Eat."

"Not hungry."

"Eat this before I fucking shove it down your throat." I growled, shoving it to him. His eyes widened as he took it off me slowly.

"I can't eat with you being in pain. That should have been me. I shouldn't have told you to come. It's my fault you got shot." He said, putting the food down.

"Bish bosh, it was in my arm and I ain't dead. I'm right here. And the fuckers dead either way, so it's fine. Bada bing bada bong." I said, giggling.

"Even when you get shot you can't act serious can you?" He said, cracking a small smile. I shook my head and ate my food, as did he.

He stayed with me the whole night until the morning, and I was grateful for that.

I didn't deserve him.

I sighed, and ran my hands through his hair.

My strap was gone, so was my guns.

"Dane who took my guns?" I mumbled, massaging his neck.

"I did, I took them before we came here." He replied, his eyes closing.

"Go to sleep." I mumbled, leaning forwards, kissing his head.

And he did. He fell asleep straight away.

I couldn't help but have a bad feeling about tomorrow, and whenever I had a bad feeling, it turned out to be pretty fucking true.

I leaned my head back on the bed, closing my eyes. I fell asleep too.

twenty-five

Baby tell me when you're ready,I'm waiting,Baby anytime you're ready,I'm waiting, Even 10 years from now, If you haven't found somebody,I'll be around.

{ THIS CHAPTER IS ONLY ABOUT DOM AND HER BIRTHDAY SURPRISE, NOTHING ELSE HAPPENS. IF YOU WISH TO SKIP IT, DO, BUT IT WOULD BE BETTER IF YOU READ IT. THIS CHAPTER IS FOR YOU DOG LOVERS, LIKE MYSELF }.

Mornings had always seemed to appeal to me. As much as I seemed like a no morning please person, I pretty much was. I loved waking up to the sound of the birds chirping - and no, it happened in real life too.

Dane and I were driving back from the hospital, my arm definitely felt better. It was around 7:30 in the morning, I think. The sky was slightly dark since the December month had taken over.

I'm 19 today too. Dane hadn't wished me a happy birthday, not going to lie, I acted like I couldn't care less, but I fucking could. I sighed and leaned my head against the window. Today wasn't a particularly great day in all honesty.

"You okay babe?" Dane said glancing at me. I nodded but said nothing. I noticed the look of distress on his face when I added, "I'm tired. Being shot and all ain't fun Dee Dee." Had he forgotten? He seemed to remember pretty well last night if I do say so myself - and no, no in that way you freaks!

He chuckled and nodded.

"Dane give me your phone please?" I asked holding out my hand. He raised his eyebrows but pulled it out anyway. I pulled up The Emperor's Junction website and gave them a call, making reservations for 5 people at 6. I handed Dane his phone back and the ride was awkwardly silent for some reason. We reached my house quickly. I muttered a quick 'bye' and left. I think my siblings and mother had gone out because there wasn't anyone at home. I sighed and made a group chat with Raeni, Darya, Willow and Ocean about tonight. (A/N: Darya is pronounced as Dar-ee-yah).

"Dress formal, classy, sexy. I booked reservation at 6 at The Emperor's Junction. It's all going to be paid for so don't worry about that. Hope to see all you girls there.

- Dom."

It was quite early, 8 in the morning to be exact. I changed out of the clothes I was wearing, took a long ass shower and wore just a long tee. I pulled my hair up in a bun, and slipped on some sliders. I trekked into the kitchen, looking for anything to munch on. On the fridge there was a note from my mother.

"Dom, your brother has taken me and Diana out to a resort thing for a few days. We all wish you the happiest birthday, and your gift is waiting for you in the garage. Have a good few days, we'll definitely be back before Christmas lol!" I had stopped reading and cringed the fuck out, but carried on. "Stay safe, if anything happens call me immediately. I'll be back in no time. We all love you.

- Your family xX."

I sighed in content, that was good I guess, no one to ask me about my arm. Suddenly excited, I raced into the garage to see what my mother had gotten me, and to say I was shocked was the least.

There was a large box in the centre of the garage, with a small bow on top and a note. The box moved slightly, making my flinch. I walked up to it cautiously and quietly. I finally got close enough to read the the note stuck on top.

"Happy birthday!" Was written in cursive writing. I opened up the box to see 4 pairs of big eyes staring back up at me.

"EEEEEEE!" I squealed in delight picking up each puppy one by one; there was 4 of them. On the note was also written what breed they were; one was an Alaskan Malamute, the fluffiest fluffball I had ever seen, the next was a cute little Doberman puppy, next to the Doberman Pinscher was a beautiful caramel coloured Shiba Inu and next to the Inu, there was a beautiful white Pitbull Terrier. They were all definitely boys.

Tears of joy rolled down my face as I played with all of them. I saw out of the corner of my eye, their food bowls and water bowls and cleaning equipment, toys, and stuff was all there.

I had no idea what to name them. I led them inside and put food and water out for them. Surprisingly, they all listened very well. They already seemed to have understood what I meant by 'stand' and 'sit' and 'eat'. I was so chuffed that they weren't that much hard work. I placed them all in a straight line so I could look at their cute little faces properly and decide on names, and, they all had to be boy names. Their eyes were the lightest and most beautiful shades of green, blue, and black.

Malamute was first in line, then the Inu, then Pitbull and last but not least the Doberman.

I sat down cross legged in front of them.

"Hi." I said awkwardly, petting the Pitbull. They all barked quietly in response.

Titus was the Malamute's name I had decided on.

Trigger - such an original name - was what I chose for the Pitbull.

Virtus was what I chose for the Doberman, and last but not least, Zyron, our very on Shiba Inu. I got onto my knees, sitting on my calves looking at all of them. They had all finished eating and sent wolfish grins my way.

I pointed at the Pitbull. "Your name is Trigger." I scratched his head slightly. I then pointed at the Malamute. "Your name is Titus, you're going to be so big when you're older!" I gushed, kissing his head. I then moved onto the Doberman and pet him too. "You're Virtus. I love it." He licked my hand and yapped happily. "And last but not least you little fluff ball, your name is Zyron." I mumbled, pulling the puppy into my lap, as the others followed.

I was happy that I now had these doggos, I gave them a tour around the house and all. I just had to go to the pet's store and buy them leads, they already had their boxes in case of trips to the vet, which I was grateful for, they needed to be vaccinated and that was also happening today. I glanced at the time and smiled to myself, I had long until I had to get ready for the dinner.

I drove over to the pet's store, not before threatening the dogs that if anything was chewed on I wouldn't be very happy. I grabbed the same collars for all of them, they were black with small studs on them. They were in a badass family now, they were also badasses. The leads I chose were all the chain style leads, but the holding bit was different colours. Titus was blue, Zyron was red, Virtus was red, and Trigger was white. I grabbed a few packets of dog treats with me too.

I rushed back home, getting ready to get them vaccinated. I was so happy with these dogs. I came inside and yelled "Honeys! I am home!" dramatically, before rushing off to the garage to see them all sleeping soundly. I cooed at them and got them all to get in their boxes. I didn't want to wake them up, they seemed so peaceful! These dogs were officially my weakness.

I got them all in safely, and drove to the vets. It didn't take as long as I thought, all of them were done and dusted in under an hour, and I was glad. I took them back home and let them knock out.

I made sure their bowls and everything were full, and their water was full. I decided I would make a big shed in the garden for them later.

My heart swelled in happiness because they weren't even scared of me which I was grateful of. I was so happy that they weren't timid or anxious. Maybe they were? But it didn't seem like it.

I took a glance at the clock and it just hit 3.

I had around 2 hours to get ready.

I didn't fret because I know I would get in time.

"Guys. I got 4 puppies for my birthday. I'm squealing.." I texted on the group chat, waiting for replies.

"I'M FUCKING COMING OVER TO SEE THEM!" Willow texted back.

"SAME!" Raeni also texted back.

"ME AS WELL OMG." Darya said as I chuckled.

"You know what, get ready at my house, bring all of your stuff we have enough space." I texted smiling.

"I'm down." Willow replied.

"Down 2." Darya started.

"You know I'm on my way girl tf you thought?" Raeni texted as I laughed. I lay on the bed, laughing to myself.

I was truly happy with the people I had in my life at the moment. But I couldn't help but feel this would go spiralling downhill very soon.

~*~

UNKNOWN POV:

"Have we found her?" A gruff voice muttered, lighting up a cigar.

"Yes boss. She turns 19 today, reservations at a restaurant at 6, with 5 other girls." His shaking voice replied.

"Good. I want you to go get her and bring her back." He said, taking a long drag.

"I want her back. Dead or alive." He said, sipping his scotch.

twenty-six

I t's time to go hard or go home,One way up, no way out,I give it up, all for the family, We stay up, no bail outs,We give it up, All for the family.

"FUCK YOU! HE IS ALL MINE." Willow growled, trying to pick Titus up. He yelped and ran towards me jumping into my arms. I let out a big laugh, shoving it in her face. She crossed her arms and pouted.

"Wills you have less than and hour to get ready. We're going on a fancy girls night out. You need a babes." I said, as she widened her eyes.

"I have your brother." She said, smiling.

"Brother?" Raeni and Darya said, popping out of the toilet. I grimaced and silently shook with laughter. Ocean shook her had but had an amused smile on her face.

"Hell yeah her brother, he's so hot. Girls I swear, when you see him, you are going to FLY off of your horses. We had sex, and let me tell youuu!" She said, looking dreamy, dragging out the 'you'.

"His dick is MAS-"

"NOPE! WE ARE NOT HAVING THIS CONVERSATION ABOUT MY BROTHER." I yelped, shielding my ears. They all laughed as I grumbled cuss words, picking Trigger up. I pet him for a few minutes then put him down so I could start getting ready.

"Girls. We have under an hour to get ready." I said loudly, making them freeze.

"FUCK!" Darya shouted, running towards the toilet, Raeni took her hair cap off and Willow looked like she was going to faint. Ocean was sat there staring at her phone like a bloody creep.

"Oh dear." I muttered, shooing the dogs out. Soon it was just us 5. I walked over to my closet and looking through the dresses. I went with a red silk dress, it clung to my body at the top and flowed out into a fishtail end. It was off the shoulders, with of course, a split in the middle. I slipped it on and started working on my hair. I decided to curl it loosely, and then put it in a half up half down, Ariana style. I chose some nude Azzedine Alaia bombe 110, suede heels to go with the dress. I did my usual makeup, with a bold red lip and a simple cat eye. I made sure to get my knife and my gun strap. I strapped it to my thigh quickly and shoved the knife into a little pocket I had created especially for it.

I was done, but the others weren't as fast as I was. Their hair and dress and shoes were all on, the only thing they had left was their makeup.

Raeni had a stunning yellow dress not the bright highlighter yellow, but the pastel kind of toned down yellow that complimented her dark skin beautifully. Her hair was in tight natural 3C curls, just hanging below her shoulders. She finished off her eye makeup and applied a pretty dark purple. She paired her dress with black heels.

Darya looked absolutely stunning too. She was wearing a white long dress, that was covered in silver embellishment. The back was open, and dipped into a v, right below her waistline. Her hair was let down freely in natural dark waves. She wore Jimmy Choo's Romy 100 silver heels. Her makeup was a silver glitter cut crease with nude lipstick and of course, the base.

Willow had a hard time finding a dress for herself. I eventually told her to go with black, and boy was black her colour. Her dress was a two piece, and a silky material. The top had gold embellishment on it, it was filled with gold embellishment and a sheer piece of fabric that just showed her collarbone. Her skirt was tight fitted, making her figure look even more defined than it already was. It flurred out into a circle like round up, and she paired it with gold Carvela heels. Her makeup was minimalist, a pink nude lippy and gold eye shadow.

Ocean had a beautiful royal blue ballgown making her look like a 2018 version of Cinderella. She had dyed the blonde ends of her hair blue a few days prior, which literally completed the look. Her eye makeup was stunning, and really brang out her green and yellow eyes. She paired it with white Aldo heels, and had a white clutch with topped it all off. Her hair was straightened and she looked gorgeous, all of them did.

We were all finished just in time, and we looked like a bunch of princesses. My tattoos were out and they said it made me look like a 'fallen angel', whatever that meant.

"Picture time!" Darya squealed. "My phone can take pictures on it owns, all we have to do is pose." She said smirking slightly. I sighed loudly.

We took quite a few and then set off. We reached there pretty quick, and like all the other restaurants, everyone was in big ass ballgowns or suits.

We all strolled inside confidently, standing side by side.

"Reservations for 5 at 6 please." I told the man that booked us in. He looked at my arms rudely and glanced back at his book.

"Sorry, we have no reservations at 6. Goodbye." He said rudely, glaring at Raeni.

"I booked it already. Call the manager." I muttered, getting angry. Willow placed a hand on my shoulder and squeezed it tightly.

"Calm down. It's okay." She whispered, smiling. I nodded but said nothing.

The manager came and was utterly confused.

"I have reservations at 6 booked under Romero. Please, if you will, check the bookings again. I had called earlier." I growled, growing impatient.

Some lady and her 15 year old looking daughter walked passed me, her mother sending me a dirty look.

"Do you see the filth on her arms? Amelie? Disgusting. I bet her parents are drug dealers or something, there is no way she could afford this place." She muttered lowly, but not low enough.

"Mom! How dare you? She is minding her own business, and quite frankily, I love her tattoos." She shrieked looking over at me. I sent her a smile and she smiled back. "I'm sick of these dinner parties, I'm sick of dresses, I'm sick of my hair being tugged at EVERY FUCKING WEEK!" She roared, pulling her heels off and chucking it to the other side of the lounge waiting area. "I refuse to become what you want me to become; this picture you have of an absolutely PERFECT daughter will not work with me!" The five of us were full on grinning, her mother had her hands over her mouth in shock. "I don't want to be apart of your fantasy world mom. It's killing me. I want to wear band tee's and ripped jeans. Goodbye. I'll be at home." She said, ripping her fake lashes off and smearing her lipstick off of her lips.

"You go girl!" I hollered making her laugh. Her mother sent the nastiest glare at me.

"Also mom, when I'm of age, I'm getting both my arms tatted like hers. And there is nothing you can do to stop me. Oh, and I also like girls." She yelled, running off. I smirked and shook my head. Her mothered glared at me and ran outside.

I turned back to the guy at the booking thing.

"Can we go in yet or not?" I asked annoyed.

"What was the table b-booked under?" The manager stuttered. Why was he even stuttering?

"Romero. Now if I don't get in there within the next 10 seconds, hell is going to be raised." I growled lowly. He nodded frantically and led us inside.

"Right this way miss." He led us to a table not too far at the back, it was a little in the centre but it was fine.

"Finally!" I grumbled, sitting down. The girls laughed and sat down too.

~*~

We were halfway through eating and chatting when some waitress came out with a birthday cake and a 1 and a 9 perched on top. I groaned internally.

"Happy birthday to you, happy birthday to you, happy birthday dear Dom, happy birthday to you!" They all sung along with my traitor friends. I smiled slightly and blew the candles out. We got a free bottle of red wine, which was good.

"Thanks for coming guys." I mumbled, smiling. I was actually very happy. Out of the corner of my eye, I saw two black SUV's park up right outside the place. I couldn't help but feel weary, Willow and Ocean knew how to protect themselves, but Darya and Raeni worried me. Four bulky men walked out, heading straight inside. I then noticed two men in suits, staring at me from the other side of the room.

I rang up Axel quickly, asking him to get into the security system and shut the cameras off.

"Axel? I'm at The Emperor's Junction in New York. Tell anyone my location I swear I will rip each of your fingernails out and make you eat them. Disable all the cameras, we're going to have some fun." I smiled, acting casual.

"On it boss." He said and I cut the call.

"Guys I feel like something bad is going to happen. I have 2 guns and knife but that's all. There are 4 men coming inside and 2 on the other side of the room. Don't look." I warned as OCean ever so slightly tilted her head. "Wills and Ocean, you two know how to defend yourselves no? Darya and Raeni?" I asked, impatiently as they nodded too. I breathed a prayer and closed my eyes. My phone started ringing and I saw it was Dane.

"Hello?"

"Domenica?" He said. There was a slight, cold edge to his voice.

"Yes I'm here is everything okay? Is Rosella alright? Your mother? Did something happen?" I questions, anxiety forming in the pit of my stomach.

"We're all fine. I called you to tell you that..I..Well-" He stumbled over his words in a clipped tone.

"You what Dane? What's wrong?" I said, my hands getting sweaty.

"We need to break up. It's not you it's me. I never liked you in the first place to be honest. You were supposed to be a quick hump and dump but you never opened your legs up. Sorry. I need action, I'm a man." I winced, and felt a stab of hurt in my chest. "Well don't text, call, or look or speak about me again. We're over. I thought you knew better than to fall for a mafia don." He said, chuckling cruelly.

"Okay." I replied numbly, cutting the call off.

"He broke up with me...over the phone..." I whispered, choking on a sob.

"It's okay babygirl he was a dickhead anyways." Willow said, rubbing my back. The two me were now walking towards us, I saw a bulge on his back as the guy got up.

"Guns they have guns." I whispered manically, making their eyes widen. I rolled my shoulders back and smiled slightly.

"This is just what I need." I mumbled to myself, smiling.

The sounds of shots bounced off of the walls, as the whole restaurant went into a frenzy.

"Now girls, this is where all the anger and rage you have comes in hand. Don't think, hit, there are knifes, forks, hell even hot candle wax. Use whatever you can and do not, I repeat, DO NOT, try and get yourselves killed. And also, once you're in, you don't get out. It's time to go hard or go home." I smiled cynically, blowing out a breath. They glanced at me uneasily, but grins overtook their frowns.

"I've been waiting for some action for years Demonica." Darya said, smirking slightly, pulling out a gun. I gaped at her, making her laugh. Ocean and Willow picked up sharp knives, and Raeni pulled out two guns too.

"Whatever happens, we're sisters from now." I said, gulping down the bottle of red wine. There was 6 men now surrounding us, the whole place evacuated.

"Let the games begin!" I roared with excitement, pulling out both of my guns, letting my beast that was dying to get out, finally free.

twenty-seven

Do you think of me?And how I fell in deep when you touched my skin,Oh it's to leave our hands,Left to shivering,Didn't catch a breath before we jump right in,I don't know if we can make it out.

Grinning, while putting shots in whoever came my way, I decided that today everything could go very wrong. The other girls were managing this pretty well. Some big guy attacked me with knives and I must say he had strength. I ran over to our table quickly, got my phone, powered it fully off and shoved it in my bra too.

He roughly pulled my hair, making me wince a tiny bit, but I elbowed him in the nose, making him stumble back. Some other dudes had Darya cornered and on impulse I shot them both in the head. She threw a light smile at me, getting back to work.

I felt a sharp pain in my shoulder blade, I touched it lightly and hissed at the burning sensation. I turned around and saw a timid guy standing there with wide eyes.

"Oh Lord I am so sorry I had no idea that was going to hit you. Fuck me I'm so sorry!" He rambled, going a teensy bit red.

"You're on the other side, why are you sorry?" I said lowly, walking up to him. Tears built up in his eyes as he looked towards the SUV's.

"Can we pretend we're fighting so we're on the floor and no one is listening? Because girl, everyone hears everything round here." He said with sass.

"Sure, punch me." I mumbled, as his fist came flying towards me. I ducked and kicked his shin, making him fall, he pulled on my arm making me fall with him.

"I never wanted to be in this stupid business but this fucking guy picked me up while I was walking home from school and told me I've been recruited. I don't want to stay there. It's horrific what they do to innocent boys and girls. Please help me get out of there." He said, tearing up.

I punched his jaw lightly, making him roll on top of me.

"How do I know this isn't some bullshit act?" I said, pushing him off of me. "Prove it." I said, standing up.

"How?" He mumbled, looking around.

I saw Willow and Ocean cornered by 4 guys that I had no idea show up.

"Shoot 'em all." I grinned, handing him the gun on the floor - that was not mine.

He nodded without hesitation and shot them all in the head, one by one.

"If you double cross me, I'll torture your family in front of you. I will make you beg for your life. Do not double cross me." I growled, kicking his shin. "Go back to whatever you're doing with these lot, I promise I'll get you out. Who planned this anyway?" I asked, looking outside. The SUV's were gone?

"Some boss call Viktor? Part of a gang or something. I don't know why, somethin' about his daughter." He mumbled, making my eyes widen. My heart dropped down to my feet.

The whole place was soon surrounded by men, and the girls and I had suddenly become in the middle.

"All we want is Domenica. The rest of you can go freely." One guy with a navy suit said. He wasn't bad looking, but he was on the other side.

"Why? What do you need her for?" I asked, glaring daggers at him. He smirked slightly.

"You'll only know that once you come with us." He said, keeping his eyes on me.

"The girls go unharmed?" I asked, making Darya grip my shoulder.

"Do not! We're in this together! If you get taken we do too!" She growled in my ear. My heart swelled in pride, knowing she would give it up for me.

"Darya go, then help me get out. You know what these guys look like. I will get out alive I promise." I said. She looked as if she was thinking and then slowly nodded.

"The girls go freely now. If any of you follow them or keep tabs on them I will burn ALL of you alive. Don't underestimate me." I said confidently.

"The girls can go, and no we wont keep tabs. We only want you Domenica." He said, looking at me like a pervert.

"Guys go, I'll handle it from here. Thanks for your help." I said, smiling slightly.

They left quickly, I trusted them to make the right decisions. I turned back round, the guy was right in front of me.

"What do you want with me Zed? I'm done. I left 5 years ago." I said sighing.

"Boss wants revenge. You did kill his daughters." He said. He looked over to someone behind me and nodded.

"I didn't fucking kill his useless daughters. They killed themselves. I had a mission that night, I didn't need him to send two untrained girls to 'look out for me'. He killed his own daughters." I growled.

I felt a big pain at the back of my head, I put my hands on it to see warm blood over my hands.

"Good luck. The game's have officially begun." I mumbled, smiling. I fell, falling into a deep dark blackness.

I felt myself being carried somewhere, then thrown into a van, then thrown into a deep slumber.

~*~

I groaned as I tried sitting up, but I couldn't sit up. I tried again and it was like someone was restricting me. I tried opening my eyes but it was hard. I tried moving but all I felt was pain.

I then noticed I was chained up. It was dark and smelt rotten. I squinted my eyes at the scratched, blood stains filled walls.

"Where the fuck..?" I moaned in pain, trying to get out of the chains.

"You're awake! Finally." He said. I couldn't see him but I could hear him.

"Morning!" I chirped sarcastically. He chuckled and sighed.

"Still that same old sarcastic whore you are. How did it feel killing your gang members?" He growled as I laughed.

"ME? What! I killed no one. You killed them. You killed your own daughters Viktor, by sending them to MY mission that you knew I could handle. Why'd you do it? Why'd you kill them?" I asked smiling crazily. A loud slap echoed throughout the room. The side of my face was burning but I shook it off anyway.

"5 years ago you ran away. 5 years ago you murdered my daughters. And 5 years later here we are, I'm going to kill you." He said, laughing insanely. I felt kind of scared because his laugh wasn't normal; it was a creepy laugh coming from a grieving unstable man.

"I left England. Why are you even in America?" I asked, my eyes drooping ever so slightly.

"To find you. Ever since you left I've been trying to keep tabs on you but every time I found something it magically disappeared." I laughed again. "Who said we're even in America my darling Dom?" He grinned as my heart dropped again.

"I heard you're in contact with Mr Dane Donatti. How's that going for ya?" He said, chuckling evilly. Tears built up in my eyes but I pushed them back.

"I don't know what you're talking about. I don't know who he is either." I said coldly. He looked at me in surprise and chuckled.

I fake yawned and smiled.

"Alright honey are we getting this party started or not?" I mumbled. He flipped me off and went through the doors. I tried my hardest to get out of the chains but it was extremely hard.

"Stop moving. It wont work." A voice said, scaring the absolute life out of me.

"Jesus Christ! What the fuck is wrong with you?! You scared the shit out of me." I grumbled.

"Who are you?" The voice croaked as I sighed.

"No one. You?" I asked stupidly.

"Someone." He said, groaning. I heard footsteps and Zed came through.

"I need to go toilet, hello Zed." I mumbled yawning.

"You can't." He said curtly.

"Do you want me to bleed out all over the floor that you're walking on with blood from my vagina?" I seethed, glaring at him making him flinch.

"N-no." He stuttered, going red.

"Exactly! So go to one of the girls and get me a pad and show me where the toilets are, because God help me when I get out of these chains and see you if you don't start runnin'." I growled as he nodded frantically and took off.

"Impressive." The guy said.

I shrugged my shoulders and waited for Zed to come back. "I'll get you outta here mate." I mumbled.

"You can't, I tried everything. Got me whips for 3 weeks." He said sadly as I suddenly felt sad. He was muscular but not that muscular, probably from the lack of food.

"Do you not recognise me?" He mumbled in pain as I furrowed my eyebrows.

"Recognise you? I can't even see you that well." I muttered squinting my eyes.

"Never mind. I'm just playing with you." He mumbled, then going quiet.

Zed came back with a bag. He unlocked my chains and told me to follow him.

"Well you were shit at fighting 5 years ago, you probably still are shit. So, whatever." I mumbled, looking at me up and down. I smirked internally.

"You damn right. Stepped into a gym and they all laughed at me." I mumbled sarcastically - it wasn't half wrong.

We walked through a dark corridor, took two lefs and right, then up some stairs. None of the doors required locks.

He led me into a normal house looking place, which made me figure that me and the other boy are in a basement.

He took me to a room and shoved me into a bathroom.

"You have 5 minutes. Don't try and escape, you can't anyway." He chuckled as I slammed the door on him and locked it.

I took the phone out of my bra; they were such a dumb gang, they never properly frisked anyone.

I turned it on and saw my whole messages bombarded with texts from the girls. I texted them quickly telling them I'm okay. I pretended to flush the toilet as Zed knocked and told me to hurry up. I texted Axel and told him to track my location down and tell the girls, I gave him Willows number.

It was currently 8 in the evening.

Such a great birthday. I powered it off and shoved it back in. I washed my hands and washed my face too. I found a hairband and put my hair up. I unlocked the door and walked out to Zed sitting down on a chair staring at his phone intently.

I could just kill him right now.

He didn't even hear me coming out.

"Hello?" I mumbled.

He still stared at his phone.

I grabbed a book from the desk next to me and lobbed it at his head.

"Wake up." I said curtly. "I could have escaped." His eyes widened and glared at me. He took me back down, and I saw someone who I thought I never would see again.

"Mason..?" I gaped, looking at him. He looked up in confusion. He stared right at me, but I knew he didn't recognise who I was.

"How do you know my name?" He asked, gripping my arm. Zed was rooted in his place.

"What?" I said dumbly.

"You said my name, Mason?" He asked.

"I said hydration?" I said, making him confused.

"Who said Mason?" He asked, looking around.

"I dunno, I said hydration. Need water." I turned back to Zed and he led me back down. Mason stared at me as I was going down the stairs. We took the right then two lefts and then ended up in front of the basement doors.

I had memorised the way to get out.

I was chained up again and Zed pushed food in front of us.

"Do you know where we are?" I mumbled to the guy, not feeling hungry. I pushed my tray towards him but took the bottle of water.

"I've been trying to find out for 4 years D. I don't know where we are." He mumbled. He called me D?

"We'll be out in no time." I mumbled, my mind falling back to Dane. I can't believe he just left me like that.

I leaned my head back against the concrete wall, falling into a deep sleep.

twenty-eight

I swear I'll bite my tongue next time that you're speaking,Cause you deserve the time of day,I abused your kindness with my weakness,I threw it in your face.Way to go, way to go, what a joke,I'm a joke.

Days had gone by. I was still stuck here, not knowing when to make a move. I wasn't allowed to go to the toilet but today I needed to get into contact with someone.

"Zed I need to go toilet. I'm still on my period of you hadn't noticed!" He silently nodded his head and took me to the toilet. I was surprised at how quiet he was and why he had let me go without saying no.

"You alright mate?" I mumbled, stopping in front of the toilet. His eyes turned glossy and he shook his head a no.

"They have Adrianna. They think I'm on the other side Dom." He said, sighing.

"Well you might as well help us now? Who has Adrianna?" I asked as he unlcoked the door for me.

"Russians." He mumbled as I had an 'oh' look on my face.

"Well hope she come's back quickly." I mumbled going into the toilet.

"Wait!" He said, gripping my wrist.

"What?" I mumbled again.

"Help me and I'll help you. I'll try get you out of here, hell I'll die for you as long as you can get Adrianna out. She's only 17 Dom please." He begged, a tear dropping.

"I'll see what I can do." I mumbled, my heart feeling heavy.

I had gotten beaten up multiple times these few days, thrown against walls and stabbed. They never got any information out of me, it wasn't like I was going to rock up and give it to them in their hands. I winced at the pain in my ribs as I inspected my face.

I was ghostly pale, dark bruises encircled my eyes. I pulled my phone out and turned it on to a shit ton of messages.

One was from Dane. I could only read the first bit, but I refused to open it.

"Domenica where are you? Everyone is worr-" It didn't take a genius to figure out what the end word was. I sighed and checked if anything came from the girls.

The groupchat was active and suddenly tears had fallen down my faces.

"Domenica if you see this you've been shifted multiple times across England. Everytime I get your location, it changes again! Someone is betraying you and I don't know who it is!" She said, in a voice note.

The only person I had told to help me was...

Axel!

That fucking bitch. Of course he's still loyal to a group that killed his mother.

I was fucking fuming and asked her to track it herself. Raeni had great computer skills and Darya said she'd try.

Diana had also texted me, so did Damien. And my mother sent me about 3955 missed calls. i hoped that they were all okay, and that my dogs were also okay. I missed those fur balls. Dane had called me, my phone was buzzing slightly because the silencer was on. I ignored it and shut the phone off and shoved it back in my bra. I flushed the toilet and washed my hands and came out.

Zed was staring at the wall in front of him. I pulled him out of his thoughts by tapping his shoulder. I suddenly felt out of breath, and my chest started hurting. I struggled to allow the air to pass through where it needed to. I didn't know what was happening to me, I started coughing and I coughed up blood like that morning we went to see the girls.

Zed looked at me in alarm and rubbed my back softly.

Eventually, I blacked out.

~*~

I woke up in the same room, chained to the wall. I had more bruises over my arms, and I don't even know how I got them.

"Someone are you okay?" I croaked, looking at him. He nodded at me but looked at me weirdly and chucked a water bottle my way.

"Why are you asking me? I should be asking you. Those fuckers beat you even when you were unconscious." He growled. I was surprised, why did he even care?

"Why do you even care? I don't know you." I said coldly.

"You do fucking know me." He replied, in the same tone.

"No I don't! I don't even know who you are! You're delusional." I muttered, glaring at the chains.

"It really hurts me that you forgotten who I am Domo." He said softly. My breath hitched when he said Domo.

"Don't you remember me at all? Our tree house? The stroopwaffels you loved when my mum made them? Sneaking into my dads office to get his to his chocolate box? You don't remember any of that?" He said as tears built up in my eyes.

Memories kept replaying in my head as I finally figured out who I was talking to. I left all those years ago without even saying goodbye...

"Ricca..I'm so sorry." I said weakly.

"It's okay Domo. I wouldn't have remembered me either." He said in a weird tone.

"We'll get out of here. I promise." I mumbled as he shrugged his shoulders.

~*~

DANE'S POV:

I was going out of my mind. It had been roughly 4 days since she's been gone, and I've tried to get in contact with her but I can't.

I slammed my fist into the wall, breathing heavily.

I couldn't function without her. And I was a fucking prick for breaking up with her like that, but I had no choice.

I knew that if I had told her why I broke up with her she'd go off her nut.

I missed her tattooed arms and her plump lips. Her long black her and her brown eyes. I missed her, and I doubt she'd take me back.

"Don Donatti! I found something on the Russians! Apparently they are working with a big gang in England." Raquel said as I took the papers from him.

"Get me everyone that is in the gang. Their names and all." I mumbled. I tried to think how this would plan out. She was in a gang, but I didn't know which one.

Willow and Ocean would be happy to help, so I gave them a call.

I rang Willow first, waiting for her to pick up.

"Hello?" She mumbled tiredly.

"Willow right?" I said as she sucked in a breath.

"Who's this?" She seethed. "How did you get my number?"

"Relax. It's Dane." I said, Raquel coming back in. That was quick.

He dropped the papers on my desk and headed back out. I read what the gangs name was and apparently they were called the Black Diamonds.

"Round up the girls that were with you on the night she was taken. Meet me at my house, I'll send you the address." I ordered as she chuckled humourlessly.

"Why should I? You broke her fucking heart. I had never seen her so unhappy and so...distant at all! Why are you even helping her?" She asked softly as I sighed.

"Come and I'll explain everything Willow. Bring the other girls too, I know there was other girls there. Meet me at my house in thirty, I'm texting you the address now." I cut the call off, putting my head in my hands.

I hoped she was okay. I then called her brother. Her brother actually took over the mafia her dad was running, that's why he was gone for so many years.

"Damien someone took your sister. I've been trying to find her ma non posso. I need your help." (But I can't). He sighed over the phone.

"My papa will go mad if she is hurt. Of course I will help you, tell me what you need. Diana and my mama are so worried." He said as I nodded even though he couldn't see.

"Domenica's friends that were with her are coming in thirty minutes. You might as well come, and I know Diana is going to want to as well." I said, thinking about Domenica and how she is.

"I'll be thee soon brother." HE said, and I cut the call.

Rosella rushed into my room with a big smile on her face.

"Come sta la mia principessa oggi?" (How is my princess doing today?) She giggled and I lifted her up into my lap.

"I'm fine Dee Dee. How are you and where is Dommy? I miss her." She frowned as I hugged her.

"She'll be back tesoro." (Darling). She nodded and jumped out of my lap.

"I'm going to go scare mama! Bye Dee Dee!" She said enthusiastically as I chuckled. I couldn't help but wonder what Domenica would be with kids. Our kids. I definitely wanted to spend the rest of my life with her.

She is the first woman that I have loved romantically, after my crazy bitch of an ex.

I put my head in my hands and felt my heart hurt.

I missed her and hoped she was okay.

I was definitely going to bring her back to me...even if it meant being dead.

twenty-nine

I'm way too gold for this beef, feel like I'm Kobe,Yeah this right here is astronomical,I see you picked up all my ways, I feel responsible,They tryna say that all my problems is improbable,They keep itching at my spit, I'm diabolical,You feel me?

Days had turned into weeks, and weeks had turned into months. I had just had a mad beating before, and the fucking prick stabbed me twice! I've officially been here for a month and two days.I coughed violently, coughing up blood. I felt dizzy but it went away quickly.

I hadn't seen Zed since he told me that the Russians had his sister and that he was willing to help me.

I don't know why I didn't take my knife and do anything. Oh wait, I was chained to a fucking wall. They moved me to a different room every time that they had their 'fun'. Me and Ricca had a long ass conversations about when we were younger and the times we had together.

I sighed again, looking at Ricca sitting uncomfortably on the floor. I missed Dane, I missed Willow, Ocean, Darya and Raeni. I missed my sister and my mother.

I couldn't help but feel like they had...forgotten or something about me. I wouldn't be surprised if they had anyway.

The door slammed open, making Ricca jump in fright. Victor came out in all his ugliness and gave me the dirtiest glare he could muster.

"Alright Vic?" I croaked, smirking slightly. There was no way I was going to not annoy him. He sneered at me, and stalked over to me. I was still smiling until he slapped me. Hard.

I pouted and looked at him with big eyes.

"What was that for Vic? Not very gentlemanly of you." I said sarcastically, straightening my neck out. He punched my again making me wince in pain.

I rested my head on the wall for a second when he took a big ass swing again, the other side this time.

"Who pissed in your cheerios Victoria?" I mumbled, trying to ignore the pain in my jaw.

"The Russians don't trust me anymore because of your fucking boyfriend! They landed an attack on one of the Russian hideouts, thinking I was involved! Fucking bastards!" He roared as I chuckled, coughing violently again.

"You do realise that you're going to die after all of this right?" I said seriously.

"What makes you think that princess?" He said, crouching down to my level and gripped my hair making me look at him.

"Because I'm going to rip your fucking heart out of your chest. I'm going to dig my hands inside your throat and pull your vocal box out because the way you talk pisses me off." I stated, grinning insanely.

"You actually are insane. Anyway, I'd like to see you try you slut." He seethed, pushing a knife into my thigh. It burned like fuck, but there was no way I was going to give him the satisfaction of my pain. No way in hell.

He left, the knife still stuck in my thigh. I yanked it out, muffling a scream with my arm over my mouth. My eyes watered and I tried to clean it up with water and a piece of cloth that I had ripped off my shirt. I wrapped around my thigh tightly, to stop the bleeding.

I leaned my head back and prayed for some miracle to help us out, because at this rate, we'd probably die here. And I didn't want to die too soon.

~*~

DANE'S POV:

We stood around a massive table, and stared at the maps in front of us. We had taken a flight to England, and we were in one of my bases here.

Damien, Darya, Willow, Ocean, Raeni, Raquel, Jordan, Ali, Luca and Diana were helping me. A few of my men were also here. My brother Angelo was supposed to be here too but I had no idea where he was.

"Alright guys. Their base is most probably guarded, but not with Russians because they think he betrayed him. Thank you Darya and Raeni for that, but I'm not fully sure if they would be or not." I sent a pointed look their way as they smiled.

"The basement they are staying in is in a spacious house, guarded of course. Kill anyone who pulls something out at you; or tries to hurt you in anyway. Me and Damien and Willow will go to the basement, that is one right, two lefts and then down the stairs. Ocean and Raeni along with Raquel, and Jordan, will help get rid of any obstacles. We haven't attack the Russians but we could be wrong and they could be there, the Russians aren't very predictable. Get Dom out of there as quick as we can. If there are any obstacles, get rid of them. Some of mine and Damien's men will be with us too, for extra support. Ali will be controlling the CCTV's and stuff, you should all have your ear pieces, we also go through to back, quietly." I sent a look at Luca because the dickhead made noise even when he was sleeping He smiled sheepishly and shrugged his shoulders.

"It's been a month guys. We should have done this quicker and I'm sorry we couldn't but the Russians could still be there. The guns, knives, ammo everything is out set up and out, take what you need. Take medical kits too. We set off 00:00 in the night. Try not to get killed please. And girls, I know it may be a little gory for you but please don't hesitate to take a life." I said, as they nodded.

"Kill or be killed guys. Let's get ready." I mumbled as they took what they needed. Damien patted me on the back and thanked me for helping his sister. I hoped that this would all plan out nicely, and that it would go according to plan.

But deep down I knew that something was going to fuck it up.

Or should I say someone.

thirty

Customising diamond chains,Man we was lost and had to find away,Smoking on gelato, these Laboutins got the sparkles,I started with half O's with dreams to be a narco.

Soft murmuring took me out of the sleep I was in. I always had been a very light sleeper, and I could ever so slightly hear what they were saying. I glanced at the broken, but working clock that hung above the door. Victor said he wanted me to count every second that I was hear, being beaten and stabbed until someone came to save me; he was absolutely one hundered percent sure that NO ONE would risk their lives for me.

And so I was I. I had no hope anymore, the hope I did have died down after being her for a month.

I tried to move but I had been stabbed severely, and my thigh was not making it any better. I glanced at Ricca and he looked troubled in his sleep, but I didn't wake him up.

"Dane isn't coming after her! They broke up." Victor said furiously, I could just make out what he was saying since I always had to have a good ear.

"He is coming! Trust me. He is he gathered everyone today at one of his bases. I know, I was there." I suddenly felt furious, someone was betraying him but the most shit part was that it came out very muffled, and I couldn't exactly hear the voice, but only make out what he said.

I glanced at the clock and it had just hit 11 in the night. I couldn't help but feel utterly anxious, as if something bad was going to happen.

Zed opened the door, and he was battered and bruised. I gasped as he wobbled over to me.

"T-they killed Adrianna! The R-russians!" He sobbed, shutting the door behind him.

"Oh Zed. Come 'ere." I mumbled as he sobbed in my arms. He was my friend at one point, and I knew how much his family meant to him.

"I'll help you, I'll do whatever as long as the Russians and Victor is dead. He told him their l-location." He hiccuped as he now sat next to me, his head on my shoulders.

"I'm chained Zed, there isn't much I can do." I muttered quietly. I heard a shring a ling, like keys.

"Not anymore." He said smiling softly. He held out the key and dropped it in my hand.

"Take Ricca too. He's been here far too long. The keys are the same because this dumb fuck of a gang is far too idiotic to actually act like one. I don't even know why we're one of the biggest ones. And Ricca, I got shot trying to save you and get you out of here." Zed said as Ricca's glare softened. He turned around and pulled his shirt up, a bullet would moulded into his skin.

"Thanks." Ricca muttered looking the other way. It now turned 11:15, and I don't know what I was waiting for, but, I was waiting. We all heard footsteps, Zed shoved the key into my bra, and acted like he wasn't just crying at ran over to the door.

"Don't try anything stupid because you two fuckers aren't getting out of here." He sneered as Victor came in.

Victor patted his back and Zed left, not before turning around and winking.

"Two of my bitches!" Victor said, clapping.

"I'm not a bitch." Me and Ricca said in unison.

"Shut the fuck up! You are what I tell you you are!" He sneered, punching Ricca in the stomach. The man didn't even flinch,

"Alright Victoria, don't get your panties in a twist." I said, smiling coyly. He glared at me but did nothing.

"I can't wait to see your rotting bodies in here." He sneered, stalking back upstairs and slamming the door behind him. I let out a sigh of relief, and looked at Ricca who looked a little pale.

I took the keys out, very fucking hardly can I add, and tried to unlock myself. After around a fucking million goes, I was out. I stretched my arm out, and watch the clock hit 11:30.

I stalked over to Ricca, unlocking him too. He immediately engulfed me into a big bear hug. I patted his back awkwardly and chuckled.

"Didn't know you missed me that much Ricca." I teased, smiling. He flicked my nose and snuggled his head in the crook of my neck.

"Don't get too alarmed, I know you love Dane. I'm gay." He mumbled, still his face in my neck.

"I don't love him." I said, lying through my teeth. He chuckled and patted my head.

"Whatever you say Domo." I flipped him off and reached in my bra to pull out the knife. My dress was now covered in blood and dirt and literally looked like rags. I glanced at the clock again, and there was 15 minutes left till 12.

I sat back in the place I was, pretending that I was still locked up, as did Ricca. And I did shove my knife back in my bra, I took it out for no reason. I tried turning on my phone but it was fucking dead.

I silently hoped that we were getting out of here today.

~*~

DANE'S POV:

Anxiety filled the pit of my stomach. I wasn't scared, I was worried about Domenica. I had no idea whether she was there; or whether this was some kind of set up trap thing they used to lure us in.

I checked my guns were fully loaded. I also told the others to check too. I prayed that nothing would go wrong. We were currently outside, surrounding the basement, Damien and my men everywhere.

"Alright guys I just hacked into the cameras, and the place is mostly filled with women and little kids. No sign of Victor or anyone else." Ali said through our earpieces.

"Alright, just tell us when to go." I whispered, pulling the safety on my gun. I glanced around and saw 5 big trucks, which was unusual, I didn't think anyone would show up.

"Russians." Ali muttered through the earpiece. Everyone muttered shit. Everyone.

"Stronzi. Questa e una impostare." (Assholes. This is a set up). I growled lowly as everyone sighed.

Around 40 men came out of the trucks, and what pissed me off even more, was that they were heavily armed. We didn't have very many men with us. Around 28 I think.

"We're still going ahead with this guys. We can't let Domenica down. In the name of the Father, and the Son, and the Holy Spirit. Amen." I mumbled, crossing my heart and hoping to die - for Domenica.

I glanced at the watch on my wrist, and it was 4 minutes till 12. I took a deep breath in and exhaled silently.

"We all ready?" I asked as everyone murmured a yes.

"Remember guys, it's kill or be killed." I mumbled, now 2 minutes left.

30 seconds left now.

20 seconds.

10 seconds.

5 seconds.

The whole place erupted into a massive movie like scene, bullets flying everywhere. Screams and cries in agony set the whole house alight making me smile in satisfaction.

They took my Domenica, and now I'm taking her back.

<h1 style="text-align:center">t h i r t y - o n e</h1>

And I'll tell you all about when I see you again, We've come a long way, From where we began, Oh Ill tell you all about it when I see you again, When I see you again.

THIS CHAPTER CONTAINS SUICIDE, AND DEATH. PLEASE SKIP IF NEEDED. IT IS RIGHT AT THE END.

~*~

DANE'S POV:

"FUCKING SHOOT AND RUN!" I roared at everyone, racing down to the basement. I saw Victor and he tried shooting at me but the bullet strayed. I laughed at his failure and carried on trying to find the basement.

"Mr Donatti! What a pleasure!" A thick Russian accented voice said, stopping me in my tracks. I turned around and smirked coldly.

"Vladimir. Nice to see you." I said, waving my right hand slightly. Someone tried shooting at him but he was pushed by his guards and the guard shot whoever they thought had done it.

"All of you Italian bastards are dying here today! Vopros ne zadan!" (Not a question asked!) I chuckled lightly at his statement and shrugged my shoulders.

"This is our business, it is what we die for. Anyways, so long Vladamir." I mumbled, Darya shot him in the head, Raeni and Ocean putting holes in his guards.

I nodded at her as a thanks and raced to the basement. I was in a dark corridor and I finally found a door. I pushed it opened, well tried to but it didn't work.

So I shot the locks.

I pushed open the door to see Domenica tied to a chair, and looked as if she was going to pass out anytime now. So was another guy right next to her.

"Untie them quickly, Victor is coming!" Ali yelled in my ear piece.

I rushed over to Domenica and untied her.

"Dane? Is that you?" She said, squinting.

"Yes it's me baby." I mumbled, pulling her out of the chair. I made a move to go back up but she refused.

"Untie Ricca." She said. She stretched and popped her shoulder back in or some shit, she also screamed in pain. She shook it off and stood up straighter.

This Ricca boy thanked me and stretched out too.

I chucked them both guns, but Domenica was limping. Her hair was matted with blood, her dress in fucking rags, she had bruises and cuts everywhere. I couldn't help but hate myself for this happening to her.

We ran back upstairs but was stopped by some bulky as guys. Ricca and Domenica shot all of them without a blink.

"What?" Ricca said as I raised my eyebrows at him. I shook my head but carried on trying to find the rest of the gang. More of the Russian men started piling in and I started to become a little conscious of what we were doing.

We practically declared war with the Russians for killing their mafia leader.

I sighed but carried on shooting whoever came in my way.

A little girl with blonde hair and pretty brown eyes gazed up at me as tears filled her eyes. She looked 7 or 8.

"I can't find m-my m-mama." She said, wiping her eyes. "Help m-me please?" She asked as I felt somewhat sat for her.

"Sorry darling but your mama isn't with us no more. You can come with me though?" I said, crouching down to her level.

She pondered on it and thought about it for a bit. She eventually nodded. I scooped her in my arms and continued to try and make my way out of danger for her. I got to the front door and saw our van parked up.

"Go run to the black van, you're going to see a boy tell him Dane sent me. Go." I pushed her as she took off. She was pretty fast.

"Dane watch out!" Domenica yelled as I turned around and got punched.

"This is all because of you!" A man with an English accent shouted as I winced. I kicked his knees making him fall and punched him twice, lightly. He flipped us over and threw punches anywhere he could.

"Victor get off him. He can kill you easily." Domenica said boredly as I pushed him off of me.

He suddenly had a gun pointed at Domenica and shot her thigh, the same leg she was limping on.

"You motherfucker!" She cursed, trying to stop the bleeding. He suddenly froze, then fell to the floor. Blood pooled around him, a knife sticking out of his back.

All I saw was girls and one girl that was with the Bulgarian mafia lord.

"Thank you." Domenica said as she leaned against the girl.

"No, thank you. I finally built myself an empire because of you." She mumbled as she helped Domenica move out.

"Wait! Don't fucking move anyone!" I looked around and saw blood and bodies everywhere. It was literally like a slaughterhouse.

Ricca, Ocean, Willow, Raeni, Darya and Raquel were all standing together on one side. Me and the new girl, Diana and Domenica were standing on the other side. Damien quickly pointed his gun at me and pulled the trigger. I thought it would hit me but it hit someone behind me that was going to shoot me. Damien rushed over to his sister and helped her stand, as did Diana.

Our eyes were trained on the person in front of us that was currently pointing a gun at Domenica and her brother.

"Jordan? What the fuck are you doing?" I mumbled lowly as Ali yelled into my ear.

"HE IS WORKING ON THE OTHER SIDE! THIS WHOLE TIME! FUCK!" He roared in our earpieces as Willow glared at him.

Darya stepped forwards with tears in her eyes.

"Jordan?" She whispered, taking cautious steps towards him.

"Don't fucking move!" He yelled, making her flinch. He had this...crazed look in his eyes.

"What are you doing Jordan? Now isn't the time to pull jokes." Raquel said, laughing awkwardly.

"This isn't a fucking joke! I'm going to kill her. This was all a set up, a fucking plan!" He roared making everyone in the room flinch.

"Jordan. What did I do?" Domenica said, without an ounce of fear in her eyes. She slowly trodded over and stood right in front of him.

"You killed them! It was all your fucking fault." He said, tears now stream-ing down his face.

"Killed who Jordan?" She asked as he waved his gun about like a maniac.

"My parents! That night! You got into a car crash and then your ugly little whore of a sister got kidnapped." He laughed without humour. She flinched but glared at him. "The car your murderer dad spiralled into was my parents car. It was their anniversary." He said, wiping a tear. A look of realisation clouded her face as she clenched her jaw. "I got a call. We couldn't even press charges because your druggy father had influence over the fucking cops. All of you guys are dirty! I'm going to kill you all. I'm going to kill all of you." He said as she looked around boredly.

"Are you finished?" She said, looking at him.

"No. No I'm not." He said, circling her. "Let's move onto the topic of your brother why not?" Damien's eyes widened as Domenica looked at him weirdly. "Your brother has been lying to you these past years. Going to university? Hell no. Studying? Majoring? Finding a fucking job? Oh no Dom. Oh no. Your brother took over your dads mafia. You think that he's been doing all this," He waved his hands around, "This massive shit ton of work and doctoring shit. He's been fucking keeping your dads mafia going on." He screamed at her as she shrugged.

"I know. Do you think I'm that dumb that I wouldn't know what my OWN brother is doing? Now Jordan, you could have told me you know. You could have told me that it was our car that was already hit, hit your car too. You knew all about it didn't you? The magical disappearing of the breaks? Didn't you?" She said, her knife twirling in her fingers.

I had no idea what was happening.

"W-what?" He stuttered, looking flushed.

"You know exactly what the fuck I'm talking about. You gave Armarni Diana didn't you? I knew it didn't add up. Hell you even replaced the fucking body you sick fuck!" She roared as he flinched back.

"They killed Mya. They fucking raped her in front of me and I COULD NOT DO ANYTHING ABOUT IT. Do you think I wasn't going to retaliate? Your scum dad's men did that to her in front of me." He said, falling to his knees. I had known that his sister was raped and killed, but by Domenica's father?

"It wasn't my papa's men, it was the Russians. They wanted you to hate us, now you do. They USED you Jordan. You were a puppet in Vladimir's game and look where you landed. You betrayed Don Donatti, his friends and your fucking family." Damien spat, anger radiating off of him. "Maybe if you had come to me I could have helped but no, you decided to go fucking sell me sister off and turn into a fucking psycho." Damien was now in front of him.

"Damien, he isn't stable. Leave it." Domenica said, pulling him back.

"Jordan I'm sorry about your sister. But I'm not sorry about your parents, technically that was your fault. How did you even take the breaks out of my parents car? It was your fault, if they had the breaks your parents would still be here." Domenica said softly. A look of guilt and sadness came over him as his body shook as he sobbed.

"I'm sorry. I was so alone and all I could think about was revenge. My head wasn't straight." He mumbled as he started muttering shit to himself.

"We trusted you." I murmured as I walked up to you. "We trusted you Jordan. And this is how you repay us? I helped you. I gave you a home, a job, friends, a new fucking life. And this is how you repay me?" I said, chuckling. Everyone looked at me wearily as I crouched to his level.

"You should have known better. Now because of you, I trust no one in the room. I thought you were my brother. I gave you everything. Money, bitches, cars. EVERYTHING." I roared, trying to control myself. I was fuming, this stronzi had the audacity to double cross me then say he's sorry?

"And for what? You do realise in the end they were just going to kill you? DO YOU?" I yelled, making everyone flinch.

Domenica's soft hand gripped mine.

"He's hurting. Relax." She whispered. She let go of my hand and took a step back, knowing not to get involved.

"I'm sorry Dane I couldn't think straight. I didn't know what to do." He said, standing up.

"You could have come to me. I'm your fucking brother. You could have come to me and we could have avoided all of this. Now what do I do?" I asked as he picked a gun up. Instantly, everyone was pointing a gun at him.

He chuckled and smiled sadly.

"Don't worry. I'm coming to you mom, dad and Mya. I'm coming." He said, holding a gun to his head.

"Jordan! This isn't how to go about it. We know you're hurting. Put the gun down, we can figure this out." Darya pleaded as he shook his head a no.

"Jordan please. Your parents wouldn't have wanted you to do this. Put the gun down." Domenica said softly, reaching up to the gun.

"DON'T COME CLOSER!" He said, making her flinch. She raised her arms in a surrendering way and took a few steps back.

"Goodbye guys. Thank you for everything. I know I shouldn't have done this. I'm sorry Diana, I shouldn't have done that to you. Sorry Darya, but you was just bait. I used you to get to her, I knew you two would become friends. No hard feelings. Dane I'm sorry. I know I'm not stable and I abused your trust. I don't want to stay here, I have no family or nothing. Bye guys." He said, taking a deep breath in, and pulling the safety.

Darya choked back a sob as Raquel tried stopping him.

"C'mon bro. We your family. What is you doin'? Put the gun down Jord." He begged as Jordan closed his eyes.

"I'm sorry. Until I see you again, guys. I love you all. I think." Was all he said then a loud bang echoed throughout the whole house.

His body immediately fell into Raquel's arms, blood seeped through his head. I rushed over and checked his pulse, and there wasn't one.

Even though he abused my trust, he was still family. And family means everything in the mafia. My heart swelled in pain when Darya started crying. Domenica had a distant look on her face.

"We hold the funeral tomorrow. No strangers, just us." Domenica said, limping away into the car.

I picked up his body and we all soon set off home.

I watched my brother take his life.

Tears built up in my eyes as I pushed them back down and lay him on the seats.

Soon, ll of us went home. Domenica went her way, without sparing a glance at me and I went mine. I sighed.

I cleaned up his body and showered and freshened myself up. I bought him to the mafia hospital so he could be checked over in time for the funeral.

I headed back home, wondering how I was going to win Dom back.

My life was currently a mess and I didn't know how to clean it up.

I sank in my bed sheets and popped two sleeping pills, that allowed me to fall into a silent slumber.

thirty-two

I wished you, the best of, All this world could give, And I told you, when you left me, There's nothing to forgive, But I always thought you'd come back, And tell me, all you found was, Heartbreak, and misery. It's hard for me to say, I'm jealous of the way, You're happier without me

PLAY THE SONG WHEN DANE'S POV COMES. I WROTE HIS POV WHILE LISTENING TO THIS.

Weeks passed slowly, my wounds were healing. As much as I tried to erase the image of Jordan doing that I couldn't.

Me and Ricca was in a good relationship, he was now our bestfriend. Our 5th member, the girls took a strong liking to him too.

It took all of my might to ignore Dane. As much as I wanted to, I couldn't. Hell, I think I loved him.

The funeral for Jordan passed quickly, and he was buried near his family. I still couldn't get the image of him shooting himself in the head. It hurt me, a lot. Darya was finding it hard to cope, but of course we were with her forever.

It had literally been me and the four girls for the whole time I was ignoring Dane.

I missed him so much, it physically hurt me.

It was currently 6 and we were going out clubbing, so my mind could be at ease from Dane. Everywhere I looked I saw him. I had no motivation whatsoever with anyone. School passed as normal days, my grades flying high. Even Damien was worried.

I refused to speak to anyone other than the girls, Ricca and my family too. I wasn't ready to come into contact with anyone that had contact with Dane.

I felt so sick...every time I looked at him in the hallways, or passing him outside, or seeing him play football. It hurt so much.

I was currently getting ready for the club, I was round Darya's, Ocean, Willow, Raeni and Ricca were here too. I wasn't in the mood to look pretty or nice or whatever. I just couldn't be asked. I had no energy. And all I wanted to do was drink everything away.

I was still mad, furious, angry and hurt at Dane.

His words were so harsh, and the fact that he had the audacity to laugh made it worse. I hadn't been this hurt in my life after Diana and father left.

"We need to break up. It's not you it's me. I never liked you in the first place to be honest. You were supposed to be a quick hump and dump but you never opened your legs up. Sorry. I need action, I'm a man."

"Well don't text, call, or look or speak about me again. We're over. I thought you knew better than to fall for a mafia don."

I shouldn't have fell for a fucking mafia don. I was so mad at myself. I told myself that I wouldn't catch feelings for anyone when we moved here, but I did.

"Domo? You okay?" Ricca said, sitting down next to me.

"I don't know Ricca. I don't know." I mumbled, putting my arms around his waist and snuggling into his chest. Tears built up in my eyes and before I knew it, they fell freely.

I had a good long ass cry, and Ricca did nothing but console me which I was very grateful for.

Eventually we got up and got ready. I threw on a black Thrasher crop top, and some white skinny jeans. I pulled out some red Nike Air Force 1's, and took out my leather jacket. I let my hair down, and ran my fingers through them.

I didn't do much for makeup, I lined my eyes and put on some strong wine red lipstick. I spritzed perfume on and pulled my gun and knife out, and of course, brang them with me.

The girls and Ricca came out looking fine as ever. Raeni was wearing a short pink dress, Ocean was wearing ripped jeans and a crop top like me, Willow was wearing a cute overall, and Darya was wearing a two piece.

Ricca was wearing a button down top, short sleeves, and striped pants. His earring was in and he had a few necklaces around his neck.

"Ricca you sexy hunk! Would totally let you dip your dick in me if you weren't gay." Willow said, trailing a finger down his chest.

"The only person that is dipping their dick in you is me. Get your own bitch Ricca." Damien said, wrapping his arms around Willow who blushed.

I chuckled and we soon left to the club. People were scattered everywhere, in short skimpy dresses and unbuttoned shirts. The sign was bright and glowing; it had 'Déjá Vu' in bright neon font.

We headed into the club with ease, we didn't get searched surprisingly. The girls and Ricca immediately went to mingle, and I went to the bar.

"Give me your strongest." I said curtly at the bartender as he smiled lightly and nodded. He sent a shot glass towards me, filled with apple juice coloured drink. I immediately downed it, grimacing at the way it burned my throat, but fuck it, it was nice. I asked for more and more until black spots clouded my vision. They came and went.

The door slammed open, and 6 hot ass men strolled through.

"Damn." I whistled, downing another shot.

"They're pretty hot." The bartender mumbled, a blush gracing his freckled face.

"You a b-boy right? I have a friend c-called Ricca and he's gay and needs some action. He's a little dominating but y'all balance eachother out!" I giggled, calling Ricca here.

"Shot please!" I yelled happily, as he sent one my way. I downed it and tried to get up. I nearly fell but someone helped me steady myself.

"Thank you stranger!" I mumbled, smiling.

I wobbled over to the girls and saw them socialising with some other girls.

"Hi!" I chirped as they all looked at me with confused faces.

"Sseee that's my best frriend! Her name is Dom. She needs to get laaaaaid." Willow said as all of them giggled.

Out of the corner of my eye, I saw someone glaring at me.

"Er..Dom you might want to come with me." Darya said hastily. She wasn't drunk. She didn't drink.

"W-why I am happy!" I shrieked, grabbing the bottle of Hennessey off the table and downing it.

"Don't! Don't turn around." She said, her eyes pointing at something.

"What wh-" My sentance was cut off, as I did turn around. I wish I hadn't.

There was my boyfriend, locking lips with some bitch on his chest. I immediately turned right back round. Darya's eyes softened at me.

"Don't worry, he's a bastard Dom." She said, rubbing my arm. I rubbed my eyes, everything was hazy. Jealousy ignited in my body as I marched over towards them.

Dane's eyes widened as he pushed her off of him.

"Here you are, swapping spit with some girl while I'm drinking my love away for you." I said, laughing without humour. "How could you? How fucking could you? I tried to fucking love you a-and cherish you but you chucked it all back into my face? How could you?" I muttered tears falling. The girl looked at me in pity.

"I'm sorry I didn't know he had a girlfriend!" She rambled as I smiled sadly and stopped her.

"I'm not his girlfriend darling. I'm nothing to him. It's okay, carry on." I mumbled looking him in the eye. A flash of hurt clouded his eyes but was soon replaced with a cold, icy glare.

"I don't love you, get over yourself. You're not even that special." He said, his voice sending shivers down my spine. The girl gasped and glared.

"I should have never kissed you, prick! Fuck off!" She roared, stumbling off. She gave me a quick hug and whispered a sorry. I picked up the Ciroc off the table and gulped it down.

"I really fucking hate you Dane Donatti. I hope you never find love, the type of love that I would have given you. I hate you." I said, tears falling again. I walked away back to the bar, downing the strongest stuff they had.

Someone gripped my arm and twirled me around into their chest.

His chest was hard and...nice. I looked up at him, he had stubble on his chin and his hair was swept back. He had a strong jawline and pointed features, and his eyes were fucking beautiful. Dane was glaring at the both of us but I didn't care.

"Hello.." I said, tears in my eyes. He looked down at me angrily, but with humour.

"I've seen you before somewhere but I don't know where. Let's get out of here." I mumbled, pulling him along upstairs to the rooms.

He happily complied and followed.

I pushed him into the room and took my shoes off. There was a bottle of strong vodka on the table, which I also took.

"What problems are you drinking away darlin'?" He said, as I lay back on the bed, as did he.

"I-i don't know. I'm not sure." I giggled, taking another swig. "What's your name pretty boy?" I mumbled as he laughed.

"Hassan. And yours?" He asked as I smiled.

"Dom." He nodded.

"I'm such an idiot. I fell for someone I shouldn't have. I don't know how to get out of it now because I think I might even love him. I fucking love him." I mumbled, choking a sob back.

"I don't know what I did wrong. Am I ugly?" I asked, taking another swig.

He shook his head a no as I laughed. "So why would he want to break up with me Hassan? What did I do? Am I prude for not giving him sex? I'm not good at relationships. I tried hard for this Hassan and it got thrown back into my face."

"Thanks." I mumbled as he threw his arm around me.

"Well pass me the bottle, I need a drink too." He said, taking the bottle as I pouted.

"My girlfriend of 5 years broke up with me. I was loyal and I loved her to bits. I don't know where I went wrong either princess." He mumbled, taking a gulp. I wrapped my arms around his waist as he sighed and rested his cheek on my head.

"I love him so much Hassan. Honestly. I just saw him downstairs eating some pretty girl's face. I don't know what to do Hassan." I said, crying now.

"It's okay princess. He'll realise what he lost, he doesn't seem like a dumb man." He muttered, staring at the wall.

"Your girlfriend will realise that she lost a good man like you too. I hope she realises her mistake Hassan. Thank you." I mumbled, now snuggling into the sheets.

"It's okay princess. Go to sleep." He said, pulling me into his chest.

We were just sleeping, and I was fine with that. I couldn't get the images of me and Dane out of my head.

It had been far too long for my liking to feel hurt over someone that didn't love me.

I sighed and turned around, and buried my face into Hassan's chest.

I fell into a deep slumber, the images of me and Dane clouding my thoughts. I hope he finds someone that is willing to give him the love I had, because I'm not willing anymore.

I was done.

~*~

DANE'S POV:

When she told me she hates me, I felt my heart break into pieces. I felt frustrated that she didn't know I was doing all of this for her. I followed them both up the stairs, there was no way in hell I was allowing this prick to do anything funny with here.

I sat in front of their door, listening to their conversation.

"I'm such an idiot. I fell for someone I shouldn't have. I don't know how to get out of it now because I think I might even love him. I fucking love him." She said, her voice hoarse.

"So why would he want to break up with me Hassan? What did I do? Am I prude for not giving him sex? I'm not good at relationships. I tried hard for this Hassan and it got thrown back into my face." I could hear the sadness in her voice as my heart clenched in pain.

"My girlfriend of 5 years broke up with me. I was loyal and I loved her to bits. I don't know where I went wrong either princess." The guy said as she sighed. At least he didn't want to get in her pants.

"I love him so much Hassan. Honestly. I just saw him downstairs eating some pretty girl's face. I don't know what to do Hassan." She cried as I felt tears in my eyes. I was so sad and heartbroken too. I loved her too.

"It's okay princess. He'll realise what he lost, he doesn't look like a dumb man." He said as a tear fell down my cheek. "I'm so stupid. What the fuck is wrong with me?" I said to myself, putting my head in my hands.

I stayed there for the rest of the night. They both fell asleep I think. I was so unhappy the past few weeks. I didn't know where to turn. It was either me protect her by breaking her heart, or let her get killed.

"If you don't breakup with her we'll kill her and her family. She's making you weak. This finishes on her birthday, or else. I know you do not want to test me, son." Whatever he said, kept replaying in my head. I don't know what I was doing. I was a lost fucking cause.

I didn't kiss the girl, she kissed me, and just as Domenica turned around her lips were on mine. Damien did sock my in the nose for breaking her heart.

I love you Domenica. Forever and always.

thirty-three

I had all of you, Most of you, Some and now none of you. Take me back to the night we met

Seven months later...

Seven months.

Seven months since Dane had broken up with me. To say I had changed wasn't an understatement. The girls from Armarni's little ring had helped me build an empire. It took seven months of grief, sadness and anger for me to build this. We were now one of the strongest gangs in the world; if not the strongest. We weren't a mafia, but we were a family. The girls had started working for me and I had payed them a good amount. The older ones finally got into universities, and colleges and bought their own houses. My summer house now only had around 20 girls. The younger girls all shifted into the summer house after the older ones left. A few went back to England, and Columbia and Puerto Rico. I was very happy that they had finally found their feet.

Our cartels, drugs, weapons, money, business everything was running greatly, and without a doubt I was famous now. Of course I had to cover the 'gang' stuff with a normal business. I owned Romero Enterprises. I saw myself on the headlines all the time; youngest female billionaire. I had a few restaurants around too.

All of this in seven months to myself and the girls, and Ricca.

Everyone including my mother said I had shut everyone out, and became cold. I couldn't see it.

I still love Dane, unfortunately. I tried not to but I couldn't. And it had been a long time since I had seen Rosella either. I tried extremely hard to try and stay away from him.

Damien had stayed in New York after I was taken, he said he wanted to be there to protect me.

"Boss you have a meeting at 3 with Mr Shelton about the co owner of Shelton and Co. Is that okay for you?" One of my employees, Khadijah said. She was a very hard working worker, I had utmost respect for her.

She had to manage time for work and being a single mother. I was empathetic, but I didn't let it show. I gave her good pay and also gave her a house and a car.

"That's fine Khadijah. Bring me up a black coffee, no sugar. Please." I said coldly as she hummed in response. Diana had her grades flying high, she had all AP classes now. Mother found a job she loved and Damien took care of the other business while I was taking care of this one.

I missed my father, but I knew he would be proud of me.

My phone started blaring as I saw Willow's name on my screen.

"Hey boo!" She chirped, I could feel her energy from here. She now was in the process of creating her own fashion and makeup line along with Darya and Raeni. Ocean was now studying to be a software developer for Apple.

Life was perfectly imperfect.

"Hello? Are you there? Earth to Dom?" Willow said over the phone.

"Hi yes I'm here. What is it you want?" I mumbled, Khadijah bringing my in my coffee. I smiled a tight-lipped smiled as she left.

"We have a meeting with Violeta the Bulgarian Mafia Dona, about the shipments." She said as it dawned on me.

"Fuck, what time?" I asked, sipping on my coffee, putting her on loud speaker. I flipped through some of the Enterprises papers as she mumbled something.

"Sorry what?" I said. "I didn't hear it, repeat." I took another sip of my coffee, sighing in bliss at the taste.

"In 45 minutes.." She trailed off as the coffee in my mouth spluttered out.

"45 FUCKING MINUTES! AND YOU DECIDE TO CALL ME NOW?" I roared as the outside office were all staring at me. I turned around to the view of New York and composed myself.

"Willow, you are cooking for all of us today." I said. She tried protesting as I shut her up.

"Do you want to wash the fucking dishes bitch?" I whispered yelled as she muttered no.

"It's Alina's birthday today. Please make it she was asking before. Party starts at 6." She mumbled, trying to get out of it.

"Good. Cooking it is, and I'll try be there." I said, cutting the call off.

I glanced at the time, it was 1 at the moment. I had another meeting at 3, then at 6 I had to go home. I straightened my blazer out and pulled my hair into a high pony tail. The Rolex on my wrist read 1:03, and I had to start making a move quickly. Since I was already ready, I called Willow to asked if Violeta could be available now.

"Hello boss!" She said as if I wasn't just talking to her.

"Ask Violeta if we can make the meeting now. I don't have enough time on my hands. Text me straight away, pronto." I said, cutting the call off. I gulped down the last of my coffee and headed out. My employees smiled at me as I kept my face black and nodded at whoever did.

"Boss! Mr Shelton said that he can't make it at 3. He asked if we could push it to 4?" Khadijah said wearily, as if I was a time ticking bomb.

"Tell him, I said 3. I am a busy lady I don't have enough time on my hands. Also tell him, he'd be losing a great deal of money if he lost this deal. Work your persuasive magic Khadijah." I said curtly as she nodded and went back to her office.

"She can meet you now, she is free. Meet her at La Pierre." Willow had texted me as I sighed in relief.

I walked out into the car park and got into my sleek black Maserati. I drove quickly to the restaurant to see her getting out with body guards by her. I had my gun in the back of pants, I wasn't worried. I stepped out and she greeted me with a smile.

"Don Dom! A pleasure! It's been too long!" She said in glee, hugging me.

"And you Dona Violeta. How are you doing?" I asked as she shooed her bodyguards away.

"The business and everything is going well, thanks to you. I would have still been stuck wit that Alex prick." She grumbled rolling her eyes. I chuckled lightly. She walked into the restaurant, I followed behind her.

Suddenly my phone started ringing, I took it out as she turned around raising her eyebrows.

"Sorry, you go ahead, I'll be there in 2." I said, smiling picking it up.

"Khadijah! I'm in a fucking important meeting! What is it?" I said harshly as she sighed.

"Shelton said 3 is fine boss. Although..never mind actually. Don't worry, sorry for troubling you." She said as I cut the phone. I growled in frustration. I put my phone away when a sweet little girl was staring at me. I raised my eyebrows at her.

"Sorry, you look like someone I know." She said politely. That voice...I had heard it somewhere.

"Who do you know kid?" I asked, crouching to her level. She looked around 8 years old.

"My old friend, Dom. She left me a long time ago. I'm still waiting for her, I know she'll be back." She said sadly.

My breath hitched in my throat as I studied her face. Pointed nose, hazel eyes, long hair.

"Sorry my mama is calling me. See you soon. I'm Rosella by the way!" She chirped running off to Rebecca. My eyes widened at her as her did to me.

She smiled softly and sadly. I quickly smiled back and turned away into the restaurant.

"Sorry for that. Duty calls." I said, grinning crookedly.

"Down to business then." She said as the waiter came.

"What can I get you ladies today?" He asked politely, smiling.

"Can I get the lobster and shrimp with the rice and white wine please." I asked, nodding to Violeta so she could order.

"Steak and red wine please. That would be all." She finished as he nodded and walked away.

"How have you been holding up darling?" Violeta asked, looking at me with worry in her eyes.

"I'm fine." I said curtly, sipping on the water.

"Domenica don't you dare!" She seethed as I smiled lightly. She was like an older sister I never had.

"I don't know Vio. I'm drowning myself in work to get my mind of whatever happened. I don't know." I mumbled sighing.

"Dane looks like shit. He has bags under his eyes, a shit ton of stubble. Nonetheless, still hot. If I didn't like girls I'd tap that." I glared at her playfully.

"Really?" I asked, picturing him in my mind.

"Yes darling. He's gone extremely cold and ruthless, though, I must warn you." She said as I raised my eyebrows.

"Someone asked him about you and he ripped his shoulders out of their sockets. He definitely still loves you." She said, smiling softly.

"I still love him too Vio." I said, as the waiter came back with our food. "Every day I try not to think of him, and the worst bit is, is that I start to love him more every single day. I have no fucking idea why." I said, chucking lowly at myself.

"It's okay. That's what love does to you I guess. Trust me Domenica he still loves you to bits. I can see it in him. Have you ever thought that maybe, there was a reason he had broken up with you babe?" She asked, sipping her wine as I shoved a shrimp in my mouth.

"No." I muttered, "He could have fucking told me. He could have told me and if he did I would not have one fucking problem splitting up with him. He's so fucked." I slammed my fist on the table, anger igniting in me.

"Calm down Domenica." She said, pushing my wine glass in front of me. I gulped it down and leaned back into my chair sighing.

"I'm a mess without him Violeta. I don't know what I'm doing." I mumbled, putting my head into my hands.

"It's okay Dom. Don't worry." She said soothingly as I sent her a thankful smile. We ate in a peaceful silence, which was good because I hadn't eaten since yesterday.

"Down to business." I said, wiping my mouth lightly. She nodded and sipped her wine, as I did.

"The Mexican's have no problem with our shipment through Mexico as long as we don't get caught." She said as I nodded.

"How much is one shipment?" I asked, gulping my wine.

"46,000,000 for weapons including ammo." She said as I nodded.

"Do you trust the Mexicans?" She asked as I nodded without hesitation.

"That day I got shot, he agreed straight away with my idea. I'm sure I could persuade him to allow 20 shipments through Mexico." I mumbled, smiling. She nodded and laughed lightly.

Her eyes suddenly widened, looking at something behind me.

"Don't! Don't turn around. Look at me, act normal and like your better than everyone else. Dane is right behind you. He smiled at me curtly but he's trying to figure out who you are." She said, sipping her wine acting normal.

My breath hitched in my throat, and I could feel my heart wanting to jump the fuck out of my chest.

"Dona Violeta. It's a pleasure." His silky, husky voice came through. Tears built up in my eyes as I clenched my tattooed hands on the table.

"Who is your friend?" He said as if he knew it was me. I still hadn't looked at him, but he was very fucking close.

"Oh her, she's a beauty isn't she. Her name is Domenica Romero. Sure you've heard of her." She grinned cynically making me glare at her. I sat up straight, unclenched my fists and smiled fakely.

"Hell Mr Donatti." I said boldly as his eyes softened on me.

"Hello Domenica." He said, his gaze still on me. Vio was right, his eye bags were bad, he had stubble but it looked cute and the curls on his hair had gone longer. He also looked much, much muscular.

"How've you been Domenica?" He said, his eyes set on my lips.

"Fine, Mr Donatti. I have businesses to run, it was great catching up Dona Violeta but I must be going now. Mr Alamanzer should be expecting my call, if not, Damien's. Have a good day, the both of you." I mumbled, getting out of my seat, walking extremely quickly to the door.

"Domenica! Wait!" I gripped the handle of the door, tightly, trying to calm myself.

"Are you okay Mr Donatti?" I asked, smiling FAKELY.

"Please don't be so formal with me Domenica. I miss you so much." He said, his voice breaking. It took all of my might to not cry.

"I'm sorr-" I started to say as he cut me off, taking my wrist and dragging me outside.

"Dane what the fuck? You can't be doing that now the paparazzi are everywhere!" I seethed, as he pushed me into a small alleyway.

"Meet me at the roof tops on top of Santebello's gym. I promise I will explain everything there. I promise. If you don't come...I'll take that as my asnwer of no, but I will do everything I can to get you back. I'm done being afraid. Please Domenica. I've missed you so fucking much." He said, hugging me.

I didn't want myself to be stuck in his embrace but I couldn't make myself get out of it. I ran my hand through his curly locks and we stayed in that position for a few minutes.

"I need to go, I have a meeting." I said, pulling away.

"Romero Enterprises huh??" He teased as I chuckled.

"Bye Dane." I said, sighing. He waved and watched my go to my car. I couldn't help but feel as if I was being watched.

"Ready to go Miss Romero?" My driver, Walter said.

"Yes Walter, lets go." I mumbled, leaning my head against the window.

We soon got back into my building and made my way to my office. It was currently 2:30, and the meeting was at 3 so I had 30 minutes to freshen up.

I sat in my chair, recalling the events that had just happened. I couldn't help but also feel like I had made a decision that felt right, but so wrong.

I was stuck, and I needed help out of this.

There was only one person that I wanted to speak to anyway and that was my dad.

thirty-four

- -

We're only getting older baby, And I've been thinking about it lately,Does it ever drive you crazy?Just how fast the night changes.

The meeting with Mr Shelton went well, he immediately signed the papers over which made me extremely happy. I couldn't get Dane off of my mind, and I think everyone realised.

"Boss? Boss? Boss? BOSS!" Khadijah yelled as I snapped out of my daze.

"What?" I snapped as she looked down.

"Sorry, I was wondering whether you wanted your coffee. It's 5:15..." She said, gulping. I felt bad for her, I didn't need to take me tensions out on her.

"Sorry Khadijah. Go tell everyone that they can go home, and yes please do bring my coffee and then leave. Thank you." I mumbled, leaning on my desk, facing towards the New York view.

"U-uh right away boss!" She said, running out. Her hijab nearly flew off of her head, it made me chuckle. She was a very hardworking mother, and was actually 23, with a beautiful heart.

I was 19 with an ugly heart.

A few moments later, Khadijah returned with my black coffee with no sugar, and a few files in her hand.

She put it down with the files as I thanked her. She was still standing there.

"Is there something you need Khadijah?" I murmured, looking through the files.

"N-no. I - I well, I thought that...well...oh fuck it." She murmured underneath her breath making me chuckle.

"I know your younger than me but you look really I don't know, sad? Or tense? I mean I came to ask well I got your coffee too. I just wanted to ask whether you are okay boss?" She asked timidly. My heart swelled in happiness that someone who I don't even know well asked me whether I was okay.

"To be honest, no Khadijah," I closed the files and looked at her, "But I will be. You can go now, your two little boys will be waiting." I said, smiling timidly. "Give them my love." I mumbled as she smiled brightly. "They miss you, they ask about you, you know." I smiled, feeling good. "I'll make my way soon Khadijah. Go home now, I'm okay, thank you." She nodded and pursed her lips.

"Well boss you know where I live and everything so, just stop by if you want. I make a mean tea." She grinned childishly, her grin contagious. Khadijah was very beautiful woman, dark skin, big plump lips, big eyes, a gorgeous figure. She was extremely pretty.

"I will one day Khadijah. Leave now, shoo, go have some you time." I mumbled, shooing her away. She smiled and yelled a bye, leaving me in my building by myself.

I sighed and got to work. My phone pinged which was unusual, I got a new phone and had like 5 contacts.

"Come at 11 on the dot. Santebello's gym roof top. Dane." It said as I furrowed my eyebrows.

"Don't worry about how I got your number. I am a mafia don after all." He sent, with a smirk emoji. I sighed and put my phone away.

I carried on doing my work, whatever I needed to do I did. I felt a little peckish and headed down to the cafeteria.

I needed to be at Alina's at 6. I grabbed a sandwich and went back to my office. I packed everything up and took my laptop and shoved it in my bag.

I had finished school earlier since I had to manage this business. I headed out to my car park and asked the watchman to lock up everything.

Walking outside was nice, the breeze was free and it felt good. My phone was blaring as I dug in my bag to try and fish it out.

"What?" I snapped, picking up not looking at the caller ID. It was quiet for a few seconds when I was going to turn it off.

"Dom? Are you coming?" Alina squeaked in a small voice. She was frightened, I could tell.

"Yes darling I'm coming. I'll be a tiny bit late though. I'll be there as soon as I can okay?" I said softly, making her squeal in delight.

"Alright! Hurry it is nearly six!" She said, cutting the call. I chuckled and got into my car. I had to get her gift, I had asked a jeweller to carve her name into gold and make it into a necklace, and I had to go collect it.

I went down to the jewellers and saw my personal jeweller standing there with a grin on his face.

"I had a feeling you would stop by today Dom!" He said, pulling something out of the desk thing underneath.

"18 karat gold plated with 461.2 round S12 VG cut grey diamonds. Pretty thing ain't it?" He said, pushing the necklace towards me.

"I love it. I need to take it now," I glanced at my phone, it was 50 past 5. It took me half an hour to get home. "I'll take it, package it up nicely." I said hastily.

"On it boss!" He said, pulling out a pretty red pouch and carefully placing it inside.

"Here you go, come again!" He said, putting it into a fancy little bag.

"Thank you Mani, the money will be put in your account. Thanks." I smiled, rushing out. I hopped into my Maserati and tried getting to Alina's house as quick as I could.

She was turning 17.

I reached there at 6:30, it wasn't too late. I knocked on the door thrice, to which Mina, a girl from the ring, had opened it.

"Come in!" She said, ushering me inside. Loud music was blasting throughout the house and balloons were everywhere.

I walked inside the living room to see all the girls laughing, holding non-alcoholic beverages, looking very pretty. I walked in quietly, they were all focused on the movie playing and Alina herself.

"Hey guys." I muttered sheepishly, smiling.

"Dom!" They all yelled, around 50 girls running towards me and tackling me into a hug. I fell on the floor with an 'oomph', the girls around me laughing.

"PEOPLE TOWER!" Dren yelled, jumping on top of the girls. Soon we had made a girls tower, with me right at the bottom and it started to get difficult breathing.

"G-guys. Can't b-breathe." I wheezed, Alina sensing my uncomfortable state.

Finally, the girls had gotten off of me as I straightened my blazer out.

"Thanks for that girls." I said, glaring playfully.

They all chuckled and we headed to the backyard, that was quite spacious. We all sat round the little campfire imitation things.

"Happy birthday Alina. I hope you finally find what you're looking for in life, you're not a little girl no more." I said, as she smiled tearfully. "These past seven months has been rough for all of us, but I'd like to thank you for all the commitment, hard work, happiness and overall good will you guys put into the businesses. I couldn't be any happier." I said as they all threw their arms around each other. "I got you a gift Alina, it's not much but I think you'll like it." I mumbled, pulling the red pouch out.

"There is no need for that Dom! You gave me a house, a future, a career, an education. Safety. I don't need this trust me! I'm forever grateful for all of this," She waved her arms about happily, tears rolling down her face, "I don't need anything more. Thank you." She said, flinging her arms onto me.

"Think of it as a 'thank you' gift for helping me. Open it up." I said, I was excited.

She pulled out the necklaces and held it delicately in her hands, smiling ever so widely at me. She immediately engulfed me into a big hug. I put it on for her as she thanked me a shit load of times.

The rest of the night went past slowly, we were just talking and eating and drinking. It was fun. We sang Night Changes by One Direction together and surprisingly it was very good. Apparently it showed us that we're getting older way too quickly.

But the only thought on my mind was Dane.

thirty-five

Only half a blue sky,Kinda there but not quite,I'm walking round with just one show,I'm half a heart without you.

Thoughts were floating around in my brain, about what Dane was going to even say. I was definitely nervous, I didn't know what to expect.

These past few months I had become extremely cautious, of everyone and everything around me, I took guns just in case. I made my way to the gym, it was 10:50. I walked inside quietly, a few people were working out, it was a 24 hours a day gym.

I made my way upstairs, and up the spiralling stairs. My hands were clammy, I wiped them on my suit trousers and took a deep ass breath in, pushing the roof door open. I looked around and spotted him sitting right at the edge of the roof, very far out. Sudden panic filled me as I rushed towards him as quietly as I could, so he didn't get scared.

"I know you're behind me. Come sit." He said, making me jump.

"O-okay." I stuttered, sitting down next to him. Seven months later, and he still made me stutter. I sat next to him, closely. I could feel his body warmth from here. He shuffled closer and pulled my into his side. I didn't pull away, I had missed this.

"I wanted to start of saying I'm sorry. I'm sorry for letting you go like that. I'm sorry for causing you so much hurt. I'm sorry for my prick actions. I'm sorry for leaving you. I'm sorry for acting like I didn't love you." He said, resting his cheek on my head. I choked back a sob as he continued, "I'm sorry for breaking your heart, I promise I didn't want to. I had no choice. My father...he didn't like that I had finally found someone I could love, and marry and start a family with. He thought I was getting weak. He thought I wasn't able to handle the mafia with you being in my life, so he told me to let you go. Or else he'd hurt you. And I know my papa, he will hurt you. He's sly and conniving, and I didn't want anything to happen to you mia regina. I don't know what I would have done with myself if you had gotten hurt because of me...the months you were gone were hell." A tear strolled down his cheek as I wiped it quickly. "I couldn't eat. I couldn't sleep. I couldn't talk to anyone without snapping. I was going crazy because you weren't with me. There wasn't a day that passed and I didn't think of you. I tried hard to try and forget you but I couldn't. Diana punched me." He said, chuckling making me crack a grin. Tears had now fallen and he wiped them with the rough pad of his thumb and stared at me. "I'm so sorry Domenica but I can't stay away. These past months have been hell. I want you back. I'm so sorry. I love you. Ti amo." (My queen. I love you).

I couldn't help but cry my eyes out as he hugged me. I was so overwhelmed and I had no idea that he actually missed me and it wasn't his fault. As much as I wanted to blame him, I couldn't.

"You should h-have told me. I wouldn't have minded or anything. I w-would have helped you. You fucking idiot. I love you so much." I said, slapping his arm as he hugged me tight to his chest.

"I love you Dommy." He said, kissing my hair.

"I love you too Dee Dee." I mumbled, burying my face into his chest. I pulled away and admired his face.

He leaned in slowly, making my eyes wide in realisation.

"WAIT!" I yelled, pulling back. He raised his perfect eyebrows at me. "You still l-like me right?" I asked, blood rushing to my cheeks. He let out a throaty laugh and shook his head a no.

My heart dropped.

"I love you. I literally just told you I love you Dommy." He said, brushing his nose against mine. I smiled, looking at the stars in the sky.

Again, he leaned in slowly and quickly he attached his lips to mine. It took me a second start kissing back because he bit my lip. I got up quickly, and led him back to the gym and into the changing rooms, the stalls were separate - fortunately. He locked the stall behind him and immediately pushed my up against the wall, attacking my lips. The kiss was fast paced and emotional. My hands made their way into his soft curls, gripping them lightly as he moaned in delight. His eyes snapped open as he gripped my chin.

"I love you." He said, making my insides explode.

"I love you too." I mumbled quickly, crashing my lips against his again. He was like a drug, and I sure as hell couldn't get enough. His hands made their way up my body, slowly grazing my breasts and up to my neck. He started trailing kisses up my neck and to my jaw. I moaned in pleasure as he started sucking and nipping at my neck, that was definitely going to leave a hickey. He claimed my lips again, and it was my turn to leave marks on him. I kissed his neck ever so softly and made my way up to his jaw and on to his cheek, planting a chaste kiss there. I made my way back down to his neck as his scent intoxicated me, lifting my into a new ass high. I licked, kissed, nibbled on his neck leaving my marks. I kissed down his chest, and to his waistline. He sucked in a breath and put my hair up. I kisses his now erect member through his joggers, making him throw his head back.

I pulled his joggers and boxers down at the same time, his dick hitting my nose. My eyes widened at his size.

"Holy shit." I muttered as he laughed a deep throaty laugh.

"Suck princess." He commanded as I wrapped my lips around the tip. I swirled my wet tongue around the tip of him, as he moaned. I deepened his length in my throat, sucking and flicking him with my tongue. He gripped my head as he forced my down his whole length, making my eyes water. I kept bopping my head up and down on him until I felt him shudder and shoot his warm seed down my throat.

I guess I was doing well for someone who hadn't done this before.

He moaned ones more as I ended it by removing my mouth with a 'pop' at the end. I pulled his boxers and joggers back up for him, standing up to his height, my cheeks coated with red.

"You did so well for me princess. I love you." He praised, pressing a chaste kiss to my lips as I smiled lightly.

A few short kisses later, we pulled away, panting.

"We should do that again sometime." He said as I nodded.

"Yeah, we should. Let's go." I mumbled, walking out of the stall, him trailing behind me. We exited the gym and the cold, crisp breeze immediately made itself known.

I unlocked my Maserati and got in as did he. I dropped him off quickly, and there was a comfortable silence between us.

"I want to take you out tomorrow. Dress fancy." He said as I nodded.

"Bye." He said as I waved. I watched him go through the gates of his house, then I left to go to my apartment.

I had moved out of the house seven months ago, weirdly. I never thought I would have.

My apartment was big and spacious, it got lonely but it wasn't too bad. I unlocked the door and threw my bag and everything down and made my way to my room. I put on some soft music on, and let if flow throughout the apartment. I hopped into the shower and showered quickly, then changed and did my night routine skincare stuff. I glanced in the mirror and saw a big red hickey on my neck.

"I have to cover that up now." I mumbled to myself, putting my hair up into a bun.

I went back to the main room, pulling out some cookie dough ice cream, and putting on a movie. I had settled on my first movie to be To All The Boys I've Loved Before, it was so cute. I was engrossed in Lara Jean and Peter Kavinsky, when I started to drift off to sleep. I had made sure to set my alarm for work tomorrow, but I wouldn't mind hitting snooze.

I fell into a deep slumber, Lara and Peter still playing.

I smiled softly at today's events. I finally had him back, and I couldn't be happier.

thirty-six

I'd climb every mountain,And swim every ocean, Just to be with you,And fix what I've broken,Oh, cause I need you to see,That you are the reason.

Sitting at the meeting table, everyone applauded at my new found ideas. A fundraiser charity ball was also coming in sight.

The past few weeks have been good, the business sales have gone up very well, from both sides. More and more people are investing in it and I couldn't be happier. Dane and I did go out and we had a lovely time.

Today I was going to meet Rosella and Rebecca again. I was nervous definitely. It was currently 14 minutes past 3, and I was at the meeting and it had just ended. I was going to meet them at 5:30.

"It's a pleasure doing business with you Miss Romero." One of the investors said. He was hot, but not as hot as Dane. He had sandy blonde hair, blue-y green-y eyes and a cute smile.

"And you Mr Jacobs." I said, winking. He laughed and shook my hand.

"See you around Romero." He said, leaving. Khadijah was sitting by my side, fixing her hijab.

"He's easy on the eyes no?" She said, smirking at me. I laughed and flipped her off, we did actually get closer ever since she started working.

"I need to leave at now, I have a...meeting." I mumbled, thinking about Dane. She wiggled her eyebrows at me and I flipped her off again. "Tell everyone to finish up and leave by 5. Y'all can go have some time to yourselves." I said, gulping down my coffee. She nodded and carried on working, as I headed out to the car park to go home.

I had driven my Maserati as always, it was shining in all its glory. My beautiful baby. I made my way over to their mansion, and it took an hour from where my workplace was. I was wearing a black high neck mesh con dress, and I paired it with the So Kate black suede Louboutins, and the black Versace Medusa cape jacket. It went together pretty well, and I didn't look bad. My hair was in its tight curls, and my makeup consisted of mascara, foundation, highlight, contour and wine red lipstick.

I put their address into the GPS and made my way through New York.

~*~

I reached their mansion at around 5:45. There was a lot of traffic and I had already called Dane and told him. The guards let me in immediately and I parked my car up quickly.

I knocked on the door thrice and a maid opened it up, smiling softly.

"Miss Romero?" She said, in a questioning tone, it wasn't rude though.

"That's me." I said curtly, waiting to be let in. She nodded and smiled again and let me in. I breathed in the scent of home made cookies and vanilla. I missed this scent.

Rebecca came out and pulled me into a tight hug. She sniffled a few times before releasing me.

"You have no idea how much I missed you. And thank you, so much." She said, holding my hands.

"For what?" I mumbled in confusion.

"Ever since you and Dane started speaking again, he's gone back to how he was before. He isn't loading himself with work, he's not distant...he's..happy." She finished, gazing at the wall. I smiled but I couldn't bring myself to say anything.

"Anyways!" She said, snapping out of her daze, "How have you been my dear? I see you o the headlines all the time!" She said, grinning at me.

"I've been doing okay, the work is a ton but it's cool. I have a good team on my side." I said, chuckling.

"Mama? Who is here?" Rosella's tiny voice called out. Seven months sure was a long time, because she did look bloody different.

Taller, mature, prettier than she was before. She was totally going to be a heart breaker.

"Dommy?" She said, peeking into the room as she looked at me with wide eyes. I nodded and opened my arms up as she ran into them.

"I missed you! Where did you go for so long?" She asked, pulling back from the hug.

"I had some work to do Rose. But now I'm back!" I said, grinning as Rebecca smiled full on.

We chilled for a bit, talking, eating, watching movies. It was pretty nice. I had missed them both. The other family members smiled politely but didn't attempt to talk to me.

It was around 9 in the evening, when Dane turned up.

"Mama I'm hooooome!" He sang, dropping on the couch smiling weirdly. He hadn't seen me, I was in the kitchen making some hot chocolate.

"Mama. How do you know you're like really in love?" He asked, randomly. It made my heart and mind race. Rebecca winked at me and sat next to him.

I decided to quietly make a mug for him too.

"When the person you think you love makes your heart race, and makes you feel like you're on cloud nine. When they cloud your thoughts and is literally all you can think about. You feel like you're high on their love. Don't get high though or else I'll smack the shit out of you." She said, making my stiffle a laugh. "It's the best feeling in the world my love. When you're happy for them no matter what. When you finally realise you love someone, you become a better person. You're there for each other and whatnot. Why though?" She asked, as I mixed hot chocolate powder in 4 mugs.

"Mama I love Domenica so much." He said, making my heart race. He put his head in her lap as she stroked her hair, it was nice to see such a good mother and son relationship. "She makes me happy. She's all I ever want. I'd swim every single ocean in the world to be with her mama. If she isn't happy, I'm not happy. She is so caring..and nice, and such a good person. If I lose her I don't know what I'd do. I love her so much. I want her to have my kids, and my happiness, and everything she never had before. I know I've done some pretty bad shit in the past mama but I swear I'll never let her cry because of me ever again. I love her. I want to marry her in the most beautiful islands in the world. I could stare at her for the whole day and not even get bored, that's how serious I'm talking." He said, smiling like crazy. I topped the hot chocolate with marshmallows and cream and quietly brang them out.

"Well I love you too. Marriage can wait though, we're still quiet young. And, I wouldn't mind if you had my kids." I said, trailing off as he sat up looking embarrassed. A sweet red blush coated his cheeks as he glared at his mum.

"You never told me she was here?" He whisper yelled, his tone going up every word. I laughed really hard as did she. His cheeks went red as hell, which was extremely cute.

He scowled playfully but did come and hug me.

"Hi." He said, gazing into my eyes.

"Hi." I mumbled, giving Rebecca her mug, Rosella came down and took one too.

"Dee Dee!" She yelled happily, hugging his legs.

"Princess." He said, kissing her cheek. I gave Dane one and I also had one. We sat there, watching movies, Dane occasionally kissing me. Rebecca soon put Rosella to sleep, and slept herself and it was just me and him. We headed out to Macy's diner, where I met Maliha.

We ate, and catched up with each other. It was nice, and refreshing.

Soon, he dropped my home but did stay round.

We snuggled into my bed, not saying anything. It was the best feeling. I couldn't help but feel like everything was getting better.

And it was.

It felt great.

"I love you." I mumbled, kissing his forehead as he smiled cutely.

"I love you too." He said, planting a soft kiss on my lips.

He fell asleep, as did I, in each others arms.

thirty-seven

Maybe you weren't the one for me,But deep down I wanted you to be,I'll still see you in my dreams,All the things I did for you,Just wasn't it for you.

"Noah! Get me my fucking file now!" I roared at my temporary PA. Khadijah was off because her two little boys were sick, and of course I wasn't going to tell her she wasn't allowed to get time off work. A ginger haired, green eyed, tall and well built boy came stumbling through my office doors, throwing me a sheepish grin.

"Sorry! I got caught up." He said, unapologetically. I glared at him as he sent a cheeky grin back.

"Noah, please stop slacking," I grumbled, pulling my hands down my face, "I can't have you being known as the laziest employee I have. I built this from nothing and I wont let the bullshit media drag it down because you Noah fucking Arabel are acting like a doof. Please suck it up." I said, softly but sharply as guilt clouded his eyes.

"Sorry boss. Promise from today I'm on my grind." He said, mock saluting make me shake my head in humour.

"Now go schedule my meeting with Mrs Vina at 12 at noon on Friday, next week. HIGHLIGHT NEXT WEEK NOAH." I yelled as he jumped, his notepad falling as I chuckled. He glared at me but I flipped him off. "Move my meeting with Shelton and Co for 1 on the following Tuesday. Pick up the files from the seventh floor about all the newly enrolled employees, also, get me a cup of black coffee." I said curtly as he scribbled in his notepad. "No sugar." I said, shooing him as he shot me a wink. I sighed and leaned back into the comfort of my soft chair.

It had been a few weeks since I had been to Danes, visiting regularly anyway. Damien had decided today here from now on, Diana was doing great at school and mother was just being a mother. A nicer one at that.

Funnily enough, me and Dane are on the right track too. We've been doing really good actually. We got back together, it took like two weeks but we did it. His birthday is coming very quickly, next week actually. It's currently August, we broke up in December. His birthday is on the 26th. I didn't know what to give him, but I did have one thing in mind...

My phone rang a few times, I left it ringing, not wanting to talk to anyone.

Soon enough, my finger and eyes started twitching, my leg bounced up and down as I desperately tried to get the ringing to block out.

I have had enough.

I lunged forwards to my phone, not looking at the caller ID and putting it on speaker as I went through some files.

"Whatever it is you're annoying me for, you have only a few seconds before I make your whole life an entire living hell. Speak." I said curtly, skimming over the monthly costs of food in my building.

"Dang bitch? The fuck you raging for? Giving me a whole ass heart attack with your British self?" Ricca said over the phone, I could imagine him frowning.

"Sorry Ricca. I'm just busy and stress and business isn't easy." I mumbled while chuckling as he made an aw noise.

"We ain't had no bonding time these past few months, the girls and I decided to have a little get together at my house, we're also having a sleep over. Please come, tomorrow is Saturday and no one is going to get hurt if you don't attend one day of work." He said, I could imagine him pouting.

"Ricca.." I trailed off as he started chanting.

"Please." He said.

"I can't."

"Why?"

"Because I work."

"You have people to cover you."

"Still."

"You're coming."

"I can't."

"Why?"

"I literally just told you."

"I don't care. You're coming. BE at mine at like 6. See you there. Bye bitch." He said, cutting the call off. I groaned and threw my phone on the table sighing.

"You could do with that sleepover miele." My head whipped up at his voice, a smile gracing his face. (Honey).

"Dane!" I squealed, getting out of my chair, running towards him. I wrapped my arms tightly around him as he chuckled and kissed my head.

"BOSS! I'm so sorry! I tried telling him that he needed an appointment but he didn't bloody listen! And boy, he can run." One of my employees, Jayden wheezed, glaring at Dane. "Holy shit. He's your babes ain't he? I'm so sorry! I didn't know! Please don't fire me this is literally my only source of income. Other than stripping..." He trailed off as Dane's eyes widened. I stiffled a laugh as he stepped closer to me. "Anyways please don't fire me! Sorry sir but please don't barge through again like heck, you could have asked me to called boss. Jesus." He finished making me laugh, full on.

"Jayden, this is Dane. My boyfriend." I said, holding Danes hand. His eyes widened as he he scratched his neck awkwardly.

"Well shit." He muttered, making me laugh again. "Sorry dude. I didn't know. Maybe if you TOLD ME, I would have. Anyways I need to go deal with those raging girls talking about some big mafia don Dane Donatti or something. They said they saw him but I didn't? This is why I prefer the male sex." He grumbled as his eyes widened on the floor again. He looked straight at me, with a straight, emotionless face.

"Your babes is Dane Donatti and he's standing right next to you right?" He asked as I nodded slowly.

"You know what I think my mom is waiting for me downstairs. See ya later boss!" He yelped, running out of my office.

"Well...that was something." Dane said, laughing as I nodded. He wrapped his arms around my waist and snuggled his head into the crook of my neck.

"I missed you." He said, muffled.

"I missed you too. Now let go, I have work." I said, pulling back. His grip tightened as he smirked.

"Work can wait. Let's grab some food." He said, pulling my outside.

"I need to get my phone and purse and stuff! Wait!" I yelped as he had already dragged me outside of my office.

"You don't need your purse or your phone. I'm paying and I haven't got my phone either. Just me and you. And the money." He said, kissing my cheek. I blushed heavily, knowing people were watching us.

'They're so cute!'

'I'm happy for boss! She deserves it.'

'Isn't he a mafia don?'

'He's hot and so is she, they're going make cute ass babies!" One employee said as Dane said thank you to her. We walked out to a cute royal blue Maserati.

"Macys?" He asked as I nodded smiling.

I really loved this boy.

"I love you." I said, reaching over, placing a playful kiss on the corner of his mouth as his eyes darkened and his jaw clenched.

"You okay there babe?" I drawled, making him grit his teeth.

"Shut your pretty little mouth before I pull over and take you right here." he said, his voice raspy. I chuckled as he zoomed off.

Out of the corner of my eye I saw a big lorry coming towards us. It was swivelling and turning in all directions.

"Dane baby watch out the lorry!" I said, as his eyes widened, swerving into another lane. My heart rate shot up as more cars started swerving, trying to get away from the big ass lorry.

"I love you Domenica." Dane said, trying to get control of the car.

"I love you too Dane." I said, tears threatening to fall out. He hand't gotten control of the car, and there was a van coming towards us too. I hoped that nothing would happened to either of us, when glass shattered and all I saw was specks of blood on my arms.

I fell into a bottomless dark pit of nothing, little patterns clouding my vision as a throbbing pain erupted in the back of my head, and I lost consciousness.

thirty-eight

She's falling in love now,Losing control now,Fighting the truth,Trying to hide,But I think it's alright girl,Yeah I think it's alright girl.

DANE'S POV:

All I could hear was rapid beeping and loud voices. It made my ears and head hurt. My body felt heavy and I think it hurt, but I didn't know because it felt sort of numb. I tried opening my eyes but they were glued shut. I tried to move but my arms and legs felt like they were chained to an uncomfortable bed.

"Call the doctor! He's moving!" A woman's voice echoed throughout the daze I was in.

"Hello?" I tried saying but nothing came out.

What even happened? Why was I here? Where was I?

"It's okay mio figlio, it's okay. I'm here now, mama is here." She said as I felt soft hands brush hair out of my face. I finally opened my eyes to people moving fastly, and white walls.

"Mama?" I said, blinking quickly, trying to adjust to where I was. Finally, I could see clearly.

There was needles attached to me, tubes in my nose and my arms were covered in little scars. My face and head hurt too.

"Mama what happened?" I asked her as tears gathered in her eyes. "Where's Rosella? Mama what happened to me why am I like this? Where is Domenica?" I said in confusion. I was at her work place and we were going to get food...

Suddenly all the memories came rushing back to me, vivid images overtaking my train of thoughts, making my head hurt. I screamed in agony as a piercing pain stabbed me repeatedly in my head.

It all stopped abruptly.

"Domenica? Where s Domenica? She got hit we got hit where is she?" I tried getting up but there was needles attached to me.

"Dane bro, you need to calm down." Damien said as I shook my head furiously.

"NO! I NEED DOMENICA! WHERE IS SHE?" I roared, pulling the needles out of my arms, and swinging my legs over the bed and onto the floor. I ripped the tube out of my nose, and it made me get light headed but I shook it off. I got up, just to fall back down.

"Sir, you need to lay back down, you're hurt and haven't walked for 3 days. Please sit back down." The doctor said softly as I glared at him.

"I need my girlfriend. I will not sit down until I see my girlfriend. Where is she?" I asked him quietly, feeling the anger inside me bubble up.

"Dane baby please. I'll take you to her just sit down and let the doctor treat you okay? I promise we'll see her in half an hour." Mama said, pushing me back onto the bed softly. I nodded in content.

The doctor stabbed a needle in me, making me immediately fall back into a deep slumber.

BACK TO DOMENICA'S POV:

Everything was dark. I tried moving but I couldn't. I could hear faint beeping and faint voices but I couldn't move, my body felt extremely heavy.

I tried moving and it worked a little bit.

I opened my eyes and all I saw was a white room. There was four girls, two boys, and one lady standing in front of me, crying.

"Hello?" I croaked, as the lady rushed over to me, telling me to relax. She was touching me and I didn't like being touched.

"Sorry please don't touch me." I croaked, a sudden pain happening in my head.

She backed away and stood there quietly, watching me.

"Hello Miss Romero, I am your doctor. Would you like some water?" A lady said softly as I nodded.

She handed me a opened bottle, and I took several large greedy gulps of it, letting the water soak in. I coughed and straightened myself up, taking deep breaths.

"I'm sorry but why am I here?" I asked, looking at my tattooed arms that had needles in them, and a few bloody scratches. There was bandages on my torso, and my legs.

"Who are you guys?" I said, looking at the people in front of me. They didn't seem like a threat but I had to be cautious.

"Why do you guys have American accents? I'm still in England no? Unless you are an American doctor that came here? Can I get some answers please?" I grew frustrated at the lack of answers.

"Do you not remember any of these people in front of you?" The doctor asked, with pity in her eyes.

I shook my head a no, as the lady started sobbing. I felt bad for her, I had no idea why she was crying either.

"Sorry miss was is something I said?" I mumbled pathetically, feeling bad she was crying.

"No, no honey. Don't worry. You don't remember me Domenica?" She asked. She felt familiar, but I couldn't remember where.

"Who is Domenica?" I asked confused.

"You! You are Domenica? What the fuck Damien what is wrong with her?" A girl wailed, clutching onto one of the boys.

I started to panic I had no idea what was happening. The lady wiped her tears and sat down next to me.

"Domenica is your name honey. I am your mother. You got into a car accident, and it seems like you've forgotten your memory. We live in America now, not England honey." She said, gripping my hand.

I couldn't help but take her word for it.

I nodded slowly and looked at the girls and boys.

"Who are those people?" I asked as she smiled sadly. She pointed to the boy that the girl was holding, crying

"That is your brother, Damien. The boy next to him is your bestfriend, Ricca." She said as I nodded. Ricca smiled softly, and Damien came sat down next to me.

"The girls, are your bestfriends." She said, they all smiled sadly at me too. "The one with red hair, is Willow." She pointed at the girl who was crying. I smiled and waved, as did she. "The one next to her with the blue hair is Ocean." She said as Ocean waved.

"Nice name." I muttered. She thanked me and looked away, a tear falling down.

"The one next to Ocean is Raeni, you met her at a ball." She said, pointing to a darkskin girl. She was very pretty, but looked like she hadn't slept in days. I smiled as did she.

"And lastly, that is Darya. You also met her at the ball." My mother said, pointing at the tall, brown skin girl with dark hair. She looked like Jasmine from Aladdin.

I smiled as she waved.

A girl came stumbling into the room, making me jump in fright.

She looked like my mother and Damien. I took in her unruly appearence as she launched herself onto me.

"Oh my god Dom you're awake! I thought you.." She choked on her words as I looked at my mother for help.

"Alright Diana get off her, I need to explain stuff to you." She said as the name Diana repeatedly showed up images in my head.

"Diana...Ana..." I murmured, trying to remember who she was. My head started hurting as I grit my teeth in annoyance that I couldn't remember anything.

"Sorry, that's my other daughter, your sister. She didn't know you had lost your memory." Mother said as I nodded slowly.

"Do I have a father?" I asked slowly as she shook her head a no.

"He left us when you were young my love. Don't worry though." She said as I nodded again, not ready to remember anything.

"Sister...Death?" I mumbled awkwardly as small words formed in my head. I shook them off and sighed.

"When can I get out?" I asked the doctor as she smiled softly.

"Later, we just have to run some tests." She said as I nodded, AGAIN. I sighed and felt like something wasn't right.

The door opened quickly, revealing a very good looking man.

He had curly hair, he was strongly built, the features on his face was chiselled and pointed. His lips was big and plump, and his eyes were the most beautiful colour I had ever seen in my life. HE was wearing grey basketball shorts, and a tight white tee. He looked hot.

"Holy shit." I muttered, making the girls chuckle. "W-who are you?" I stuttered idiotically, he was fucking intimidating.

"What do you mean Domenica? It's me Dane? Your boyfriend?" He said in confusion, taking cautious steps towards me.

Boyfriend? I had a boyfriend?

"Sorry...I don't have a boyfriend. I think you got the wrong girl." I said, pursing my lips. Just then another woman came in, a little girl trailing behind her. I couldn't see the girl well but I saw the woman. She had this homey feeling.

"Domenica my dear, how are you?" She asked, smiling.

"I'm fine thank you ma'am." I said back confused. How did she know me?

"Mama? Who are these people?" I whispered as she kissed my temple.

"That is your boyfriend and your boyfriends mum. You did have a boyfriend, you just can't remember my love." She said as I raised my eyebrows.

"Oh." I muttered, messing with my hospital gown.

"You don't remember me Domenica?" He said, standing in front of me, looking at me with love.

I bit my lip in shame and shook my head a no. He sucked in a breath and took a step back.

Tears rushed to my eyes, these people knew me and I had no idea who they were. I couldn't help but feel guilty.

"This is all my fault. If I had left her to do her work and not taken her out this wouldn't have happened. Fuck! Why am I so stupid!" The guy called Dane roared, punching a wall in the process. His chest rose up and down quickly, and his eyes darkened. I felt bad for him and I couldn't help but cry,

"I'm s-so sorry. I c-can't remember anything. I'm s-sorry." I hiccuped, tears freely flowing. He gazed at me with tears in his eyes as my brother escorted him out the room.

"Honey none of this is your fault. Don't worry, you'll be back to normal in a few months. Don't worry honey nothing is your fault." The woman said, rubbing my back soothingly. My mother thanked her as she went outside to take a moment.

I didn't even know my mothers name.

There was a little girl in the corner of the room, staring at me weirdly.

I recognised her...I helped her on the plane...

Planes? I gripped the side of my head as a throbbing pain hit me. I steadied myself and took a deep breath.

"Rose..Rosella?" I said, pointing at the girl. Her mother and the girls looked shocked.

"Yes, honey, that's my daughter. Rosella, come here baby." The lady said to her as she took timid steps towards me.

"Hey Dommy." She said quietly, hugging me.

"Hi Rosella. How are you?" I asked as she smiled. She gave me a thumbs up.

The doctor came back in and told everyone to leave.

"You got into a car crash and you have partial memory loss. Don't worry, your memory will be coming back gradually. Don't try to remember any-thing too hard, it can cause harm to your brain. Take these tablets twice a day for your ribs and pain." The doctor said as I nodded gratefully.

"That boy, he said he was your boyfriend. All he claimed to do ever since he woke up was see his Domenica. He really was your boyfriend darling. I guess this is like a second chance to fall in love all over again darling. Give the man a chance." She said, winking as I chuckled lightly.

"He is easy on the eyes." I mumbled, blushing as she laughed, throwing her head back.

"That he is." She winked at me and took the needles and stuff out of me.

"You can go home now, I'll be sending the tests results in a few days time. Until then, stay safe darling." She said as I nodded. I got up, and steadied myself easily. I changed my clothes quickly in the bathroom, there was no mirror. I couldn't remember what I looked like, but I had a load of tattoos.

I walked outside, the smell of antibacterial hand gel hitting me. Only my mother, brother and sister were outside. I had guessed the rest of the people had gone home.

"Come on honey. Let's get you home." She said softly, as I nodded gratefully.

The ride 'home' was quiet. We lived in a cute neighbourhood.

I was shown to my room, it was filled with paintings and drawings, instruments and posters of cars and bikes.

I liked it.

I threw myself onto the bed, hoping that I would eventually remember everything. I couldn't get my mind off of the guy though. He seemed so heartbroken that I couldn't remember him.

I drifted off into a deep slumber and hoped for better days, and my memory.

thirty-nine

Lose yourself in the music, This moment you own it, You better never let it go, You only get one shot, Do not miss your chance to blow, This opportunity comes once in a life time bro.

Raindrops had surfaced on the pane of my window. I watched the dark sky magically produce droplets - yes, I know about the water cycle and that, but I decided to take more of an...creative approach to it. I loved listening to the little drops of water hitting the ground, and I sure as hell loved dancing in the rain. It was six in the morning, before school. I wonder how I was like in school before. Willow and the girls were going to pick me up, and help me familiarise myself again.

My head throbbed in pain as vivid images of a car and lights and cars swerving rapidly appeared. Bright lights clouded my vision as I head a distant voice calling. IT sounded like my own voice but I wasn't sure. I couldn't quite grasp who was driving, but Dane had said it was him. I gasped for air, my throat closing up.

"D-damien!" I wheezed loudly, trying to get someones attention. I was in my room and Diana, Damien and were probably all in their respected rooms.

I dragged myself to the bathroom, trying to steady myself against the sink. I dook deep breaths in and out, and took a pill. Pain shot up in my ribs and lower back as I collapsed onto the floor, black dots clouding my vision.

"FUCK! Domenica! Wake up! Dom!" Damien's voice echoed throughout the room, or was it my ears.

All of the images disappeared, the throbbing pain in my head disappeared, the tightness in my throat had also disappeared.

I took a greedy gulp of air, sitting up right.

"You okay Dom?" He asked, looking at me sadly. I nodded quietly and thanked him.

"Sorry for that...I don't know what happened. I saw cars..and lanes and more cars swerving. I was in the passenger seat and I couldn't quite make out who was driving." I mumbled feebly, feeling weak.

"It's okay. Let's get you up." He said, picking me up softly. I leaned on him for support, he helped me back into my room.

"I'm sorry for that Damien." I mumbled, tears rushing to my eyes. His eyes hardened as he sat me down.

"Don't be sorry for something you have no control over it's fine. Get ready for school, the girls and Ricca are coming to pick you up." He said smiling. "I made waffles. Your favourite birthday cake and strawberry flavoured ones." He said as my mouth watered.

"Gerrout I have waffles to eat! Shoo! And Damien?" I said, making puppy dog eyes. He narrowed his eyes at me but smiled playfully.

"What?"

"I want sprinkles and maple syrup on it too." I said, slamming the door on him, his chuckles echoing throughout the corridor.

I got ready quickly, I did shower quickly, and pulled out my outfit. I took out a leather jacket, black ripped jeans, Yellow Nike air force 1's and a yellow crop top. As I was changing, I studied my body for quite some time.

I had small scattered scars all over my body, some of them covered by the tattoos. I had one tattoo from my upper arm till my shoulder that I loved; it was a rose bush thing with thorns. I also had tattoos on my hands, they were also my favourite. My ribs were still bandaged, they were such a disgusting colour. They hurt but I could deal with it. I re-wrapped the bandages, hissing slightly at the amount of pressure I had unintentionally put on.

I put on some mascara and lip balm, and pulled my hair into a messy ponytail.

I put on a cute pinky ring, it had a gold tiger on it. Pretty badass.

I spritzed some perfume on and ran downstairs with my backpack. I dropped it and waltzed into the kitchen, to see Damien and Diana talking quietly.

"Alright guys?" I mumbled, sitting down at a plate of waffles. They nodded quietly, not saying anything. "Don't sound like it. Whats wrong?" I mumbled with a mouth full of waffle.

"Chew with your mouth closed Dom." Diana said in disgust, wrinkling her nose up. I swallowed my bite and stuck my tongue out at her.

I finished up quickly, the door bell rang thrice. I opened it up to four girls that look as I did, we were all wearing leather and I bloody loved it. Ricca was also wearing leather.

"Fuckin' dream team us." I mumbled, taking the keys off the rack for my car.

"Dom...I don't think you should drive." Damien pleaded softly.

"It's okay Dame. I'll be fine, trust me." I mumbled, smiling tightly and heading out.

"Right, who brang their cars?" Ricca, Darya and Willow put their hands up, Raeni was probably riding with Darya and Ocean with Willow. "Race y'all to school?" I asked, smiling mischievously. "It's 45 minutes till 8, lessons start at 8:10. We take the long route to school. You guys up for it?" I said, swinging my keys between my fingers. "I'm taking the Lamborghini by the way." I mumbled as Ricca and Darya along with Willow grinned.

"We have our cars too." An evil glint appeared in their eyes.

"How did y'all even know I was going to plan this?" I narrowed my eyes at them as they all shrugged nonchalantly. I sighed and straightened out my jacket. Ricca had brang his Bugatti Veyron, Darya with A McLaren P1, and Willow with a Lamborghini Huracan.

"Let's get going then." I said, going to the garage as they lined their cars up.

My Lamborghini was the best. Murcielago. I pulled out of the garage and lined up against each of them. I felt like I was in fast and furious. All of their cars were on, all of them revving loudly. We were drove up to the traffic light, it was red currently but would turn green in a matter of seconds.

"Y'all ready? Y'all know the long routes to the school no?" I yelled, on either side. They nodded and revved. I smirked and connect the aux quickly and put on Lose Yourself by Eminem.

I was losing myself in the thrill.

I revved loudly, bypassers looking at our cars funny. I tightened my grip on the wheel, it was definitely dangerous to drive on the city roads but who cares. I hoped we didn't get caught by the police though.

I mentally prepared myself as I gripped the steering wheel, and placed my foot lightly on the accelerator.

Ready

Steady

Go! I told myself as the lights turned green. Darya and Ricca took off first, Willow trailing behind. Ricca used his turbo boost now? Amateur move.

I switched gears to 6 and stepped on it, zooming through the start and into the back streets as did they. I switched lanes past the cars, as I reached Darya. She was stunned to see I reached so quickly but of course, turbo'd again. I stayed at 6 and put more pressure on the accelerator, as we slowly came into town. There were bright flashing lights everywhere, people with their phones out. I took a hand off the wheel and tried to cover my face, not covering my eyes. I couldn't have people seeing me. I zoomed past all the lights and got in front of Darya and Ricca, when his engine started stuttering, his fault for using 2 turbos in like 8 minutes. Willow zoomed past, using her turbo too. I didn't use my turbo yet because that would be a waste. A family had come onto the road, making me swerve to the side quickly, the car loosing it's balance before I steadied it again.

I switched gears and let the turbo go as my car roared, adrenaline rushing through me. I stepped on the pedal and we flew, my guys. As the school started to come closer and closer, I stepped on the pedal, Willow not so far behind me and Darya besides me. I have no idea where Ricca went.

I raced through the gates, Darya, Willow and Ricca besides me as I quickly let out a drift and parked perfectly into a free parking space, before a black Maserati could come in.

I stared at the Maserati intently, feeling like I had seen it somewhere.

I turned the car and music off, hopping out.

"Well, now we know who one yeah?" I said arrogantly, laughing at them. Darya flipped me off, Ricca stuck his tongue out at me, while Willow pinched my ass.

I laughed hardly, walking into the school. It seemed pretty cool, I had actually gotten there by GPS, since I had forgotten where it was...

Of course, the typical highschool groups were everywhere. The jocks, nerds, geeks, bad girls and boys, cheerleaders, the anti-social kids etc. Willow and the rest came and stood besides me smiling softly

"If anything happens, Ricca is always going to be in all of your classes. The teachers know what happened, I think most of the students do too. If anything happens, I mean anything, call me straight away." Willow said softly, bumping her shoulder into mine. I nodded and forced a tight smile.

I saw Dane looking at me with longing in his eyes, and they were full of sadness. He smiled and waved. I waved back and sent a cheeky flying kiss. He looked surprised then smirked.

He waddled over to me with a few of his friends, they were definitely good looking.

"Hello miele. How are you?" (Honey). He asked, smiling softly, looking down at me. I smiled back at him, noticing how his eyes showed his only emotions.

"I'm okay. You?" I asked, walking into the school side by side with him. He muttered a same before passing me a distant look.

"We were dating you know. Everyone knew." He said quietly, smiling to himself. I made an 'o' like shape with my mouth, looking away.

"I mean...I wouldn't mind not getting to know you, again." I chuckled awkwardly as his eyes lit up.

"Seriously?" He said in disbelief as I laughed and nodded, standing in front of my English class room door. Ricca had been trailing behind us quietly, he also told me before that we had English first. I nodded quietly, pursing my lips. He bent down towards me slowly, whispering in my ear,

"I'll be at your house at 6. We'll go out to eat." I nodded, fighting back a smile.

We parted ways and I went to my first class.

Apparently I had a business before, but I wasn't in the right state of mind to handle it so Damien sent me home.

We had two, but I didn't know what the other one was. He said he would take care of it, and of course I took his word for it. I did trust him with all my heart, without even knowing him properly. Well I guess I knew him properly.

I walked into the class, not recognising anybody's face. I was so mad at myself for not realising who was who. It pissed me off to the max how people were looking at me, as if I was a fragile piece of glass. I scrunched my eyebrows up and kept my face emotionless.

"Guys of course you know who this is, Domenica," She said, smiling. "I'm sorry for your accident honey, get well soon. Go sit in the seat right at the back near the window." I nodded quietly, and pursed my lips.

I saw a whole bunch of boys and one boy that I sort of recognised.

My head started hurting when little images played back, showing a distorted image of his face. I sort of flipped him off, but he was genuinely nice.

He was also friends with Dane, I think. He smiled at me and waved, and I nodded my head at him curtly.

As I was walking, there was this one girl that made me annoyed, instantly looking at her I knew I probably hated her before.

She smirked at me, making me glare hardly back. I took my respected seat and hoped for the minutes of learning about Romeo and Juliet would pass quicker.

fourty

I gotta protect my heart,I gotta protect my heart,Quick CRB Check to pry up your history,Hope my boys ain't been there in the past.

Months had passed, and I still hadn't got the slightest bit of memory. I was introduced to both business's I had before, and familiarised myself with everything that had happened, and quite frankly it was pretty movie like. Me and Dane were on a great track, I fell in love with him all over again. He took me on dates, he took me on road trips, he gave me so much love. He appreciated and waited for me and I couldn't have asked for anything better.

He had made a big effort with me, which made me extremely happy. He asked me to be his girlfriend a few weeks back, and I obviously accepted. School was probably the same as it was before, I literally spoke to 5 people, Willow, Ocean, Darya, Ricca and Raeni.

Life was going good. There wasn't anything that affected me anymore - other than not remembering shit all. My gang business and my normal business were going great, and tonight there was a charity ball where our families had to attend for children's cancer. It was the other business's one though.

I was currently getting ready for the ball, mine and Dane's family were going. Of course, the rest of the girls and Ricca were too. I had decided on a loose, creamy satin gown. It was 5:45 and the ball started at 7.

I pulled out a creamy, satin floor length dress and slipped it on. I stood in front of the mirror, studying my body. I had a ton of tattoos and so many scars. Every time I ask Dane if he knows where they are from he changes the topic and talks about something else. My ribs were fully healed - which I was extremely grateful for - but I wasn't healed emotionally. I wanted to know so much more but only got a quarter of the answers. I didn't pry that much but I knew one day he was definitely going to tell me.

I didn't know what to do with my hair so I left it in the curly mess it was in. I applied light makeup, and a bold wine red lipstick too. I went with normal black stilettos, and a big statement necklace and earrings. I spritzed some Dior perfume on and gave myself a once over in mirror.

I got ready pretty quickly, and then made my way downstairs to get something to eat since I had been feeling a little hungry. On my way down, I saw Diana standing there looking beautiful in a short black dress.

"You're looking beautiful Ana." I said, smiling slightly as she blushed and laughed.

"You look hot. Dane's gonna be all over you." She said, wiggling her eyebrows. Me and her had got on with Damien very well since I returned from the hospital, it did actually feel like I've known her for years. My mother and brother also came out of hibernation.

"You look beautiful ma." I said, smiling slightly as she laughed. We headed out into our cars, I was taking my Maserati, while the three of them were going together. I connected my phone to the aux and put on CRB Check by Chip and Not3s. I sang along to the lyrics, heading towards the place where the ball was held. It was a quiet drive to the place, but I liked it. As

I got closer, there was a shit ton of people there, wearing fancy dresses and suits. The things that caught my eyes were the amount of beautiful cars that were lined up.

I pulled into the car park and parked my car in an empty space, Damien and them also followed me closely. I got out of my Maserati and fixed my dress, a few people waving at me. They didn't look familiar, but they didn't look unfamiliar. I nodded curtly at them, not wanting to engage in any conversation.

Out of the corner of my eye, I saw Dane and his family walk out of the big palace. He saw me and smiled brightly, walking towards me. I waited for my family to come out so we all walked together.

"You are beautiful Domenica." Dane breathed as he pulled me into a hug, kissing me on the lips. Willow and the girls along with Ricca had also turned up.

"Girl you look stunning!" Darya said, pulling me into a hug. I laughed and hugged her back.

"You guys looks so pretty. You look handsome too Ricca." I teased as he smirked. Dane wrapped his arm around my waist, pulling me closer to him.

"Should we go in?" He asked, not aimed at anyone. Damien nodded, his arm was around Willow's waist.

I wiggled my eyebrows at her as she blushed.

Classical music played in the background, pearls and diamonds sparkling everywhere. We signed in and went to our respected tables.

"You okay baby?" Dane whispered in my ear, sort of loudly over the lively chatter of everyone.

"I'm fine, you?" I asked as he mumbled a 'same'. A lady with strong posture and a respectable aura came to our table, with a few more girls behind her.

"Domenica! Dane! My favourite fraudulents, how are you guys?" She had a somewhat Russian accent.

"Violeta! How are you?" Dane said, standing up. I stood up too, when vivid imaged of a restaurant and the same woman in front of me flashed.

"I'm doing great! Business is great. Everything else is great." She said, smiling.

"Domenica how are you holding up?" She asked as I smiled softly.

"I'm getting there. And yourself?" I asked as she laughed.

"I'm good. We need to have a little heart to heart again, like we did before. I miss our chats." She said, chuckling as I smiled and nodded.

"Soon Violeta, soon." I mumbled as she headed towards another group of people. She had a dangerously homey feeling around her, but it wasn't threatening. She smiled softly, looking back and me with slight pity in her eyes. I simply smiled back.

I sat back down when the guy that organised the ball started talking, mic in one hand and a class of champagne in the other.

"Ladies and gentlemen, that you for showing up today! I am Arestes Viorno, your host for the night." He said, lively. The surrounding crowd applauded. "I would just like to remind you that we do have an auction going on in the other side of the building, the money that is earned will be gifted to different children charities. We aren't heartless are we Mr Donatti?" He said, looking Dane in the eye. Dane straightened his blazer out, before sending Arestes a million dollar smile.

"Of course not Mr Viorno. I have a heart of gold." Dane said somewhat sarcastically, but I believed it because it was very much true.

Mr Viorno laughed as did others and went back to talking about whatever he was talking about. I sent a smiled to Dane, pleased with his answer. I thought he was going to get angry but he didn't which was an upside.

I took a slight sip of the white wine in the glasses. "You look so gorgeous. I'm trying not to rip your dress off you right now." He murmured into my ear, leaning in close. I choked on my wine, catching some peoples attention, and luckily I played it off as a polite cough.

~*~

Mr Viorno had stopped talking, and allowed us to mingle. Our families headed over to the auction site and had a look around.

"Everything here is old, and ugly." Willow complained as my brother tried shushing her.

"I think it's cool. Like look at that beautiful painting over there." Ocean said, pointing at a painting of a bridge with blossom trees around it. "How could you not like that?" She said incredulously, making us chuckle.

"I need to find a potential babes here guys. I've been alone for way too long." Raeni whined as I swallowed my laughter, again.

"Go mingle." I said curtly, nudging her side. She swatted my arm away and pouted. Dane pulled me aside to the jewellery side, which made me intrigued. We looked through rings and bracelets and different necklaces, nothing caught my eye.

"Choose something baby." He said, looking at me.

I pretended to open a Poké ball and chuck it at him.

"I choose you!" I whisper yelled as he guffawed with laughter. His laughter died down and he stalked towards me.

"You can choose me when we leave this place." He said in my ear, huskily. Out of the corner of my eye, I spotted a shiny looking thing. I pushed him aside and stalked over to it, like a predator to its prey. I looked back at Dane to see him mingling with some guy in a flashy suit.

It was a beautiful black lotus flower, with gold designs in it. The guy selling it saw my interest in it and smiled slightly, he was old.

"Pretty one isn't she?" He said with a East Asian accent. I nodded and smiled tightly.

"How much for it?" I asked, looking at him. He stared at me for a few seconds and sighed.

"I'm a fortune teller. May I have your hand?" He asked as I nodded. He held my hand between his, and traced a few lines on it.

"You've been through some tough things haven't you?" He asked as I nodded silently.

"Something to do with memory?" He asked again as I nodded. My eyes widened at how he knew this but I accepted it anyway.

"Your troubles will be over soon. You are going to have 3 kids, all of them healthy and with good hearts." He said smiling, a father like smile. Tears built up in my eyes as I tried blinking them away rapidly. "That man over there," He said, pointing at Dane who turned to look at me, smiling. "He's going to love you and your kids very much. Don't let him go." He said I internally gasped.

"Your heart rate is going up, do not cry dear." He said chuckling, letting go of my hands. "For you, the Lianhua necklace is free. You don't need to pay me. You will do some good things in your life time. You remind me of my daughter." He said, smiling sadly.

"I can't accept that! I need to pay. Please?" I said, the feeling of not paying not sitting right with me.

"No darling do not worry, it is free. I accept nothing!" He said chuckling, pulling the necklace out of the glass cage thing. He put it into a nice black velvet box, and put it into a bag. He handed it to me and smiled.

"Thank you so much." I mumbled, my heart swelling in happiness.

"No problem. Zaijian." He said as I walked back to Dane.

"Hometime?" He whispered as I nodded. He notified out parents that we were going home due to my 'sickness'.

The car ride home was filled with sexual tension. My legs bobbed up and down until we got out of the car. He grabbed my hand and jogged towards the entrance of his house, opening it up quickly and pulling me upstairs.

We got to his room in which he immediately took his tie off, and smirked at me.

"I'm tired as fuck. I'm ill too, I'm going to freshen up then go to bed. See ya!" I mumbled, racing towards the toilet.

Luckily I had put my clothes in there before hand to change into, I stripped out of them and took a quick ass shower. I took off the remaining of my makeup and changed into the over sized tee i had and booty shorts. I slowly opened the door, and saw Dane nowhere in sight.

I sighed and smiled, walking out of the room. Suddenly, I got slammed into the wall.

Dane's face was mere centimetres away from mine, his breathing heavy.

"Hiding?" He asked as I shook my head a no. He leaned in, crashing his lips into mine. His soft lips moulded with mine perfectly. I pulled away and took a long ass breath.

"I'm tired." I mumbled, pulling him into the bed. I shut the light and got into the covers, as did he.

"Stop fucking moving you weirdo." I whisper yelled as he gasped.

"How dare you?" He said, turning his back to me.

"How dare I what?" I asked confused.

"I'm not talking to you now. Think about your actions." He whisper yelled making me huff. This grown man was acting like a baby.

It was kind of cute.

"Dane?" I said, no answer.

"Dane?" No answer.

"Dane?"

"Dane?"

"Dane you fucking prick!" I slapped the back of his had making him laugh. He turned back round facing towards me.

"I love you." He wrapped his arm around me waist, pulling me closer.

"I love you too Dane." I mumbled, before feeling a slight kiss on my forehead.

This past year has been tough, but I did get through it. Eventually I knew that whatever hardships I had come across would have settled quickly. I had a good family, a good boyfriend, mother, brother, sister.

I couldn't have asked for more.

I let a few thoughts linger about in my head before drifting off into a deep sleep, hoping to wake up to Dane's face tomorrow.

THE END!!

The End!

It has finally come to end for Dane and Domenica. I will do a epilogue, but after that I don't know if I should make a different book on the ending or whatever. But anyways, it's the end of a beautiful story.

No, Dom will not regain her memory. I don't her to remember everything to be honest.

I don't know when next I will be making a new book. Soon maybe.

Epilogue.

When I started this book, I never honestly realised that people would actually read it. I'm a girl that always had a major love for books but honestly, we are at 1.9K readers, as I'm writing this and it's fucking insane. Of course, from our own perspectives, we can never see how good some of our works are. I'm so so happy, I'm currently sitting in Costa, an English coffee shop I think, while my sisters sitting across me wondering why I'm so happy. I cannot, cannot, CANNOT, believe that this book has gotten this many reads???? EXCUSE ME???? The plot of this book has been made up along the way, so sooner or later I'm going to majorly edit everything. And once again, I thank you, my readers, my ghost readers, my voters and all of that good stuff, because without you guys I would not have had even a single read. This last chapter of Dane and Domenica will be the longest. My two beautiful babies. I was going to section them but, since this is going to take me some time to write because I'm busy with a whole load of real life bullshit, I'd rather combine them.

Anyway, I love you guys.

THANK YOU GUYS SO MUCH!

Onto the epilogue :)

Three Years Later...

The soft humming of the wind was all I could hear as I walked down the park, it was midday. Little kids giggled and screamed, running around with laughter in the park, it made a small smile creep up on my face. Little girls and boys screaming with laughter, their parents laughing too. I longed to have my own, and I think I was now ready to have a baby. Maybe it was the baby fever, Willow and my brother had created a sweet little boy, Elijah. I smiled to myself again.

I still hadn't regained my memory. I had vague bits of it, but Dane really made me fall in love with him all over again, Me and Dane were still strong, Rosella has sprouted into a mature 10 year old, and she was already breaking hearts. Diana had been going a year strong with her boyfriend, Luca. Luca, the one I ignored a billion times! My mother found a boyfriend, not really boyfriend but her colleague. Every time he came over, we teased her and she turned into a literal beetroot. Ricca, Darya, Raeni, Willow and Ocean and myself, we're still as tight as fuck.

"Babe?" I heard, not knowing whether it was in my head or out loud.

"Babe?!" It got louder as I tried smacking it away, flinging my hands towards the source of the sound.

"DOMENICA!" I jumped, Dane stood tall with a playful glare on his face. He raised his eyebrows at me, pulling my into the side of his chest.

"What were you thinking about?" He murmured as his chest rumbled. I shrugged my shoulders and smiled.

"You okay?" I said, as he nodded. He kissed my cheek, then we started to walk to the car. "We're going to the ball tonight?" I asked as he opened the car door for me.

"Yeah, Violeta and all of them are going to be there too." He said, sitting down. "Have you been in contact with the girls?" He asked as I nodded, grinning.

"Nearly all of them have moved out, gone to university, gotten jobs and apartments and stuff. Only the youngsters are left, the house you got can be put up for sale, and the summer house is still in use." He smiled, weirdly though, as if he planned something. I smiled softly and nodded at him, happy with our accomplishments. God forbid what would have happened to those girls if they were left there by themselves. We made it home, me and Dane actually moved out last year.

Our house was in between his, and mine. Business was still running, and very, very work loaded. Even though it was all fraud work, it still made me work for fucking hours.

I took my beautiful dogs with me, and they're my big babies now, my Alaskan Malamute, Titus, my Doberman Virtus, my Shiba Inu, Zyron and my beautiful Pitbull Terrier, Trigger.

"Where are my babies?" I shouted sort of softly, hearing the tapping of the floor. Four doggies ran towards me, yapping and barking.

"My babies!" I yelled, hugging all of them. Virtus and Titus was the maturest out of all of them, and preferred to annoy Dane, more than me. Trigger still was up and running, it was never too late for him to play around. Zyron was like the mature brother of the group, he'd play but also act as if he has his own kingdom.

They all barked happily, jumping onto me.

"Who are my good boys?" I baby-talked as Dane chuckled at me. I blew a raspberry at him and carried on loving my doggos.

"Baby we have a ball to get to. Get ready." Dane said, while dropping his blazer on the couch.

"What if I don't want to go?" I mumbled and flopped on the floor, Virtus by my side.

"I'm going to leave you here with the Ghoulies." He said making me gasp. "Sorry but I'm a Serpent thanks." I mumbled again, making the Riverdale reference.

I got up, put fresh water and food for the dogs and went upstairs. Dane was behind me, coming upstairs too.

He smacked my ass making my jump.

"Bitch!" I playfully glared at him and ran up the stairs faster. It turned into a race until he grabbed my shoulders and slammed me lightly into the wall. His face was a centimetre away from mine, his shallow breath and my heart racing was only what I could hear.

Even after three years, he had the same effect on me as before.

"What am I going to do with that mouth of yours huh?" He said huskily making me crack a grin.

"Nothing!" I whispered, ducking under his arms that has just been caging me and running into my room.

"I'm going to so get you back princess. Just wait." I laughed while pulling out a long satin dress in black. I quickly showered and moisturised my face. I did some makeup, and pulled on the dress. I straightened my hair and put on some black strappy heels. I had a faux fur shoulder wrap and decided to add that. I got my gun and knife thigh strap and strapped it on, for safety measures. I put on the necklace Dane had got me a year back and the promise ring he got me too. I spritzed my favourite Dior perfume - joy. I looked into the mirror and analysed my body.

The marks, the scarring everything has slowly faded. It's still there but faded.

I wish I remembered everything but I'm kind of glad I didn't.

"You are so beautiful." Dane said, planting kiss on my shoulder. "Even though they've left scars and marks, you still are so gorgeous. I'm proud to call you my girl, forever and always." He span me around, again, and kissed me passionately.

It was filled with love, and admiration.

"I love you Dee Dee." I said hugging him as he chuckled.

"I love you more Dommy." I laughed as he pulled away. I stared at him, his broad shoulders, his styled hair, his dimples, his everything.

"Carry on looking at me like that and I'm going to give you a child." He said lowly, his eyes darkening.

I dragged a finger down his chest, going closer to him, near to his ear, "Maybe you should." I said seductively, then pushing him away.

"You're being a naughty girl." He breathed as I made my way downstairs.

"We're going to be late pretty boy." I mumbled, going outside to the garage. I chose the Royce, and Dane was driving this time.

"Let's go." He said, getting into the car.

"Isn't that what we're doing kid?" I sneered playfully as he whacked my thigh.

"You're getting punished tonight babygirl." He mumbled, pulling out of the drive way.

"Yeah?" I said, putting another coat of lipstick on. I popped my lips and planted a kiss on his cheek. My lip prints were left there on his right cheek. I leaned back an admired my work.

"Now everyone knows you're mine." I said happily.

"You know, Jorda.." He abruptly stopped his sentence. "No carry on." I said, smiling, not to my fullest though.

"He always told me Scorpios are possessive and jealous." Dane said, smiling.

"And he was right bitch." I said laughing, turning on the radio. Work by Rihanna came on, making me giggle.

"Oh this my shit bro!" I yelled, turning it up. I started silly dancing, making him laugh.

"You know I dealt with you the nicest,Nobody touch me, you not righteous,Nobody text me in a crisis,"

I sang, dancing in my seat. He looked over at me and laughed, and suddenly my black dots clouded my vision as I saw vague images of the same thing, lights and cars.

"Dom! Shit fucking hell Domenica!" A distant voice yelled. I snapped out of it and took a large gulp of air.

"You fucking scared me shit!" Dane yelled, punching the wheel.

"I'm s-sorry..I h-had a vision thing." I said as my lip quivered. His eyes softened, he had quickly pulled over and gave me a tight hug. "I don't know what I'll do if I lose you a second time." He said kissing me.

"Sorry I'm fine lets go." I said, taking a deep breath.

"You sure?" He asked as I nodded.

We reached the place where the ball was held, many different gang leaders, mafia dons, godfathers and donas were. Dane got out first, and jogged round to my side, opening my door up for me.

"A Queen shouldn't have to open her car doors." He said winking as I took his hand and stepped out. It seemed vaguely familiar.

We made out way inside, people greeting us both as I kept a stoic face on. I occasionally smiled timidly at the people that I knew.

"Ah my favourite couple!" Violeta said, as she pulled me into a hug.

"Dona Vio! How are you?" I said, hugging her back as her girlfriend spoke to Dane.

"I am good! Ever since you shot that prick of a boss I have been fantabulous!" She said laughing.

"I'm glad I did that, he was a stronzo." I mumbled as she laughed harder.

"It's so good to see you. This is my girlfriend, Zaya." She said as her girlfriend pulled me into a hug. It was a cliche, Vio was the big bad bunny and Zaya was the little nerd. She was cute.

"H-hi." She said, blushing. I smiled at her as we parted ways. Ricca and the girls strolled in looking beautiful as ever.

"Dom!" They all yelled in unison, coming towards me. Ricca greeted Dane with that man-boy-friendship hug thing.

"How are my bestfriends?" I said as they all muttered a good, okay, great. Willow was with my brother, Diana behind them with Luca, and my mother with her mafia doctor boyfriend. We took our seats and let the host speak.

"Thank you all for coming! I hope you guys have a good evening, the auctions are open and close at 12, midnight. Here the organiser is going to say a few words." He said. We didn't know who the organiser was, it was a somewhat anonymous ball event.

"It's been quiet some time hasn't it?" The man said as Dane stood up abruptly. I looked at him quickly, pulling him back down.

"Dane? What are you doing?" I whisper yelled as anger shook his body.

"How the fuck did he get out alive?" He growled angrily, going outside to make a phone call. Willow turned towards the guy and let out a gasp too.

"Willow?" I said, clearly confused.

"Get up we need to leave now." Damien said as Ricca nodded and ushered us out.

"Wait! Guys! Why are you leaving?" The man said, "The party just began!" He said dangerously. I still hadn't turned around, my chair was facing towards the back of the room.

I got up and turned around to see who it was.

He seemed vaguely familiar.

"Ah Don Dom! How've you been?" He said weirdly, as I masked any emotion.

"I'm okay. Yourself?" I asked, keeping the conversation pleasant.

"There is no space for dogs like you Armani! Get out of here before our people set this whole thing on fire." A man shouted, sounded somewhat Russian.

"Oh Vanko! I forgot you were alive." The man, 'Armani' said rudely as my eyes hardened at him. Who was this irrelevant guy?

"Don Dom you look a little lost, maybe I should remind you about some things." He said, coming down the steps.

As soon as he stepped down, about 2000 guns were pointed at him. Darya, Raeni, Willow, Damien, Ricca, and Ocean all had their guns pointed at him, and were standing in front of me. Dane had now come back in and chuckled loudly.

"Oh Armani, you just don't give it a rest do you?" Dane was definitely bigger, and taller than him and right now they were standing nose to nose. "How the fuck did you get out?" He seethed as Armani laughed.

"I have resources. In about 7 minutes, this whole place is going to blow up, and the first person to die is you." Armani whipped out his gun and shot at Dane. Immediately everyone fired at Armani as blood poured out of about every single pore in his body.

"Dane!" I gasped as I ran towards him. He was on the floor, his hand on his torso.

"I think I've been shot tesoro." He rasped, chuckling. My words were stuck in my throat, bile rose up and I refused to choke it out.

My mothers boyfriend came and helped him, got him up and out to the mafia hospital. I told Ricca and Damien to go with him, we would handle it here.

Armani spluttered, laughing.

"I hope you both are dead by the time he gets to you. Trust me I will be watching." He rasped. I had no idea what he was talking about so I went along with it.

"You know, from the last time we saw each other, I would have thought you learned your lesson. But you clearly haven't. I spared you." I growled lowly, my hands itching to do some damage.

"No matter how close you are to a wild animal, eventually it will attack you." He mumbled, blood spewing out of his mouth.

"Good we're not close anymore kid." I said, pulling out my gun and shooting him between the eyes.

"Evacuate the area! A bomb is going to go off!" Willow yelled, getting everyone out. Everyone ran out, and I think there was about a minute left.

We all ran out and then as if it were a movie, the whole palace blew up. I didn't care, I got into the Royce and drove to the mafia hospital.

I ran inside and saw the registration place.

"Dane Donatti, what room is he in?" I asked the receptionist as she smacked her gum.

"No visitors allowed right now, sorry." She said. I yanked the back of her hair and brang her face close to mine.

"Tell em where my boyfriend is before I ruin you whole entire life." I growled, as she nodded frantically.

"R-room 346. Floor 2." She said as I took off.

I made it there and he was connected to an oxygen machine, his breathing slow.

"Domenica, Dane's state is okay, the bullets out. He lost a ton of blood though. Don't worry he is fine." Grayson, my mothers boyfriend said, smiling sadly at me. I nodded mutely and sat next to him. He was asleep.

"I love you so much." I whispered, kissing his hand.

He stirred before opening his eyes.

"Hello." I whispered.

"Hi." He said, his voice groggy. I grabbed the bottle of water besides me and made him drink it.

"I got shot." He said, looking at the ceiling. I nodded and rubbed his hand.

"You're okay now." I said as he nodded.

"Dom, he needs to stay for a day, then can be taken home. I presume you can attend to cleaning his wounds and stuff no?" Grayson said as I nodded. He left us and sent us both a small smile. "No funny business." He warned us, laughing. I chuckled and shook my head. Dane had fell back to sleep, and me too with him. It was okay.

We were okay.

Four months later...

"Domenica have you seen my files on the business?" Dane yelled form his study.

"No!" I yelled back, locking the door. Dane's wound healed fully, and he was back to being the scary mafia don.

I had multiple pregnancy tests with me, currently, I was in the toilet. I took one, waited it came out as positive.

Another one, positive.

Third one, negative.

Fourth one, positive.

My fifth and final one, positive. Tears built up in my eyes as I stared at the two pink lines. I was so happy, I'm fucking pregnant. We had some fun time, a few weeks back.

"Oh goodness." I whispered to myself as a few knocks came at the door.

"Baby? You okay in there?" Dane said, sounding concerned.

"Y-yeah I'm fine baby. You going to work?" I asked as he said yes.

"I'm leaving now. Bye baby." he said, leaving. That was weird, he never left without forcing me to kiss him on both cheeks.

I chucked them all in the bin, and freshened up quickly. I came out to our room and a large bouquet of red roses were on the bed, a note beside it.

"Come to my mothers house, at 4. I have a surprise, I love you. -D."

I smiled to myself, what was he up to now? It was about 9 now, so I decided to go and make some breakfast and do some girl stuff.

--

Currently it was 3, I had just finished watching Prison Break. I heard a knock on the door, and of course I was cautious so I took my gun with me. I opened the door and a two boxes were on the floor, with a red rose on either of them, a note on the bigger box.

"Wear this to my mothers house, I know you're going to look absolutely stunning. I love you -D."

I smiled, picking up the boxes. I kicked the door shut, and rushed upstairs as I only had one hour to get ready.

I lifted the lid of the bigger box, and I nearly died.

It was a forest green dress, the green colour was the most beautiful shade I had ever seen. I stood up while holding the dress, it was off the shoulder, with a long lace/mesh veil, like a cape. There was diamonds on the chest area, towards the waist area, it was so beautiful. I opened the smaller box and sat there was a pair of silver heels, waiting to be worn.

A tear fell out my eye, as I held the dress to my chest.

I really love this boy.

I did my hair, and makeup and put on the dress. I really admired myself in the mirror, and it was definitely safe to say I looked pretty.

My door bell rang now, and I went to go see who it was.

Luca was standing there looking like a whole chauffeur, making me laugh.

"Hello m'lady, I'll be taking you to Mrs Donatti's house. Let's go." He said, winking as I laughed. We left and he opened the doors for me and was being really suspicious.

"What has Dane been doing?" I asked him as he kept his eyes on the road.

"I have taken a oath of silence m'lady." He said cheekily making me swat his shoulder.

"Please?" I asked.

"Nope."

"Tell me!"

"Nada."

"I'll give you candy."

"I have diabetes." He deadpanned as I bursted out laughing. "Shit sorry."
We reached his mothers house, and I saw the lights were all off, and there
was rose petals leading up to the door.

"Shall we?" Luca said, taking my hand.

"We shall." I said, smiling. He led me to the door, and it was really quiet. It
opened by 'itself' and I walked through.

"I need to blind fold you now honey." He said as I sighed and agreed. My
sense heightened, I could hear shuffling and giggling and a big thwack.

"Ow!" Ricca shrieked as I muffled laughter.

"Domenica." I heard Dane's velvety voice.

"Mhm.." I said incoherently.

"From the moment I saw you at school, I instantly knew I wanted you.
I knew that I was going to have you too." He said, I heard a course of
chuckling, making me laugh too. "When you punched my nose, that was
probably when I fell in love with you. From then. Then you helped my ma,
Rosella and me in general. Because of previous events, I never thought I
would ever love again. And I never thought I would ever find a girl as good,
nice, caring, loving, scary and as beautiful as you Domenica." I laughed
at the scary part. "I've put you through so much. You lost your memory
because of me," He sniffled, and I stopped him right there. I put my hands
out to touch him and conveniently he was standing in front of me. I made
my way to his face and gripped it, I felt wetness around his cheeks.

"That was not because of you. And you know what I'm happy it happened, I've forgotten so many things I probably wouldn't have wanted to
remember if I hadn't, I got to know my best friends properly and more

importantly, I got to fall in love with you all over again. It was meant to be." I finished, A tear rolling down my face, the wetness seeped through to satin blindfold.

"Back to what I was saying.." Dane said after a minute.

"I have loved, and cherished every single moment with you. And I wanted to say I'm so fucking sorry for breaking up with you on your birthday. Anyways, what I'm trying to say is that I love you. I never wanted to put my heart on the line, but now that you're here, I have no idea what happened to me. Literally. You've made me a different man to what I was before, and I know for a fact it affected everyone around me. You've made a better version of me and I can't thank you enough for it. I know with you around my little sister and my mother have been the happiest I've ever seen them, and I want to thank you for being in my life. You bring me to my knees, all the time. I will never ever get tired of waking up to your face, to listening to your lectures, to you. I love you so much." My blindfold dropped as I saw all of my family standing around a heart of roses and candles.

"So please give me your hand in marriage, and let me marry you. Will you marry me Domenica?" He said, he was on one knee in front of me, with a beautiful ring held open.

"Yes. A million times yes!" I said, tears flowing freely as everyone clapped and cheered. He put the ring on me and kissed me with so much fire and passion.

"Sorry guys!" I yelled, as Dane tapped a spoon on a wine glass.

"I actually have a little announcement myself..." I mumbled, tears gathering in my eyes again. "I took a few tests...and they were two pink lines." I said, my mother and sister and Dane's mum and the girls crying in glee.

The boys were so confused, making me chuckle, then it dawned on them.

"Really?" Dane said, standing in front of me with tears in his eyes. I nodded, tears flowing again.

"You have an STI?" Ricca yelled as he looked at me and Dane in horror. I couldn't help but laugh, Damien whacked the back of his head.

"Ow! That's the second time!" He grumbled making me laugh.

"No Ricca, I'm pregnant." I said, making his eyes widen.

"Oh my God! I'm going to be an uncle! Shit!" He said running over to hug me. Dane was staring at me with an unknown emotion in his eyes.

"Really?" He asked again.

"Yes you oaf! How many times do I say it?" I said, hugging him. He picked me up and swirled me around before planting a bazillion kisses on my face. His hand went to my stomach, as he bent down and kissed it.

"Our little family. I love you Domenica." He said, kissing me.

"I love you more Dane." I mumbled, kissing him back.

The news was cracked, and we were all having a good time. This is what I wanted, and it was what I got. I think my father would be proud of me. I know it would never be goodbye for us, and I know we're going to see each other again. I'm waiting on it.

"The most important people in my life are in this room right here, right now. And I want to thank all of you for being here. The money will come and go, but the love for the family wont, as Dominic Toretto said. We've been through things as a family, as different families, as our own people. This love is going to be here forever. Jordan, I love you. I know you're up there somewhere. I love you guys. Mi familia." Dane said as everyone sniffled and clapped.

"I love you." I said, looking up to him.

"You know I'll always love you first mi regina." He said, planting a soft kiss on my lips.

This may be our last ride, but not for now. I now know what family is. I know now that I love these people and they love me.

Jordan, I love you too.

Until we see you again.